for emma sophia price olsen – w.a.

A TEMPLAR BOOK

First published in the UK in hardback in 2003 by Templar Publishing
This edition published in 2005 by Templar Publishing,
an imprint of The Templar Company plc,
Pippbrook Mill, London Road, Dorking, Surrey, RH4 IJE, UK
www.templarco.co.uk

Illustration copyright © 2003 by Wayne Anderson
Text and design copyright © 2003 by The Templar Company plc

First softback edition, second impression

ISBN: 1-84011-594-7

Designed by Mike Jolley
Edited by Marcus Sedgwick

Printed in China

The Dragon Machine

written by **Helen Ward**

illustrated by **Wayne Anderson**

templar publishing

george noticed his first dragon on a wet Thursday.

The more he looked, the more dragons he saw!

unseen, ignored and overlooked
the dragons went unnoticed...

...just like george.

Dragons perched on the telephone wires,

they sat amongst the dustbins.

They chased butterflies through the tulips.

They played havoc with the cat.

they sank the water lilies in the pond.

eorge fed them delicious stale biscuits and smelly cheese.

and then
the trouble began.

The dragons followed George everywhere.
George spent more and more of his time cleaning up
muddy footprints, tidying untidiness and saying sorry
for breaking things he had not broken.

George's dragons were becoming too troublesome
to stay unnoticed for much longer.

something had to be done.
George went in search of some advice.

The dragons
followed George to the library.

He consulted the Encyclopedia of Dragons.
There were dire warnings: never feed a dragon;
never let a dragon into your home... too late.
There were tragic tales of dragons discovered
and captured... too sad.

And there was a map of the place
where dragons belonged.

A great wilderness unnoticed
and overlooked and safe.
But george would have to
show them the way.

HERE BE
DRAGONS

george drew plans for a machine.

the machine had a beginning,

a middle,

and a tail end...

..an undercarriage,
        and beautiful wings.

        george hammered in the last nail.
He packed delicious stale biscuits and smelly cheese
    and himself into the dragon machine.

The machine lumbered, engine
ticking gently, into the night sky.

And the dragons followed.

The machine clicked
and whirred over the sleeping town.
It rattled and clunked
over the moonlit fields and woods.

The dragons followed.

It clattered and banged
and crashed into the great wilderness.

The dragons followed.

George was so tired he went to sleep
in the wreckage of his dragon machine.

By morning, all the dragons were gone.

There was an emptiness all around
and inside George.

And an emptiness at home where
george **should** have been.

They searched the town.
They searched the fields.
They ventured into the great wilderness
looking for george and found him among the
broken pieces of his dragon machine.

george and his dreams of dragons went home.

Everyone was pleased to see George,
and George was pleased to be back.
He no longer went unseen,
ignored and overlooked.

They made him a huge cake
to celebrate his return and gave
him a dog as a present.

nobody else noticed that it
wasn't a dog.

THE COMPLETE GUIDE TO
CORE
STABILITY

THE COMPLETE GUIDE TO
CORE STABILITY

3rd Edition

Matt Lawrence

A & C Black • London

First published 2003 by
A&C Black Publishers Ltd
This edition published by A&C Black, an imprint of
Bloomsbury Publishing Plc
36 Soho Square, London W1D 3QY
www.acblack.com

2nd edition 2007
Reprinted 2010
3rd edition 2011

ISBN 9781408133248

A CIP catalogue record for this book is available from the British Library.

Cover and all inside photographs © Grant Pritchard, except p208 © Shutterstock

A&C Black uses paper produced with elemental chlorine-free pulp, harvested from managed sustainable forests.

Typeset in 10.75pt Adobe Caslon on 14pt by Saxon Graphics Ltd, Derby.

Printed and bound in China by C&C Offset Printing Co.

CONTENTS

Acknowledgements   viii

Preface   ix

Introduction   x

PART ONE The Principles of Core Stability	1

Chapter 1 What is core stability and what purpose does it serve?   2

Chapter 2 The trunk muscles and mechanisms of stability   7

Chapter 3 Why is core stability important?   14

Chapter 4 Who can benefit from improved core stability?   22

Chapter 5 How to achieve core stability   26

Chapter 6 How to overload a muscle   30

Chapter 7 What you need to know before you start   37

Chapter 8 Before you begin   42

PART TWO The Exercises	45

Chapter 9 Warm-up exercises and stretches   47

Chapter 10   Stabilisation exercises   57

Chapter 11   Classic abdominal exercises   66

Chapter 12   The introduction of unstable bases   70

Chapter 13   Alternative unstable base exercises   90

Chapter 14   Stabilisation exercises within conventional training   103

Chapter 15   Hands-on partner work   124

Chapter 16   Medicine ball training   132

PART THREE   The Way Forward   147

Chapter 17   Multi-joint and plane movements   149

Chapter 18   Kettlebell training   161

Chapter 19   ViPR Training   172

Chapter 20   Suspension Training   184

PART FOUR   Alternative Training   197

Chapter 21   Alternative training and exercises   199

Chapter 22   Core stability training for specific age groups   212

Chapter 23   Abdominal training in water   216

PART FIVE   Programme Ideas and Class Structure   225

Chapter 24   The basic structure of a class   227

Chapter 25   Sample programmes   230

Chapter 26   Designing a programme for individuals   234

Appendix: SMR techniques   238

Glossary   242

References   246

Further information   247

Index   251

ACKNOWLEDGEMENTS

Firstly, I would like to thank all the guys at the gym: Jamal, Steve, Neils, Warren, Dave and Mario, Simon and Jake – thanks for all your help. Thanks also to Grant for managing to get some great photos despite a very hectic photo shoot schedule. Thank you also to my publishers, A&C Black, whose belief enabled me to write this book in the first place. And lastly, thank you to my fiancée, Michelle, not only for helping out with the photos but for her endless patience and tireless support throughout the writing of this book.

PREFACE

Since my early days as a personal trainer and fitness instructor, I have seen many fitness fads come and go; many have re-invented themselves, to return like a phoenix from the ashes, and have subsequently been forced on to an unsuspecting public.

This book is not about fads or gimmicks but aims to deliver plain old common sense with a few exercises thrown in for good measure. The purpose of writing this book is not to make you fitter, faster or help you to lose a few pounds, it is to provide a template and, hopefully, a reference guide to some of the most effective abdominal exercises around. The exercise repertoire has been developed using principles from science, sport and alternative health, and following guidance and advice from many industry experts. This book is designed not just to give you a starting point in abdominal training but rather a complete guide, allowing you, the reader, the opportunity to explore many different variables in exercise execution, progression and adaptation. You should tailor this book to your own goals and requirements rather than trying to complete every exercise. There is no definitive exercise or optimum programme – as with much of the fitness industry, everything is relative.

I hope that this book will help you not only to identify with the principles of abdominal training and programme design, but that it will also provide an insight into how to overcome the boredom often associated with exercise. Since writing this book, I have seen how the fitness industry has really embraced the concept of core stability, initially through education of instructors filtering down to health club or leisure centre members and finally the general public who, as a whole, are demonstrating their improved awareness of the importance of core stability. This awareness will only increase, especially with the freedom of information that is posted on the internet through various sites such as You Tube. All manner of tantalising exercise options are being posted by both competent fitness professionals and unfortunately egotists who just want to show off what they can do – out performing all other exercise options – whatever the cost to themselves. At one level this is a fantastic medium to see all manner of exercises, regardless how intense or demanding, but there is always the risk that for the non-enlightened enthusiast who doesn't understand the demands of certain exercises, injuries will most certainly happen as a consequence.

Either way, the internet is here to stay and communication and sharing of all exercise can and will only help to develop new ideas, exercise options and concepts. Use this book as a reference guide to re-ignite your enthusiasm not just in core training but also for the bigger picture of long-term health and well-being. Where the industry goes with core stability who knows? However, with some of the latest equipment trends and current exploration of function, one thing is certain – it will only evolve.

Matt Lawrence
2011

INTRODUCTION

As our Neanderthal cousins were setting off for another hard day at the office, the last thing on their minds was core stability, or neutral spine. They did not concern themselves with such trivialities as muscle bracing and correct posture, why should they? It was a subconscious thing! As hunter-gatherers, their lives would be focused on survival, which meant eating, procreation and protection. Most of their time was spent searching for food, and invariably killing it and getting it home. After a successful hunt, the kill would be dismembered, hoisted on to their shoulders or dragged back to the cave to be prepared for dinner. The deep abdominal muscles of the torso would have been continually active throughout all these running, carrying, lunging, dragging and lifting movements. Unfortunately, technological advancements have allowed modern-day societies to lose track of what their bodies were designed for. Through a lack of appropriate exercises and changes in lifestyle, we have created a new phenomenon: twenty-first-century man.

WHAT IS CORE STABILITY?

To put 'core stability' into its modern context, where there are now few mammoths to chase, consider how you lift shopping into the back of your car or take a baby out of a pram. The muscles of the torso are required to brace or tense briefly upon exertion, in order to stabilise the spine and assist the lifting movement, and to reduce any potential injury to the lower back.

In order to achieve this powerful torso, there is no one optimum exercise you can do; instead, a balance of appropriate exercises relative to your own goals and specific needs is required. If you think core stability is simply a matter of performing endless sit-ups, think again! It doesn't matter how many crunches you can do, these alone are not the answer. In fact the crunch, or sit-up exercise, while having a role in developing that sought-after 'six-pack', does little to improve core stability.

CRUNCHES/SIT-UPS

For many years, sit-ups or crunches were the only exercises used to train the abdominal muscles. Disappointingly, even today in many fitness magazines the emphasis is firmly on achieving the elusive 'six-pack'. How many variations are there for standard abdominal flexion? This on its own is bad enough, but also, for many years, the sit-up was performed with the feet secured. This is still one of the standard fitness tests used for those who wish to gain entry to the services and armed forces. While performing sit-ups is excellent training for the rectus abdominus (the 'six-pack' muscle), when the feet are secured the hip flexors take the majority of the load due to their relative strength and endurance in comparison with the rectus abdominus. So the exercise seems easier and more repetitions are possible.

One main disadvantage with the sit-up technique is that when you curl your body off the floor, and as you move into forward flexion of the spine, stress is placed on the lumbar vertebrae. If you lift too far, this stress can aggravate the spinal discs and joints.

Abdominal workouts based largely on flexion exercises can result in excessive shortening of the hip flexor muscles. This shortening can pull on the attachments to the pelvis and lumbar spine, which in turn can affect your posture. These muscle imbalances, if not dealt with, can have a knock-on effect on other muscles and joints, which can be detrimental to your posture, and cause pain and potentially spinal injury.

SUMMARY

- Most of us do not use the muscles of the torso in a functional way as part of our day-to-day life.
- Sit-ups alone do not enhance core stability and so will not improve your posture.
- Sit-up exercises performed incorrectly can cause more harm than good.

1

PART **ONE**

THE PRINCIPLES OF CORE STABILITY

WHAT IS CORE STABILITY AND WHAT PURPOSE DOES IT SERVE?

1

Core stability

Core stability is the effective recruitment of the muscles that stabilise the Lumbo-Pelvic–Hip complex, together with those that stabilise the shoulder girdle.

As we spend more time sitting down – in cars and at desks – our stabilisation muscles are getting progressively weaker. As we use them less and less in our daily activities, we are gradually losing the ability to activate them subconsciously. As a result other muscles overcompensate, taking on the role of the stabilisers, and this can lead to injury. To rectify the situation, the stabilising muscles need to be retrained so that the brain relearns to activate them, both consciously and subconsciously.

STABILISATION OF THE CORE OR MID-SECTION

This occurs when you can maintain a fixed position of your torso while carrying out certain activities or movements of the limbs. Good core stability allows you to maintain a rigid mid-section without other forces such as gravity affecting the desired movement.

(a)

(b)

Figure 1 Spinal joint movement: (a) bending opens the spinal joints; (b) reaching up closes the spinal joints

Some of the benefits associated with core stability training include:

- improved posture
- fewer injuries
- better agility and improved ability to change direction
- improved balance and co-ordination
- improved power and speed.

The necessity for good core stability is only now becoming widely accepted, and yet core stability training is not a new concept. Indeed, many current trunk stabilisation techniques have been developed by physiotherapists using specific rehabilitation methods to strengthen the torso. 'Pilates', created by Joe Pilates in the 1930s, was originally designed as a training format to help reduce injuries in dancers and gymnasts by concentrating on stabilisation techniques directly related to dancing. Pilates focuses on movements that require the deep trunk muscles to be activated, rather like creating a corset to help support the spine.

These days, stabilisation and **bracing** techniques to enhance core stability should be a prerequisite for exercise programmes at all levels. However, when you introduce the relevant exercises, unless an understanding of what is supposed to happen and what you are supposed to feel is taught correctly to the participant, the exercises will not have the desired result. If the participants do not have sufficient **kinaesthetic awareness** they will not benefit from the workout, and in certain circumstances are more likely to injure themselves through poor techniques and incorrect muscle control.

THE SPINE

The spine serves three main purposes within the human body – those of support, protection and mobility. It supports the skull at the top and acts like a frame, giving the ribs, pelvis and limbs a structural base to attach to. In conjunction with the ribs, it acts as protection for the heart and lungs, and for all organs in the abdomen and chest cavity. More importantly, it encases the **spinal cord**, which carries the nerves from the brain to the organs, limbs and tissues. Lastly, it provides the movement for the trunk, allowing **rotation** and flexion forwards, backwards and to the side.

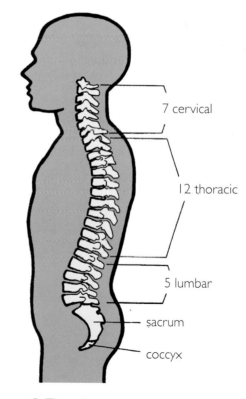

7 cervical

12 thoracic

5 lumbar

sacrum

coccyx

Figure 2 The spine

3

The spine consists of 33 bones called **vertebrae**. These sub-divide into seven cervical vertebrae (C1–C7), 12 **thoracic** vertebrae (T1–T12), five **lumbar** vertebrae (L1–L5), five sacral vertebrae (fused together to form the **sacrum**) and four coccygeal vertebrae (fused to form the **coccyx** or tailbone).

The vertebrae are stacked on top of each other, forming an S-bend, and are linked by bony projections called facet joints, which permit movement of the vertebrae, thus allowing the spine to bend and twist. The cervical vertebrae have high mobility to allow multi-directional movements of the neck, whereas the lumbar vertebrae are much wider and thicker as they have to cope with much stronger forces from many of the larger muscles that are attached to them. The lumbar vertebrae allow **flexion** and **extension**, whereas the thoracic vertebrae allow more twisting and rotational movement.

The muscles of the lower back cross the pelvis and help 'fix' the spine to the pelvis. The gluteals assist hip and leg alignment, and create the **force** needed to walk or run. Each vertebra is separated by a disc, which acts like a cushion helping to dissipate forces across its centre. It also enables partial mobility between the vertebrae allowing you to twist and bend.

Figure 3 Discs (cross section through the spine)

young, which is important because the discs begin to dry up and become brittle with age. The onset of this deterioration process has been seen to occur as early as 30 to 35 years of age.

Throughout our lives we bend and rotate the spine relative to the movements we are doing. As we flex or bend forwards, the vertebrae press on these intervertebral discs. This can displace the gel within the disc's centre, potentially forcing it to the rear. Over time and with increased flexion, poor posture and ageing, the disc can deteriorate and sometimes rupture, causing the gel inside to leak through its fibrous wall. This can create pressure on the spinal nerves and can cause deferred pain elsewhere. Often with lumbar disc problems, it is the **sciatic nerve** that is affected, normally causing pain down the back of the leg.

DISC STRUCTURE

Each disc has a hard outer casing and a spongy centre called a disc nucleus. The discs have no blood supply, but the spongy gel forming the nucleus is kept healthy through movement. Fluids are pressed in and waste products squeezed out as the spine moves and twists. Regular activity and movement of the spine helps to keep the discs

FACET JOINTS

The facet joints, together with the **muscles** and **ligaments**, help to stabilise the spine by restricting excessive movement. If you fall or receive a heavy blow the discs help to absorb some of the shock, but if the shock is severe the facet joints will be forced beyond their natural movement range and can become bruised or damaged. If the joint becomes acutely inflamed following a fall or sharp

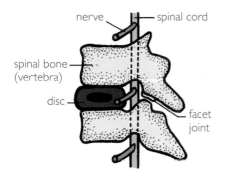

Figure 4 Facet joints (spinal segment)

jolt, it can swell and cause pressure on a nerve in the **neural canal**. This will refer pain to whatever body part the nerve supplies. It is therefore important with movements of the spine not to over extend or flex as this can cause wearing of the facet joints and lead to problems later on.

To avoid over-extending, all initial movements should begin slowly and gradually to allow for mobilisation to occur. Rapid and dynamic movement should be avoided unless sports-specific, and only following a directly relative warm-up procedure.

SPINAL COLUMN

The spinal column protects the spinal cord, which contains thousands of nerve fibres, bunched together. These nerve fibres carry electrical messages from the brain to the organs and limbs, travelling up and down the spinal cord continuously. Should something block these impulses – after an injury, for example – the electrical message will alter, affecting movement and feeling. You might feel a tingling, numbness and/or sharp pain in the area the affected nerve travels to; this might occur following a sports injury, or if you trap a nerve or slip a disc. Rest and massage can sometimes help, but should symptoms persist or if the pain is very uncomfortable it would be advisable to seek specialist advice from an **osteopath** or chiropractor.

NEUTRAL SPINE

The spine forms an S-curve when viewed from the side. The curvature in the neck, thorax and lumbar area acts much like a spring, helping to absorb much of the shock from impact activities. If the spine was straight, any impact from running, jumping and the like would create a huge shock to the head. To protect the spine we should aim to maintain its natural curve when performing a movement. Maintaining this curve allows the ligaments, spinal tissues and discs to exist at their normal length and pressure. We call this normal position **neutral spine** or say it is 'in neutral alignment'; it is approximately mid-way between the full anterior and posterior tilts of the pelvis. In other words, halfway between where the pelvis is fully tilted forwards, with your backside lifting upwards, and where it is fully tilted backwards with your backside tucked underneath. We look at how to achieve this position below.

By maintaining this neutral position you minimise the stress placed upon the ligaments and discs, especially in the lumbar region. You can practise finding this neutral alignment almost anywhere, either lying down or in a seated or standing position.

FINDING NEUTRAL WHEN LYING DOWN

Lie down on the floor, face up, with your knees bent and your feet on the floor approximately hip distance apart. Begin by rocking the hips back and forth a few times and be aware of the two extremes:

1   the pelvis tilting backwards, where the hip bones push up towards the ceiling as the lower back flattens into the floor
2   the pelvis tilting forwards as the back arches away from the floor.

Now try to find the neutral spinal alignment by allowing the pelvis to relax into a position that feels natural to you, between the two extremes.

FINDING NEUTRAL SEATED ON A STABILITY BALL

This same thing can be done on a stability ball. Seated on a stability ball with your feet together, aim to tilt or tip the pelvis forwards to increase the hollow in the lumbar spine, trying to pull the buttocks upwards. Then tilt the pelvis back, lifting the crotch area upwards to flatten the lower back. Avoid any rounding of the shoulders as you perform this movement. After finding the two extremes of movement, reduce the tilting and rocking effect to find the mid-point that feels comfortable. This is your neutral spine position.

FINDING NEUTRAL STANDING UP AGAINST A WALL

Stand against a wall with your feet shoulder width apart. Perform the rocking and tilting movements as before. As a guide, when tilting your pelvis forwards, as your lower back hollows you should be able to fit your hand into the gap between your lower back and the wall. When you tilt your pelvis backwards you should feel your lower back press against your hand as it flattens. Once again, aim to find the mid-range of this spinal movement. This is your neutral spine position.

SUMMARY

- Stabilisation of the core or mid-section occurs when you maintain a fixed position of the torso while carrying out certain activities or movements of the limbs.

- Stabilisation and bracing techniques, to enhance core stability, should be a prerequisite in exercise programmes at all levels.

- The spine serves three main purposes within the human body – those of support, protection and mobility.

- A total of 33 bones make up the spine; each is separated from the next by spongy discs.

- Poor posture over time can lead to damage of the facet joints and discs.

- The spinal column protects the spinal cord, which carries nerves to all the organs, tissues and cells in the body.

- The spine has a natural curve and works best when this neutral spine alignment is maintained.

THE TRUNK MUSCLES AND MECHANISMS OF STABILITY

2

THE TRUNK MUSCLES AND THEIR FUNCTION

Before identifying the contraction and bracing principles, we need to look at the trunk muscles and their function in more detail.

RECTUS ABDOMINUS

The rectus abdominus muscle creates forward flexion. Putting this into a non-sport-specific context, its functional role is to get us out of bed or out of the bath, which begs the question why do

Table 2.1	The trunk muscles and their function	
Muscle	Position	Function
Rectus abdominus	Runs from the lower ribs and the 'xiphoid process' of the sternum to the pubic region. It has three fibrous bands running across it and a vertical band (the linea alba) splitting it in the centre. These bands help to create the 'six-pack' effect visible in athletes and those with low body fat.	Trunk flexion, sitting up from a lying position.
External obliques	Run from the lower eight ribs diagonally to insert at the iliac crest, rectus sheath and pelvic ligaments.	Trunk stability, rotation and some lateral flexion.
Internal obliques	Run from the front of the pelvic bone to the lower ribs and into the sheath covering the rectus muscle, at an angle to the external oblique.	Major role in trunk stability and lateral flexion.
Diaphragm	A flat muscle separating the chest cavity from the abdominal cavity.	Principle role in initiating breathing by contracting and creating a vacuum in the chest cavity, which draws air in.

Table 2.1 The trunk muscles and their function

Muscle	Position	Function
Transverse abdominus (the corset muscle)	Travels from the pelvic bones and spinal muscles horizontally to the sheath covering the rectus muscle.	Trunk stability, acts as a girdle, helps create forced expiration (e.g. laugh, cough etc.), pulls the tummy in.
Quadratus lumborum	Runs from the iliac crest of the pelvis to the lowest rib and sides of your lumbar spine.	Helps stabilise the spine against lateral movement. Involved in pure lateral flexion.
Multifidus	Originates in the lower cervical vertebrae (all thoracic and lumbar vertebrae) attaching to the 'spinous process' of all vertebrae extending from L5–C2 (see the section on 'The spine' on page 3).	Bilaterally extends the vertebral column, has a controlling effect in lateral flexion, assisting stability, and is attached to all vertebrae.
Psoas	Originates on the 'transverse process' of the lumbar vertebrae. Joins together with the iliacus, which attaches along the inner surface of the pelvis. Together they pass through the groin, attaching to the top of the front thigh.	Flexing the hips and lifting the legs.
Pelvic floor	Run from the tailbone (coccyx) to the pubic bone. The front and back passages (vagina, anus and urethra) are controlled by the sphincter muscles, which lie within the pelvic floor.	Has controlling effect when urinating.
Thoraco-lumbar fascia	A large sheet of fibrous tissue surrounding the back, covering the extensor muscles. It attaches medially to the thoracic, lumbar and sacral vertebrae, and laterally to the ribs.	
Intercostal muscles	The muscles that lie in between the ribs.	Help to elevate the ribs and assist in respiration, are constantly active during speech.
Spinal erectors	Attached to the sacral and iliac crest, form a thick tendonous muscle, which ultimately attaches to the lumbar and thoracic vertebrae.	Help to extend the spine and support it during flexion activities, such as bending forwards.

the majority of abdominal exercises we see described in various magazines spend so much time on conditioning this muscle. Is the quest to achieve the elusive six-pack that important?

The rectus abdominus is essentially made up of **fast-twitch fibres**, and to work this muscle effectively we need to look at the most appropriate training methods, movement ranges and resistances to use.

TRANSVERSE ABDOMINUS

The transverse abdominus contracts constantly during all movements, irrespective of direction. It is predominantly a **slow-twitch muscle** and when acting with the obliques helps draw the navel to the spine, working together with the **diaphragm** and pelvic floor muscles. It restricts movement by the thoraco-lumbar fascia and acts to increase **intra-abdominal pressure** (the pressure inside the abdominal cavity) when required – for example, when you might hold your breath if lifting a heavy object or indeed when you cough or laugh, as the transverse abdominus contracts during any forced expiration.

EXTERNAL AND INTERNAL OBLIQUES

The external oblique creates rotation of the trunk, which is vital in many racquet and field sports. It also assists in lateral flexion of the spine and, together with the internal oblique, helps stabilise the spine from lateral forces. This happens as a result of the muscles working in opposition due to their line of movement, positioning on the body and relative angle of pull.

QUADRATUS LUMBORUM

The inner portion of the quadratus lumborum is adjacent to the spine and we use this muscle to counter any situation where the spine is being forced to bend laterally (sideways), such as when holding a suitcase or a shopping bag in one hand. The outer portion works together with the obliques during lateral flexion.

PELVIC FLOOR

The pelvic floor muscles are important as they form part of the abdominal cavity and assist in maintaining intra-abdominal pressure. This pressure can assist stabilisation (as described later) and is important, especially when lifting. Yet when these muscles are deconditioned, say after pregnancy or following severe lower back pain, the sphincter muscles within the pelvic floor can lose control of the bladder and dribble urine. This can sometimes occur when you laugh or cough.

The stabiliser muscles

The stabiliser muscles are deep supporting muscles and have various roles in torso conditioning in relation to stability, posture and specific movement. Most of them are incorporated to some extent during abdominal work, but it is important not to overwork the superficial muscles to the detriment of the stabilisers when exercising. This can create muscle imbalances, and this in turn can cause postural problems or lead to an injury at a later date.

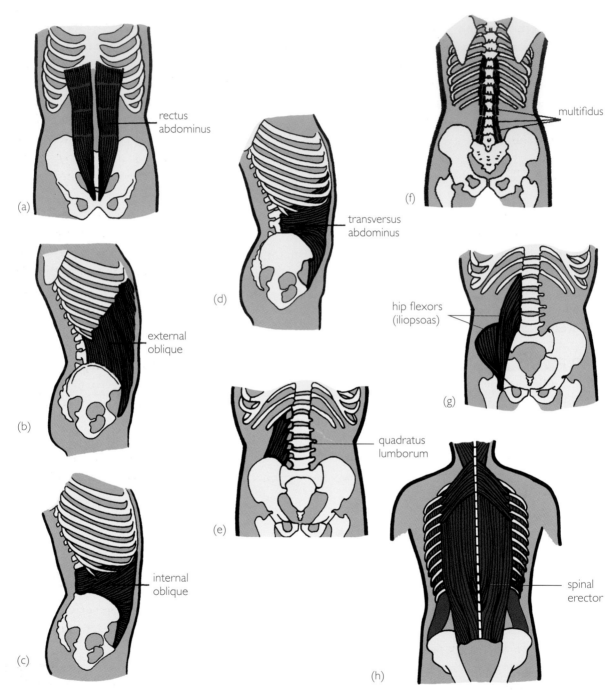

Figure 5 Muscle chart (a) rectus abdominus; (b) external oblique; (c) internal oblique; (d) transversus abdominus; (e) quadratus lumborum; (f) multifidus; (g) hip flexors (iliopsoas); (h) spinal erectors (erector spinae)

MULTIFIDUS

The multifidus helps to stiffen the spine to enable it to resist bending forces. It has a flattening effect on the lumbar curve, but following injury to the spine or after lower back pain this muscle will need to be retrained in order to restore its supporting ability.

SPINAL ERECTORS

The spinal erectors support the spine when bending forwards and backwards, and are responsible for extending the spine from a flexed position. They are powerful muscles but have low endurance and as such should be trained with this in mind. The greater the bending of the spine that occurs, and unless the muscles are firing correctly, the weaker they will become.

HIP FLEXORS

The hip flexors (psoas muscle group) flex the hip by either lifting the leg towards the trunk or, when flexing at the hip and keeping the back straight, pulling the trunk towards the hips. When the hip flexors contract, the attachments pull the lumbar vertebrae together, increasing the pressure on the discs. This can aggravate the lower back, causing pain, so make sure that when you are working the hip flexors the spine is stabilised and in a neutral position.

HOW A MUSCLE WORKS

A muscle can only contract and pull, it can never push. The fibres within each muscle overlap and pull together to create a force, which in turn pulls on the **tendons** and limbs. Consider your arm action when you drink from a glass. The muscles on the front of your upper arm contract and pull

your lower arm towards you, bending at the elbow, to lift the glass to your mouth. The muscles at the back of your upper arm relax to allow this movement to occur. If you look at an abdominal curl or sit-up exercise, the rectus abdominus pulls on the ribcage to bring it closer to the pelvis, lifting the shoulder blades off the floor. However, the rectus abdominus can only shorten so far, and when fully contracted there can be no further movement. For the spine to flex further, the hip flexors have to take over to pull the lumbar spine off the floor. The involvement of the hip flexors can aggravate the lower back, so when performing an abdominal curl you should try to minimise the hip-flexor involvement to reduce potential injury to the spine.

The trunk muscles fall into two categories:

1   those that are primarily responsible for stabilisation
2   those that are primarily responsible for movement.

However, the spine is not only supported by your trunk muscles – other mechanisms of stabilisation occur to initiate stability and maintain correct posture.[1,2,3,4]

INNER AND OUTER UNITS

We often refer to the deep stabiliser muscles as a 'corset' or 'girdle', which enables stabilisation and core stability. These muscles create what is also known as an 'inner unit' and, as we have seen, have a stiffening effect on the spine.[1,4] The inner unit muscles include the transverse abdominus, multifidus, pelvic floor, diaphragm and posterior fibres of the internal oblique. The transverse abdominus plays the major role among the inner unit muscles. It is activated prior to all movement and, in conjunction with the inner unit musculature, helps to stabilise the spine, allowing movement from the limbs. Poor conditioning of the inner unit stabilisers can lead to spinal injury and/or related pain.[3]

The primary role for the outer unit muscles is to initiate movement but some do have a stabilisation role. These are known as the global muscles and include the spinal erectors, external obliques, internal obliques, latissimus dorsi, gluteals, hamstrings and adductors. These work in unison with the inner unit musculature.[4]

As we have seen, stabilisation is achieved by the inner unit muscles, which help to co-ordinate a series of mechanisms to assist stabilisation.[4]

THORACO-LUMBAR FASCIA GAIN

As the transverse abdominus contracts, pulling in the abdominal wall, the internal oblique acts in synergy to create tension through the thoraco-lumbar fascia. This tension exerts a force on the lumbar spine helping to keep it supported and stable; this is called thoraco-lumbar fascia gain.[3,4] In principle, this process is not dissimilar to erecting a tent, in so much as the different guide ropes act together, 'as a team', to help support the main structure.

INTRA-ABDOMINAL PRESSURE

This is created following the contraction of the transverse abdominus, which pulls the abdominal wall inwards, increasing the pressure in the abdominal cavity, and forcing the diaphragm upwards and pelvic floor downwards. Holding your breath during a lifting, punching or throwing action will also increase this intra-abdominal pressure.

HYDRAULIC AMPLIFIER EFFECT

This occurs when the thoraco-lumbar fascia surrounding the back muscles and fascia forms a relative cylinder. During contraction of the back muscles a hydraulic effect occurs that assists extension of the spine from flexion.[4]

Let's put this into context and look at the movement that occurs when you lift a loaded wheelbarrow. Prior to the lift, you position yourself in the most suitable position so that your legs are next to the barrow's handles. As you bend your legs, you initiate contraction of the transverse abdominus and other core muscles to maintain stabilisation of the torso. There might be a partial forward lean, even though the legs would be performing the majority of the lift. To keep your erect posture, your back extensor muscles engage. At the point of lifting, your transverse abdominus braces, creating the thoraco-lumbar fascia gain (described above). Your intra-abdominal pressure (again, see above) would be increased both due to your transverse abdominus being contracted and possibly because you might need to hold your breath as you lift. As you lift, the forces encountered mean a hydraulic amplifier effect occurs, which enhances your back's stability. While your inner unit muscles are contracting, they are assisted by your outer unit muscles, namely the erectors, abdominals, glutes, hamstrings and back. As you wheel the wheelbarrow forwards your outer unit muscles assist with stabilisation and allow movement using the legs while the inner unit muscles work with them to counter any spinal movement.

All these mechanisms of stabilisation work as a result of the contractions of the inner unit muscles. Together with assistance from the outer unit musculature the result is a synergy of force that acts to overcome the external forces of the load to be lifted against gravity. This is essentially how core stability and stabilisation of the spine occurs.

SUMMARY

- A muscle can only contract and pull, it can never push.

- The trunk muscles fall into two categories, inner and outer – those that are primarily responsible for stabilisation and those that are primarily responsible for movement.

- Poor conditioning of the inner unit stabilisers can lead to spinal injury and/or related pain.

- Different mechanisms of stabilisation work as a result of the contractions of the inner unit muscles.

- The inner and outer unit muscles work together to create stabilisation of the spine and allow subsequent movement.

WHY IS CORE STABILITY IMPORTANT?

3

Improving your core stability can have a major knock-on effect. It can improve your power, agility and balance in sport. Strength and endurance gains in the core muscles can help improve your posture and are often fundamental to overcoming injuries to the lower back and spine. Correct bracing techniques can help you to achieve a flatter tummy, not by a reduction in fat, but rather thanks to the conditioning of the transverse muscle and other deep abdominal muscles, which, together with better posture, has a flattening effect on the trunk. Improved core stability also has a central role in controlling all movement. So, as you can see, core stability work should have a central role in all fitness programme design, as many exercises and movements will benefit. From a different perspective, any functional movement, whether related to a sporting action or a lifestyle activity, can be performed while applying core conditioning techniques and abdominal bracing. This has led to the term often associated with good core stability – 'functional fitness' (sometimes also known as 'functional movement').

FUNCTIONAL FITNESS

There has been much talk of functional fitness training in recent years, but all too often the term 'functional' is misunderstood. Functional fitness training can relate to either lifestyle exercises or sports training. To check whether an exercise is 'functional', ask yourself the following questions.

ARE THE BIO-MOTOR SKILLS BEING DEVELOPED USEFUL FOR THE DESIRED ACTIVITY?

The terms 'bio-motor' or 'life movement' skills refer to levels of power, strength, speed, endurance, co-ordination, agility, flexibility and balance, as described below.[5] To achieve functional gains you have to perform an exercise that utilises these principles relative to your sport or activity. To create an appropriate exercise plan for sport you should initially follow a basic conditioning routine. Then, gradually introduce exercises that are directly relative to movements in the sport itself. In other words, if you are following a training programme for squash, which involves many multi-directional lunge movements, it would make sense to incorporate multi-directional lunges using a bar or light dumbbells as opposed to using a leg press or leg extension machine, which also trains the legs.

DOES THE EXERCISE REQUIRE YOU TO MAINTAIN YOUR BALANCE?

Free-standing exercises tend to be functional in nature compared to machine-based exercises, where balance is not tested. When you perform a seated leg press on a machine there is little risk of losing your balance. You do not need to recruit your stabiliser muscles or adjust your centre of gravity, because your base of support remains unchanged as you sit on a fixed chair. However, when you perform a front squat using a barbell, you have to maintain your balance as your centre of gravity adjusts when you lower and raise the bar. You are forced to make tiny adjustments in your 'static' and 'dynamic' stabiliser systems in order to maintain your balance. The static stabilising system is working against the force of gravity to maintain an upright position, while the dynamic stabilising system controls the joint muscles to allow you to maintain the position of the bar while performing the desired movement.[6]

DOES THE EXERCISE REFLECT THE SPORTING MOVEMENT OR ACTIVITY?

For example, if you are a volleyball player and are training to improve your vertical jump height, you will obviously include leg exercises. Research suggests that by following generalised motor patterns of movement, the brain is assisted in developing **motor skills** relative to that final movement.[6,7] The brain remembers the movements more than the specific muscle contractions. As a result you should look at which movements, not just which muscles, are relative to a specific sporting action. So, with volleyball training, you should progress from basic muscular strength training exercises like a classic squat, to more dynamic movements like power cleans, and then introduce related jump exercises including resisted jumps using weighted vests and resisted jumping. These movement patterns resemble the end movement and so will train the nerves and muscles in a directly similar way to desired movement itself.

IS IT AN ISOLATED OR COMPOUND MOVEMENT?

To be effective, we need to move away from the idea that you should train a specific muscle solely on the basis of aesthetics (that is, to increase its size). We should consider using **compound exercises** that train groups of muscles, rather than **isolation exercises** that focus on a single muscle. Consider this: when you perform a lying triceps extension you will train the triceps, but performing a triceps dip off the end of a bench will train the triceps, shoulders and inner chest muscles. In addition, this is much closer to the kind of movement you might perform during your day, such as pushing down on the arms of a chair to help you to stand up when you have to answer the front door.

Functional fitness training for non-sports people integrates lifestyle or functional movement into a training programme – that is, it creates exercises that replicate activities you do on a daily basis, such as lifting shopping into the boot of your car or standing up from a seated position. When introducing functional fitness, either when working on your own or when teaching a class, it is wise to work with just body weight exercises rather than additional equipment, so that you can focus attention on the desired movement.

If you are a sportsperson, or are involved with training sportspeople, introducing multi-plane movements such as multi-directional lunges makes sense. But for the general population even certain conventional exercises might not have been mastered. Take, for example, a squat technique. Many participants will not lower their torso sufficiently to resemble a functional squat (a sitting position). This is because there is no guide to the lowering position. A functional fitness training technique would use adjustable-height benches so that the participants can actually 'sit down' and stand up again. For those participants who find squatting to a seated position difficult, you would need to raise the bench height slightly so they are performing a quarter-squat to sit on the bench. As they become more confident with this movement, you can lower the bench height gradually until the height resembles that of a chair or toilet seat. Consequently they will be training their muscles and their balance in a directly functional way. Everyone has to go to the toilet, therefore it is a **functional exercise!**

The goal with functional training is to combine body awareness with normal 'life' movements in a co-ordinated and structured way. Rather than focus on isolation exercises that train specific muscles, we train 'holistically', integrating groups of muscles throughout a movement that challenges your balance, improves your stabilisation and enhances your co-ordination. Before you embark on this holistic or integrated training process it is necessary to understand the science behind integrated training and this begins with the **Kinetic chain**.

The Kinetic chain is an **integrated functional unit** comprising muscles, tendons, ligaments, **fascia**, nerves and bones. All these elements need to work in harmony for optimum movement and performance. This **synergy** of working together is known as **neuro-muscular efficiency**. If there are imbalances within this unit, problems can occur, such as decreased performance, **muscle trauma** and injury. An imbalance in muscles whereby, for example, one muscle group is weak, might lead to other muscles having to compensate in maintaining or performing a movement. This is known as **synergistic dominance**.[19]

This imbalance disrupts the efficiency of the neuro-muscular system and the Kinetic chain is compromised. It is necessary to try to recondition the weakened muscle through appropriate training to help restore the balance in the Kinetic chain.

Regardless of your goals, let us not forget that all movement originates from the core and thus good core stabilisation is fundamental for all movement.

POSTURE

Good posture ensures that movements can be performed with minimal strain to the joints, ligaments, tendons and muscles, and that there is no compression on the internal organs, nerves or blood vessels. A balanced posture with a neutral spine reduces the stresses to the vertebrae and surrounding muscles and ligaments, allowing normal movement to occur without pain or discomfort. Your posture is controlled by an automatic mechanism in the brain, which responds to the feedback from messages sent by your muscles. For example, if you lean slightly to one side, the nerves associated with the muscles and ligaments send messages to your brain, which then sends out messages to other muscles to help correct this movement or stance by telling the muscles to contract to regain your posture or balance. Poor posture over a period of time can lead to disc problems (see page 4), but also to osteoarthritis in later life and, if not corrected, poor posture can exacerbate the postural conditions outlined below.

> **Posture**
>
> Posture is the alignment of the joints and muscles to assist function.

KYPHOSIS

Often, poor posture is related to muscle imbalances. Over time this can lead to joint and spinal problems. Kyphosis is an extreme example of this. Excessive slouching can cause the chest muscles to shorten and they will eventually pull on the shoulder girdle, causing a 'rounding of the shoulders' – kyphosis. This can sometimes be seen in a gym environment, where certain members train their chests excessively and have created very strong chest muscles, which have shortened. Their back training routine is not as prominent, though, and the muscles there are weak and stretched. This imbalance can lead to a rounding of the shoulders.

LORDOSIS

Lordosis is another common postural problem. It occurs when the lumbar curve becomes more pronounced. Typically, when viewed from the side, this means that the belly sticks out to the front and the buttocks to the rear. Poor abdominal tension is one causal factor, as are tight hip flexor muscles and weak back muscles. If corrective exercises are not incorporated, together with the appropriate stretches, an increased lordotic spinal curve can lead to increased lower back pain and disc problems.

SCOLIOSIS

Scoliosis is a condition in which the spine curves to one side. In many cases this occurs in childhood but goes untreated, causing problems later on. Obvious signs might be uneven shoulders, leaning

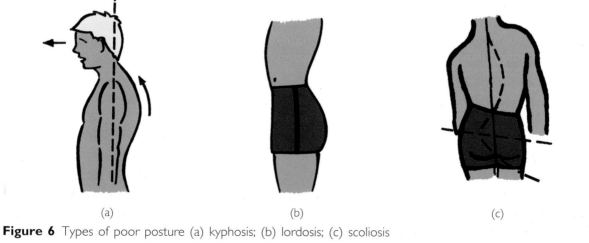

(a)	(b)	(c)

Figure 6 Types of poor posture (a) kyphosis; (b) lordosis; (c) scoliosis

to one side or having a prominent shoulder blade. Adolescent girls are more likely than boys to suffer from serious scoliosis but whether this is due to growth spurts, hormonal imbalances or connective tissue disorders is uncertain.

CAUSES OF POOR POSTURE

Some of the causes of poor posture include:

- foot problems
- incorrect footwear
- being overweight
- weak muscles
- injuries
- pregnancy
- poor diet.

Testing your posture

To test your posture, work with a friend or partner and use a vertical reference such as a plumb line or door frame. If you were to drop a plumb line down from the ceiling, or stand sideways on to a door frame, the line should go through your head, ear, elbow, hip and knee and finish just in front of your ankle joint. When looking at your pelvis from the side, the top point or 'rim' – that is, the point that is furthest forward – should be directly above the pubic bone.

Look at your partner from behind. Get them to stand with their feet 10 cm apart and view their body up and down. Check their feet to see if they have either a high arch or flat feet, as these conditions might cause compensatory effects elsewhere. Look at the creases at the back of their knees and under their buttocks to check they are similar and the same level. Look at the pelvis and hips to see if one side is higher than the other. Look at the spine to see if there is any twist or lean

to one side. Check the shoulder blades to see that one shoulder is not dominant or whether one looks higher than the other. Finally, check the shoulders and neck to look for any tilting.

The adverse effects of overworking muscles

If a muscle is overworked it will shorten, become overactive and, finally, become fibrous and not return to full length. This can have a detrimental effect on both posture and muscle balancing.

One way to test your posture is to stand upright next to a wall. Your head, shoulder blades and buttocks should be in contact with the wall and your heels approximately 5–10 cm away. Place your hand, or ask your partner to place their hand, in the gap between the wall and your lower back. This should be a relatively snug fit. If you have quite a lot of space between your hand and your lower back you have an increased lumbar curve.

It is worth recording any 'abnormalities' or 'weak areas' on a sheet so that you can compare your results when you check again after six months of training.

Before embarking on a training programme it is important first to identify your posture or alignment when performing certain exercises or movements. The positioning and alignment of your ankles, limbs, pelvis, torso and head throughout the movement will identify any **postural deviations** caused by muscular imbalances you might have.

Muscular imbalances occur when one muscle is tight or weak in comparison with its opposing muscle group. For example, if the hip flexors are tight and the gluteal muscles are weak, this can cause the pelvis to tip forwards causing a lordotic curve in the spine. Before performing an exercise such as a squat, it would be important to establish a better postural alignment of the pelvis. Appropriate stretching exercises to reduce tightness in the hip flexor muscles, together with the correct strengthening exercises for the gluteals, hamstrings and lower back, will help to improve the alignment of the pelvis.

There are different ways to test for postural alignment and specific muscle imbalances. An example of a **screening test** is shown below:

OVERHEAD SQUAT TEST
STARTING POSITION AND ACTION

- To perform this test, begin in a relaxed position with feet shoulder-width apart and parallel.
- Extend your arms straight above your head with upper arms next to your ears.
- Perform the squat exercise by bending the knees and lowering yourself down to a near

sitting position before straightening your legs and returning to the start position.
- As you perform this exercise, try to ensure your knees are in line with your feet but that they do not go over and in front of your toes as you squat down.
- The hips should remain level and, as you lower yourself down, your arms should remain in the same line as the start position, extending above your head.
- You should get a qualified trainer to observe as you perform this task and get them to look at any postural deviations, starting at the ankles and working their way up to the head.
- The trainer should observe you performing repeated movements or repetitions, viewed from the front, the side and from the rear to assess all the possible imbalances and you should perform 10–15 repetitions.
- You could ask a friend to observe you, but they might not identify all the areas of misalignment and thus miss potential muscular imbalances you might have.

Table 3.1	Tips for improved posture
Technique	Action
Correct lifting techniques	Bend your knees when lifting something, and avoid bending your back as you lift. Brace your abdominals and use your legs to provide the power when lifting. When carrying objects, keep them close to you. Try not to overload shoulder bags as this will cause you to lean to one side when carrying.
Sleeping techniques	Avoid sleeping on your front. If necessary, when sleeping on your side, place a pillow between your thighs.
Using the telephone	Use a speaker-phone or earpiece so that you do not have to balance the receiver between your neck and shoulder.
When sitting	Knees should be level with or just above the hips. Place a rolled towel or firm cushion behind you to provide lumbar support.
When walking	Walk tall, keeping your head up and your shoulders back.

This is one of the most common screening tests used when identifying muscular imbalances as it identifies many potential 'weak' areas within one exercise. Having performed the movement in front of a trainer or colleague, some of the observations might be that your feet flatten as you squat or even that you come up on to your toes, or perhaps your knees move closer together. Maybe your hips tilt to the left or right as you lower down or maybe you cannot maintain your arms extended above your head and they come forwards in front of your head. These are all signs of muscular imbalances and can be potentially explained in Table 3.2.

If your soleus muscle (the muscle behind your ankle and at the rear of your lower leg) is tight, you will not have full range of movement around the ankle joint and so you might not be able to squat down without rising up on to your toes. If your knees come closer together as you squat, it might be that your adductor muscles are tight or that they are trying to assist in the movement because other muscles, such as your quadriceps and gluteal muscles, are relatively weak. Perhaps you have a stronger right or left leg, which you try to use more when performing the movement. This can cause a tilting of the pelvis. If you cannot maintain your arms in an overhead position as they drop down and forwards, this is likely to be because you have much stronger and tighter chest muscles in comparison to your back muscles such as the rhomboid group or infraspinatus.

Screening tests are useful when embarking on a new training plan as it is important not to over-train muscles that might already be tight. For example, if someone has very strong and tight hip

Table 3.2	Screening exercise test – squat with arms overhead		
Area	Observation	Possible reason	Possible rectifying actions
Ankles	Heels come off the floor	Tight soleus	Stretch soleus muscle
Knees	Knees abduct	Tight glutes/piriformus	• Stretch piriformis and gluteus medius • Strengthen adductors
Knees	Knees adduct	Tight adductors/weak glutes	• Stretch adductors • Strengthen glutes
Pelvis	Pelvis tilts forwards	Tight hip flexors/weak glutes	• Stretch hip flexors • Strengthen glutes
Pelvis	Pelvis tilts back	Tight glutes/weak hip flexors	Stretch glutes
Pelvis	Pelvis tilts to one side	Stronger/weaker muscles in one leg	Apply flexibility and strengthening exercises accordingly
Shoulders	Arms fall forwards	Tight chest muscles, tight latissimus dorsi and/or weak rhomboids/teres minor/infraspinatus	• Stretch chest and latissimus muscles • Strengthen rhomboids and teres minor/infraspinatus
Head/neck	Head pushes forwards	Tight neck flexors (sternocleidomastoid)	Strengthen neck extensor muscles

flexors causing an increased lordotic curve in the spine, it would be foolish to perform leg lifts and/or abdominal crunch movements that could exacerbate the situation. A stretching programme to reduce the tightness in the hip flexor muscles, together with core strengthening exercises for the torso and also for the weaker gluteal muscles, would be the solution.

SUMMARY

- Core stability can improve your power, agility and balance in sport, and can help improve your posture, helping to overcome the effects of injuries to the lower back and spine.

- Improved core stability has a holistic role in all movement.

- The term 'functional exercise' describes the integration of movements that relate directly to lifestyle activities, or sports-specific movement.

- Posture is the alignment of the joints and muscles to assist function.

- Kyphosis is a condition where there is an increased thoracic curve.

- Lordosis is a condition where there is an increased lumbar curve.

- Scoliosis is the curvature of the spine laterally.

- The Kinetic chain is an integrated functional unit comprising muscles, tendons, ligaments, fascia, nerves and bones. All these elements need to work in synergy for neuromuscular efficiency.

WHO CAN BENEFIT FROM IMPROVED CORE STABILITY?

4

Improvements in core stability are of benefit to everyone, from new exercisers to regular fitness enthusiasts, from high-level athletes looking for that extra 'edge' to the elderly or those recovering from injury.

Include core stability exercises in any exercise programme. All too often, basic exercise programmes focus solely on machine-based gym exercises. While it is important for the new exerciser to train on equipment that requires minimal stabilisation and thought (as the technique needs to be learned first) as soon as the exerciser feels confident performing the exercises then adaptations should be made to encourage more functional movement. The introduction of free-weight exercises is one way to encourage the engagement of stabilisation muscles. As confidence grows, more advanced drills can be introduced.

If you look at various training regimes it can appear that they apply totally different principles. However, if you look a little closer they are actually very similar.

Firm foundations

Every time you create an exercise regime, think of the human body as a house. It doesn't matter how strong your brickwork and joists are if your foundations are not solid. A house built without firm foundations will have no support and has a strong chance of collapsing. Similarly, if an exercise regime does not incorporate core stability work, you won't see optimal strength and conditioning gains.

If you consider the four different disciplines of dance, martial arts, sport and yoga (as shown in Figure 7), all have varying amounts of rhythm, fluidity, focus and applied power, depending on the discipline. You might think that the abdominal training within each discipline would be very different, and to a certain extent it is. First, bracing and stabilisation are important parts of dance training and yoga, with many positions and

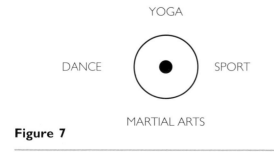

Figure 7

stances that require exceptional balance and which therefore incorporate stabilisation conditioning techniques.

Much of the appropriate training in martial arts also comes from indirect training – for example, when 'taking' or 'throwing' a punch one needs to brace or tense the abdominals in order to minimise any pain felt or to gather optimum power respectively.

Now think about a tennis serve, volleyball spike or chest pass. Without optimal bracing or contraction of the transverse abdominus, albeit with a small but rapid contraction of the rectus abdominus, there would be no power. We often think of the transverse abdominus as the muscle that controls intra-abdominal pressure and assists with forced expiration – well, think of the vocalisation and functional grunting you hear at a ladies' singles tennis match!

So, as you can see, the transverse abdominus and deep core muscles are highly active in all four of the disciplines described. The inner circle reminds us that while the specific training for all four disciplines will vary, there will still be a core requirement of abdominal training that is very similar.

THE ELDERLY

Research indicates that it is never too late to start exercising. Cardio-vascular and strength gains, together with body fat reduction, improved posture and greater mobility have all been achieved by people in their sixties, seventies and eighties. However, an important issue when devising a conditioning programme for an elderly person is that of balance. Injuries sustained from falls as a result of poor balance are the leading cause of deaths in people aged 70 and over, yet this figure can be drastically reduced with the appropriate dynamic conditioning and stabilisation activities. Interspersing conditioning exercises, which strengthen the legs and lower back, with balance and stabilisation drills, is one answer. Introducing exercises using stability balls is another. Incorporating dynamic movements like balancing on one leg or throwing and catching a ball is a very effective way of training the stabiliser and neutraliser muscles of the trunk. Other functional activities would include t'ai chi and even dancing – anything where balance and mobility is tested, provided that the trunk muscles are actively working to assist balance and to protect the spine.

PREGNANCY

During pregnancy, the growing child causes the abdominal muscles to stretch so that its growth is not restricted in any way. The large muscle at the

Sport's foundation

Core stability exercises should be incorporated into training for all sports and life in general. It is only when we look into the different requirements of each discipline that we need to be more specific in our training. With this in mind, if we can replicate the movements of a sporting action, applying the appropriate resistance in a controlled manner, we will be on the way to training the muscle functionally and directly, relative to that sport. If we can enhance core conditioning within the training programme, then increases in power and agility will follow.

Figure 8 Diastasis in pregnancy

front of the torso, the rectus abdominus, has the ability to stretch vertically but its horizontal, or lateral, stretching ability is limited. As the child grows, the rectus abdominus actually splits in the centre, along the linear alba. This process is called diastasis. The extent of this split is dependent on many factors, such as having a large baby, or twins or triplets, in comparison to the size of the woman's pelvis. The diastasis is often enlarged in women who seldom exercise and whose abdominals are relatively weak, or in those women who have not followed a conditioning routine for their abdominals following a previous pregnancy.

Doing abdominal exercises during pregnancy is perfectly fine, but after the third month (first trimester), pregnant women should avoid exercising when lying flat on their backs. When a pregnant woman lies on her back, the weight of the baby puts pressure on the large vein that returns blood to the heart, and the artery that carries blood to the baby. This could cause reduced blood flow and lead to dizziness, light-headedness, or even possibly fainting, and potentially cause problems for the child. Pelvic tilting and abdominal hollowing or bracing exercises (drawing the navel towards the spine) can be performed in a

seated or standing position, as feels comfortable. Exercises should also be avoided in a prone, or face down, position as the pressure will be too great on the foetus. However, abdominal exercises on all fours are fine, unless the weight of the child causes the spine to be pulled out of neutral alignment and pain is felt in the lower back. Abdominal hollowing and bracing movements can be performed lying on the side as this puts less strain on the back.

If you have access to a gym environment with adjustable cable machines, it is perfectly fine to incorporate resistance training as long as you have used these machines previously and before becoming pregnant.

If you are confident of correct posture and muscle bracing then rotational, pulling or pressing exercises using the adjustable cables are fine. Again it is important to remember the emphasis is to work with a resistance that causes mild fatigue and, as you progress through the pregnancy, modifications to these exercises will need to be in place. Other body weight exercises are also suitable providing your technique is not compromised by your 'bump' and that you are sensible. It would be wise to consult with a trainer for a personalised programme specific to your own needs rather than just do a few exercises for the sake of it. However, a general programme can be found on page 235 in Part five.

Following childbirth, pelvic floor exercises (the pulling inwards and tightening of the pelvic floor muscles) and abdominal hollowing can be introduced within the first week (three to four days after giving birth), provided there were no complications. These contractions can be practised throughout the day to help restore tone to the pelvic floor and abdominal muscles. Exercises such as pelvic tilting and lower-back stretches to help reduce any exaggerated lordotic curve can be introduced during the first few weeks. Other movement-related exercises, such as rotations and trunk flexion (see pages 47–49), should be avoided until the rectus abdominus muscle gap has narrowed to approximately 2–3 cm (this can be measured by using your index and middle fingers together, and pressing them gently into the gap).

SUMMARY

- Core stability training is of benefit to all regular exercisers – without it, strength and conditioning gains are affected.

- The introduction of free-weight exercises is one way to encourage a new exerciser to engage his/her stabilisation muscles.

- The elderly can also benefit from performing movements that encourage core stability, and this can help improve their balance. Injuries sustained from falls as a result of poor balance are the leading cause of deaths in people aged 70 and over.

- Abdominal exercises that work on the pelvic floor muscles and core stability are of benefit both during and after pregnancy if sensible precautions are taken.

HOW TO ACHIEVE CORE STABILITY

5

The biggest problem when teaching core stability, both in a one-to-one setting and group exercise environment, is that participants in general have very poor muscle awareness and many cannot identify with all of the principles.

People's ability to identify and then contract the transverse abdominus still seems to be the biggest limiting factor. Remember that this is a learned process! To initiate the transverse contraction, you begin by drawing the navel inwards, towards the spine. A useful analogy would be to imagine you are trying on a pair of jeans and you have to pull in your abdominals to zip up the jeans. Visualisation terminology might be to 'think thin'. As you do this, engage the pelvic floor muscles by pulling in and tightening. Aim to contract the muscles of the anus and then initiate contraction of other muscles around the vagina or penis, much like the contraction that occurs if you are stopping yourself from urinating. This contraction should then be held while maintaining correct breathing throughout.

In a group environment, it is imperative to educate each participant as to exactly what is supposed to happen and what they are supposed to feel. One of the best ways to do this is using a hands-on approach so that each participant will feel their muscles contract as they aim to tighten and brace the core stabilisers. On a one-to-one level, hold your participant's abdomen with them so that their fingers press just above the hips with finger tips approximately 5 cm away from the navel. By pressing this area you are most likely to feel the transverse abdominus contraction. If you are working in a group, or are on your own, position yourself so that the spine is in a neutral position, either lying, seated or standing, and then initiate the transverse abdominus and pelvic floor contractions, allowing your fingers to feel the abdominals tighten as you do so.

Important

This careful and monitored teaching of the basic contraction of the core stabilisers is vital, as otherwise some participants will not identify with the contraction required and will just breathe in and hold their breath!

Having identified and learned the appropriate bracing and stabilisation techniques, the next stage is to apply these with varying degrees of difficulty. This can be through holding the spine in neutral while the limbs perform certain movements, or maintaining a neutral spine as the entire body is rotated or moved.

It is important to train the stabilisation muscles first, as these are invariably slow twitch (have greater endurance) as opposed to the superficial, global muscles, which are predominantly fast twitch (have less endurance, but have greater capacity for growth). This means that the global muscles will not tire as quickly. Once you, or your class, have grasped the mechanics of stabilisation, and understand the relative intensity and duration of contraction required, you should look at functional exercises that involve movement bias and varying degrees of functionality. These exercises train the muscles in a similar movement to a specific sporting action, requiring elements of flexion, extension and rotation.

UNSTABLE BASE TRAINING

When you embark on a core stability training programme, for a class or for yourself, you must remember that many exercises will be brand new and will therefore require careful description, demonstration and checking. The learning curve time you need to allow is longer than you may be used to, to make sure the necessary information has been understood.

As muscle awareness improves and stabilisation techniques can be performed with relevant ease, only then is it time to progress. This means looking at specific goals and applying the abdominal conditioning exercises accordingly. For instance, you could incorporate proprioceptive drills (those that train balance and dynamic movement, see below). You can include certain

equipment aids such as stability balls and wobble boards to achieve this.

The right focus
Remember that abdominal muscles are active in almost every movement we make, so they can be trained to a certain extent in all activities as long as the focus is appropriate.

EQUIPMENT

Stability balls, wobble boards and Reebok Core Boards™ can be very effective and fun ways of training core stability. They require the stabiliser and neutraliser muscles to be activated, to perform movement without losing form or balance (the neutraliser muscles work in synergy with other muscles, counter-contracting to maintain form).

This sort of equipment can be very beneficial from a sports-specific perspective because if you can successfully apply a specific sporting movement using an unstable base, your core muscles will be trained to maintain form. As a result, you are creating a solid foundation to work from when you apply the same movement when doing the sport. A stability ball can train the abdominal muscles through a greater range than they are normally worked, and because of the instability the core muscles are required to be active throughout all movements to remain balanced. Wobble boards and Reebok Core Boards™ both have their advantages, as many different exercises can be performed that train dynamic balance and require bracing techniques to maintain a controlled posture. (See pages 91–97 for exercises that use this equipment.)

PROPRIOCEPTION

Proprioception is the way that the body reacts and recovers from being unbalanced. Any external force, such as gravity, a strong wind or an unstable floor, can cause the body to lose its balance for a moment. The muscles are constantly providing feedback to the brain about their surroundings and forces acting on them. The brain sends messages via the nerves to the muscles on how to respond and when. This two-way process of internal feedback using sensory awareness and muscle and joint sensitivity creates this complex system of proprioception.

Think about walking up some stairs carrying a heavy load. The increased weight might throw out your natural centre of gravity slightly, causing you to have to adjust your stance or movement to stay balanced. If this fails at any point you might need to hold on to the wall or take a step back, for example. Supposing you are out walking your dog along the sea front, a gust of wind disrupts your balance and you grab hold of a railing. This external force of wind acts against your body, causing your muscles to have to 'think' to stay balanced. This 'neuro-muscular awareness' can be improved through training. Training on an

Figure 9 Bus surfing

unstable base can teach your stabiliser and neutraliser muscles to respond rapidly, improving your overall balance and co-ordination.

Putting this into context, think about the balance and proprioceptive training that occurs when you put your socks on one at a time while standing up. Then consider the same movement, but performed with both eyes closed. Incorporating balance drills into your life can make training more fun, and it is an excellent way to apply the stabilisation control you need to a fully functional activity.

PROGRESSING

As your stability training progresses, and you start to do body resistance exercises, external resistance exercises or use an unstable base (stability ball etc.), you should start to introduce stability

---

Bus surfing

Why not try this functional core stability exercise the next time you are on a bus? Quite simply, the task is to stand up on a bus, or on the tube, without hanging on to anything, bracing your abdominal stabilisation muscles throughout, to assist your balance.

If you are good nobody will notice. If you are OK at it you will look like a surfer. If you are bad ... well it's a great way to make friends!

No limits

Once you have got to grips with the principles of core stability and can see how beneficial specific exercises can be, then the only limiting factor is your own imagination!

exercises to your resistance training programme. Your programme should intersperse machine-based exercises with stabilisation exercises. So, in your workout, gradually replace some of the machine exercises with free-weight exercises. Then incorporate functional strength movements and resistance exercises using a stability ball to encourage functional strength and stability gains.

Abdominal exercises can be split into three distinct camps:

- training for aesthetics
- training for specificity
- training for core stability.

The latter two feed off each other, as, within a sporting context especially, specificity of training often requires core stability awareness in order to perform a certain movement. Progressive resistance can be applied but the resistance should be geared towards the activity itself. If aesthetics (looking good) is the goal, then a combination of factors is needed. Correct diet and **aerobic** exercise are the first priority, to reduce body fat stores,

while training needs to focus on hypertrophy (increasing muscle size), and so progressive resistance and **overload principles** should be used. Different forms of resistance can include **cables, resistance tubes**, medicine balls and weights (see pages 105–123).

SUMMARY

- To contract the transverse abdominus, begin by drawing the navel inwards, towards the spine, in a hollowing or bracing action: 'think thin'!

- When you are training the abdominals it is important to train the stabilisation muscles first, as these will tire less easily.

- Unstable base exercises, using stability balls and wobble boards, require the stabiliser and neutraliser muscles to be activated to perform movement without losing form or balance.

- Proprioception is the way that the body reacts and recovers from being unbalanced.

HOW TO OVERLOAD A MUSCLE

6

HOW A MUSCLE GROWS

When you work a muscle the stimulus or force acting on it causes a breaking down of the muscle proteins and forms tiny tears in the **muscle fibre** and connective tissue. During the rest period new proteins are built up and the connective tissue repaired. This causes the muscle fibres to grow back thicker and stronger. This increase in size is the result of an increase in the number of filaments within the fibre bundle and an increase of muscle proteins. This increase of cross-sectional size is called **hypertrophy**.

Hypertrophy depends on many factors, including the type of training, diet, rest periods and genetics of the person in question. The emphasis with stabilisation work is endurance; however, in certain sporting disciplines it can be argued that using strength training with the stabilising muscles is also important, to help deal with the intensities placed on the body when doing the sport.

STRENGTH, ENDURANCE AND POWER

When training a muscle or muscle group you should always do so with the desired outcome in mind. Is your goal a sports-specific one? Are you training for strength and power, or to enhance function and/or muscular endurance?

Muscular strength is the force required by a muscle to overcome a resistance. Maximum strength is the ability to perform one complete **repetition** of an exercise.

Muscular endurance is the ability or capacity of a muscle to repeat a movement continuously before it tires – for example, performing a bridge-position exercise and maintaining perfect form for a long period of time or, alternatively, being able to perform an endless amount of sit-ups on a stability ball.

Power is the ability to overcome a resistance at speed or with force – for instance, when throwing a medicine ball.

CONTRACTION EMPHASIS

There are three types of contraction available to the muscles. You will usually be performing exercises that are either movement based (**isotonic contractions**) or static (**isometric contractions**). **Isokinetic contractions** generally require advanced machines that control the speed of movement when force is applied.

Isokinetic

The isokinetic machines found in advanced sports gyms and laboratories keep the movement speed constant regardless of the force applied by the muscles. This can enable greater recruitment of muscle fibres to perform the movement. It is unlikely that you will encounter any of these machines in most everyday health clubs, yet isokinetic principles can be incorporated into some of the 'hands-on' and partner-work exercises, provided that great care is taken to avoid any unnecessary injury.

Isometric

During an isometric exercise the muscle stays the same length while contracting, so there is no shortening or lengthening when it contracts against a fixed resistance. (There is no change in the joint angle either.) This is what happens to your deep abdominal muscles during all 'bracing' movements. This contraction also happens with many balancing or holding exercises, such as the abdominal bridge (see page 61) or partner twists (see page 125). While excellent strength and/or endurance gains can be made with isometric work, these gains are only achieved through that specific range of movement. When you perform isometric work during stabilisation exercises, correct breathing is vital to avoid an increase in **blood pressure**.

Important
Never hold your breath during an isometric contraction. Breathe steadily to maintain adequate oxygen levels throughout.

Isotonic

An isotonic exercise is where there is muscle shortening or lengthening as you lift or lower a resistance, and there is movement about the joint(s) involved. For example, if you are performing a sit-up movement, the rectus abdominus and hip flexor muscles will shorten and create flexion of the trunk and, to a certain extent, of the hips. Isotonic movements fall into two types: concentric and eccentric contractions.

A **concentric contraction** is where a muscle shortens against a resistance – for example, the biceps muscle will shorten and the angle of the elbow will reduce as a weight is lifted against gravity. If you consider an abdominal exercise, the rectus abdominus shortens as you begin an abdominal curl.

An **eccentric contraction** is the reverse of a concentric contraction and occurs when a muscle lengthens against a resistance. During the lowering phase of a bicep curl, the joint angle of the elbow increases and the bicep muscle lengthens as the weight is lowered, against gravity, back to the start position.

Muscles are 30–40 per cent stronger in the eccentric phase of a movement. It is often effective to set up an exercise in which the participant cannot perform a full rep (i.e. both eccentric and concentric movements) by assisting the concentric phase but by controlling the eccentric movement under load, e.g. eccentric curls, partner-assisted full press-ups.

RESISTANCE

The most common type of resistance used is constant resistance, where the load doesn't change (for instance, body weight, a barbell or dumbbells). However, it is important to think about where the

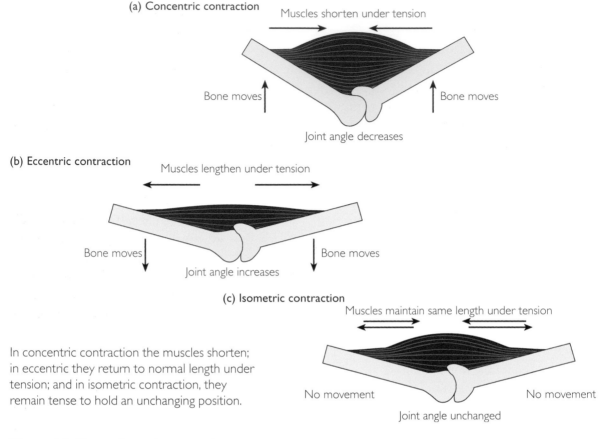

(a) Concentric contraction

Muscles shorten under tension

Bone moves

Bone moves

Joint angle decreases

(b) Eccentric contraction

Muscles lengthen under tension

Bone moves

Bone moves

Joint angle increases

(c) Isometric contraction

Muscles maintain same length under tension

No movement

No movement

Joint angle unchanged

In concentric contraction the muscles shorten; in eccentric they return to normal length under tension; and in isometric contraction, they remain tense to hold an unchanging position.

Figure 10 Types of muscle contraction

resistance is in relation to your movement, and whether gravity affects this. If you are using resistance equipment such as body bars, hand weights, medicine balls and so on, gravity plays an important role – that is, because gravity always acts as a downward force, you must work against gravity, moving in an upward direction, to work your muscles effectively. Alternatively if using your own body weight you must lift or push your body upwards against a fixed object (for example, pull-ups on a bar or press-ups on the floor). However, sometimes when using your own body weight the resistance will not be sufficient to

achieve a suitable overload. If this is the case, you must increase the effort by adding extra resistance or looking into additional methods of achieving **overload** (see pages 30–36).

Any exercise that requires the resistance to be moved 'across' gravity will place the overload on a muscle other than the one that is creating the movement. This is usually a stabilising muscle working isometrically to maintain the limb position against gravity (for example, performing a chest-press movement while standing, using dumbbells instead of a cable machine).

Variable-resistance exercises can be performed using a 'variable-resistance tool' such as a resistance tube (a flexible tube that causes resistance to increase as it is stretched). Also, certain types of weight machine, which use pulleys on a 'cam' system, have a variable-resistance effect. With this type of machine, the weight, in effect, increases or decreases during the movement phase as the pulley travels over the parabola-shaped cam.

The advantage of using an adjustable cable pulley machine is that you can perform many movements while standing, so the direction of movement is not restricted by the forces of gravity. However, as you move the pulley handle and so lift the weight, **cross-gravitational forces** are created that pull on your torso, trying to move it out of position. The trunk stabilisers have to contract sufficiently to maintain correct form and allow you to complete the repetition. As a result, many more muscles are 'called into action' than is the case when using a bench or fixed weight machine.

PROGRESSIVE OVERLOAD

In order for a muscle to respond successfully – whether to achieve endurance benefits or gains in strength and/or size – the overload or resistance placed upon it has to continually challenge the muscle. As the muscle responds, it gets stronger and/or has better endurance, so if the overload remains the same the muscle will not be stimulated optimally. This is why the amount of resistance used or the duration of the exercise needs to be continually increased in order to provide a suitable overload for the muscle. This form of continual intensity change is classed as **progressive overload**.

Increased overload to the abdominal muscles will vary according to the level of specificity required. Unless the activity is sports related and requires specific resistance or speed-related movements that require optimal bracing and stabilisation, the usual way to train the stabilisation muscles is to keep the intensity relatively low but to increase the duration, to create an endurance training effect.

Neuro-muscular adaptation

When the brain has to learn a new task or skill, such as a new exercise, the nerve pathways that tell the muscle to contract need to be developed. Depending on the complexity of the movement, this motor unit development might require some practice. This is known as **neuro-muscular adaptation**.

When introducing stabilisation exercises into your workout regime, the number of exercises to incorporate, together with the frequency with which they are to be performed, will vary from person to person – everyone has different goals, time restraints and fitness levels. As with any form of training, the most important thing is to blend the new stabilisation drills into your current regime when you are ready, remembering not to introduce too much too soon or increase the relative intensity of any drill before you are fully able to progress.

REPETITIONS/SEQUENCING

The number of repetitions and the order in which they are performed will increase muscle overload by working similar or opposite muscle groups in sets of repetitions. The following are descriptions of some common methods.

Pyramiding

Performing a set of exercises, then increasing the resistance and performing a second set with fewer repetitions. On the third set increase the resistance again and perform this set again with fewer repetitions. This kind of training is usually geared to the development of strength and size. Rather than increasing the resistance, you could increase the duration to create the overload.

Super-setting

Super-sets involve, for example, performing a set of exercises on one muscle group, and then immediately performing exercises on another muscle group. This works with opposing muscle groups, such as a chest exercise followed by a back exercise. Alternatively you could work on one group of muscles only, but follow one exercise with a different movement – for example, a lateral raise followed by a shoulder press. If working the abdominals, you might perform a static stabilisation exercise (e.g. the bridge/plank) followed by a dynamic power exercise (e.g. medicine ball throw to floor).

Pre-exhausting

This method of overload is similar to same-muscle-group super-setting, in that you might perform a lying triceps extension to exhaust the triceps prior to performing a press-up that works the chest, shoulder and triceps. As the triceps are pre-exhausted the chest and shoulders have to work harder.

When you are planning an abdominal training routine, it is important to incorporate many principles of overload, including both full- and partial-range exercises using external resistance – either gravity based, variable resistance (tubes/bands) or 'hands-on' techniques – to create the appropriate intensity. Power movements, proprioceptive training, functional and **dynamic stabilisation** (stabilisation using an unstable base) should be incorporated for both variety and specificity. The exercises can be sequenced in a multi-set approach, using super-sets (two exercises at a time), tri-sets (three exercises) and giant sets (four-plus exercises).

Focus on technique

As always, the emphasis should be on correct focus and technique of each repetition, not just on completing the set.

Recovery

When planning an abdominal training routine, stabilisation exercises should be interspersed with dynamic movement drills and strength/power drills, allowing the appropriate recovery time after each set that will allow each muscle to perform to its optimum level. In a class-based situation, this recovery will vary from person to person, depending on their fitness level, and also according to the sports-specific goal. Generally, however, 20–40 seconds is usually sufficient between exercises.

TEMPO/RHYTHM

The speed of the movement is very important. Too fast and this could cause injury due to near-ballistic work (i.e. an over-emphasis on the influence of gravity), also the full range of movement might be impaired. Generally, slower movements are preferable as they reduce the chances of momentum taking over, and so allow pure muscle contraction.

Power training

When you are training for power you should remember the principles of inertia and momentum, and how speed can also be a useful tool. Every static object has inertia and every moving object has momentum. Excellent power gains can be achieved by applying greater force during linear movement repetitions (e.g. clap press-ups, squat jumps, medicine ball chest passes). Before introducing power exercises, you should be very comfortable with the ability to brace your core muscles to create a firm base of support. These power moves often require greater recruitment of fast-twitch fibres and this, together with appropriate strength training, can lead to greater hypertrophy of the muscle.

EFFECT OF LEVER/BIO- MECHANICAL CONSIDERATIONS

In addition to certain weight training machines, which use 'cams' and pulleys, you can change the effort required to perform certain exercises by increasing/decreasing the length of the lever used – for example, a press-up performed with your thighs resting on a stability ball is much easier than with only your toes resting on it. Certain body adjustments can intensify the exercise due to bio-mechanical principles and leverage.

In some movements there can be 'sticking points' where you are at a **bio-mechanical disadvantage** and, consequently, in order to complete the required number of reps you will lose technique or have to cheat to complete the movement. This can happen during a sit-up movement on the floor, where your body is too heavy for your abdominal muscles to lift it through the full movement range required and you 'cheat' by throwing your body weight forwards (i.e. using momentum rather than muscular strength). If you find yourself in this sort of situation, you should consider changing over to other exercises or machines.

PROGRAMME DESIGN

In writing this book I have tried to steer away from absolute training protocols here as this book is geared to be more of a smorgasbord of core stability exercises and principles. There is no one definitive solution to any exercise programme because everything can only ever be relative. The relativity factors are the desired goal, the equipment available, the time and intensity of training and also the ability of the participant in question. However, it is important to remember the integrated training principles as mentioned on page 16, and the need to identify any imbalances that you might have before you begin a total body programme. Failure to do so is likely to restrict your progression and will potentially cause injury.

Everyone is individual and what appears simplistic to one person might be difficult for another. For a truly structured programme, always seek the advice of a reputable trainer at a local gym. Some highly regarded training institutions are the CHEK Institute, the National Academy of Sports Medicine (NASM), the National Strength and Conditioning Association (NSCA) or the American College of Sports Medicine (ACSM) to name but a few.

For a structured programme, it is important to initially identify corrective exercises to strengthen weaker muscles and to help stretch tighter ones. This helps to re-address the balance and synergy within your body. This should be followed by integrated stability exercises, which should challenge your stabilisation muscles and help improve your balance, reactions and strength and challenge your cardio-respiratory system as well.[20]

As your core stabilisation improves, the focus moves to more strength-related exercises, interspersed with more advanced compound stabilisation exercises. The final phase is the power phase and should only be followed when a high level of core stability has been achieved. These exercises require increased power demands and incorporate advanced stabilisation drills throughout, according to your own goals or the specific demands of a particular sport.[20]

SUMMARY

- Muscles have to be 'broken down' in order to grow.

- Several different muscular contractions are involved in resistance training.

- In order to create overload, sufficient and appropriate resistance must be applied.

- There are numerous methods of overload available to train a muscle. For effective gains to occur, the increases in overload should be graduated in small increments, utilising the different methods discussed in this chapter. This is classed as progressive overload.

- Neuro-muscular adaptation in the muscles and nerves occurs when a new skill or movement has been learned.

- Changes in resistance, repetitions, sets, speed and lever length can all affect the intensity of the overload.

- Generally, full-range controlled movements will provide the best training effect. However, if training for a specific sport, your exercise should mimic the desired sporting action as closely as possible.

WHAT YOU NEED TO KNOW BEFORE YOU START

7

WEIGHT CONTROL, DIET AND EXERCISE

Weight control is simply a matter of creating an energy imbalance, which forces your body to burn fat stores for energy. Everyone has a metabolic rate, which regulates the speed at which they digest, absorb and utilise the food they consume, converting this into energy which then powers the relevant organs and tissues, allowing growth and repair, and fuelling our day-to-day existence. The basal metabolic rate (BMR) is the rate at which you burn energy (calories) when you are doing nothing – for example, if you were to lie in bed all day and rest.

TOTAL CALORIC EXPENDITURE

Everything else we do, from shopping, going to work and cleaning the house to doing an aerobics class, uses extra energy that is burned off, or expended. This is classed as your total caloric expenditure. In simple terms, if you consume more calories than your total caloric expenditure, you put on weight. If you expend more than you consume, you lose weight. Core stability training, for all its positive effects, will not necessarily help you to lose weight.

In conventional resistance training, research indicates that by increasing your muscle mass (hypertrophy, see page 30), you can increase your resting metabolic rate. This is because muscle requires more energy (or calories) just to exist than fat. So the more muscle tissue you have the more energy is used up to feed it. As a result, your basal metabolic rate is increased. However, a weight-training programme will not burn as many calories as a cardio-vascular workout, so it makes sense to increase your total caloric expenditure through some form of cardio-vascular activity.

CARDIO-VASCULAR WORKOUTS

Basically, the more intense your cardio-vascular workout, the greater the duration and the greater the frequency, the larger the number of calories expended. However, as with any intense workout regime this can lead to injury. As a result there is no optimum workout programme as everyone has different levels of fitness and experience. It is also worth mentioning that not everyone has the same time available, or the same motivation to exercise. My general recommendations for weight loss are therefore to eat carefully, train wisely and rest thoroughly.

AESTHETICS

If your goal is to achieve the elusive six-pack then, basically, you need to reduce the body fat that surrounds those muscles in order to see them. Once you understand the principles of weight loss explained above then it should simply be a matter of correct diet and exercise. Unfortunately there is one other aspect to take into account: genetics. You are born with a predetermined blueprint, your DNA, which decides everything about what you are. While exercise and diet can affect the way you look, they can't alter your genetic make-up.

BODY TYPES

Your parents provide the genes in your genetic make-up. These genes are arguably responsible for many things, including your level of athletic ability, your intelligence, musical talents and the way you look. Looking at body type, this is why some people are naturally thin and others have a more rounded physique. There are three general body types, as described below.

ECTOMORPH

Ectomorphs tend to have long limbs, and are often tall and slim. Their hips and shoulders are generally narrow and, due to a faster metabolism, many complain that they cannot build muscle and gain weight. If I think back to my school days, ectomorphs were often the tall gangly ones who weren't necessarily that co-ordinated but had long limbs and were often pushed into sports where their height was an advantage, such as basketball or high jump.

MESOMORPH

Mesomorphs are the 'natural' athletes. Distinct characteristics are broad shoulders, a slim waist and a muscular athletic look. They seem to be able to put on muscle and lose weight relatively easily. At school, as I remember, mesomorphs seemed to be good at anything sporty and often excelled in team sports.

ENDOMORPH

Endomorphs have a more rounded look, with larger chests and waists. In women these are the classic 'pear' shape. They can gain weight easily as the body tends to store fat more readily. Weight training is always a great complement to a workout but the training emphasis should really be on cardio activity for this body type. You might remember the classic endomorph from school. They would often be the one who was a little fatter and tended to tire more quickly. They would be the last ones to be chosen when deciding the teams for games, yet were the first chosen for the scrum in rugby!

Most of us are a combination of two of these body types, and characteristics from each will be more or less prominent throughout our life.

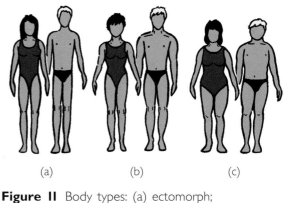

(a) (b) (c)

Figure II Body types: (a) ectomorph; (b) mesomorph; (c) endomorph

CONTRA-INDICATED EXERCISES

There really is no such thing as a contra-indicated exercise, rather every exercise has relative risks according to the person performing it and the desired goal. For example, a gymnast has to perform many twists and turns, leaps and stretches as part of their sport. The training needed to achieve a high degree of strength, and the gymnast's body movement, will be very different to that of the average gym-goer. For a gymnast to achieve a gold medal there will be many different movements that they need to master. Some of these movements will have a high risk of injury, yet, for the gymnast, they are fundamental in training to achieve that gold medal.

As a regular exerciser, or fitness trainer, you also have a choice of exercises that may cause subsequent injury. You have to decide whether performing a specific exercise is appropriate to your fitness level, or the fitness level of your class, or whether another exercise can be substituted that will provide a similar training effect, but with less risk of injury.

When you are choosing an abdominal exercise, consider the benefits of a specific exercise against the potential risks. With this in mind I have described below two 'classic' abdominal exercises that have been popular over the past 30 years.

STRAIGHT-LEG SIT-UPS

When performing a sit-up, initially the head is lifted off the floor, engaging the neck and abdominal muscles. The abdominals contract further to bring the ribcage towards the chest. This reduces the relative lever length of the upper body. As you curl further forwards the hip flexors begin to contract to lift your back off the floor; however, due to leverage issues, if the legs are straight this compromises the hip flexor involvement. In a straight-leg position, the hip flexors lie parallel to the spine, which means they are mechanically disadvantaged, such that their leverage ability is minimised. In this position, when the hip flexors contract they pull directly on the spine and can cause the lower back to arch.

In the past, the classic sit-up was performed with your legs straight, lying on your back, face up, with your hands clasped behind your head. The movement was often demonstrated by pulling on your neck muscles to sit up and bend forwards to touch your elbows to your knees. This is unnecessary movement, as the full sit-up serves no functional purpose and causes excessive stress to the lower back.

The bio-mechanics of leverage means that the abdominals are active for only a small part of the movement before the hip flexors take over. For this reason, full sit-ups should be discouraged. There has been a resurgence in the use of straight-leg abdominal exercises in recent years; however, the movement range of this classic abdominal curl technique has been drastically reduced.

When performing a sit-up or flexion exercise of any nature, the main issues are that the movement stimulates the main flexion muscle – the rectus abdominus – optimally (i.e. you train muscle through an optimal range relative to function, specificity and relative overload).

DOUBLE LEG RAISES

The double leg raise has been used for many years as an exercise to train the abdominals. The action is to lift the legs off the floor and either to hold them or lift them to a near-vertical position. The muscles responsible for this movement are the hip flexors, as they attach to the lumbar spine and the top of the thighs. They contract to lift the legs and, in doing so, pull on the lumbar spine, which can increase its lumbar curve. In addition, the hip flexors can tilt the pelvis, which can pull the lumbar spine out of alignment.

In the past the double leg raise was performed as an endurance exercise, holding the legs 15–30 cm off the floor for upwards of 30–60 seconds. This would place great stress on the lumbar spine and, with minimal knowledge of effective stabilisation, injuries were likely.

Wherever possible, especially when introducing stabilisation exercises to a class environment with varying ability levels, it is recommended that the legs should be bent when held against gravity to reduce the lever effect, and so the intensity and subsequent risk factors. Initially it might be necessary to work one leg at a time, again to minimise any potential for injury.

A word of caution

There are certain exercises in this book that do allow for a double leg raise – however, these are only to be attempted by the most advanced athlete. Provided that the spine is maintained in a neutral position, and there is no compression of the discs or damage to the ligaments, then holding a double leg raise is justifiable.

POPULAR MYTHS
ELECTRICAL MUSCLE STIMULATION GADGETS CAN CREATE A DEFINED TORSO

Electrical muscle stimulation (EMS) has been used in rehabilitation settings since the 1960s to help stimulate muscles that have suffered nerve damage. Electrodes are attached to the skin and a small electrical current passed through them to the underlying muscles. The stimulation from the electrical current has helped to prevent atrophy or shrinkage in a number of patients in the clinical setting. The fitness industry is always looking for a quick-fix solution and, often, similar EMS products are advertised, proclaiming their ability to create a solid six-pack and attractive torso within weeks. It seems that just 10 minutes a day will reduce your body fat, narrow your waistline and give you a rippling set of abdominals with little or no effort! As with many of the 'fitness products' on the market, there is often little or no research to support any claims made by the advertisers and, let's face it, if it was that simple, everyone would have a six-pack!

SIT-UPS WILL HELP SUPPORT THE SPINE

The muscle responsible for performing the sit-up exercise is the rectus abdominus and, as previously discussed, when it contracts it creates forward flexion of the spine. It is a mobiliser muscle and provides little support for the spine. Spinal stability can be enhanced by the strengthening of the core stabiliser muscles of the inner unit and the postural muscles attached to the spine.

PERFORMING ABDOMINAL EXERCISES WILL HELP REDUCE THE WAISTLINE

By incorporating stabilisation exercises into your workout you can gain improvements in posture, and doing movements where the transverse abdominus is actively bracing to maintain correct form can have a flattening effect on the torso. However, the only way to reduce your waistline is to decrease your caloric intake and/or increase your cardio-vascular activity to essentially burn more calories than you consume. The resultant energy deficit will result in your body utilising more of your fat stores for energy. There are no exercises that will spot-reduce or remove fat from any one area.

SUMMARY

- Your basal metabolic rate (BMR) is the rate at which you burn energy while doing nothing.

- By increasing your muscle mass, you increase your metabolism. When exercising, the greater the intensity, duration or frequency of your workouts, the greater the amount of energy that will be used.

- Body types fall into three categories: endomorph, mesomorph and ectomorph.

- When considering any exercise always question the potential benefits it might deliver compared to the potential risks.

- Sit-ups alone will not reduce your waistline.

BEFORE YOU BEGIN

8

As with any new exercise routine, always check with your doctor that there are no reasons why you should not embark on a new programme. Perhaps a previous injury might be aggravated by some of the exercises, or a joint problem or muscular condition could cause you pain in certain positions. Also, it is important to identify any imbalances you might have and introduce corrective exercises to recondition any muscles that might restrict your progression. Once you have received your doctor's all-clear then you can work your way through this book, but try to avoid skipping exercises or chapters.

It should be remembered that, as with any exercise routine, there are no quick-fix solutions. Exercises need to be learned through practice, concentrating on each and every repetition. Only when you have learned the correct method of stabilising for a particular exercise should you move on to the next. Use this book as a continual reference to remind yourself of the correct bracing techniques, breathing and related postures.

The exercises in Part two demonstrate numerous core stability exercises and principles, beginning initially with minimal equipment. The section progresses to incorporate unstable base training and then how these principles can be used with more conventional exercises in a gym setting. I have included hands-on training and medicine ball exercises towards the end of this section to look at alternative overloads and include more dynamic movements, many of which are used within sports-specific drills.

Part three introduces a total body perspective of integrated functional exercises that will challenge both your strength and your stabilisation capability, throughout the movement. These exercises really test your core function and so it is important that you are confident with bracing techniques as you work your way through this section. Having identified with unstable bases and overload principles, this section sees the introduction of kettlebells and newer industry concepts such as ViPR Training and Suspension Training. These concepts on their own really challenge the dynamic of human movement and core stability, taking the concept of integrated function and whole body integration to a different level, working in a totally three-dimensional or multi-planar way. The cross-gravitational forces created by dynamic kettlebell exercises and ViPR training really challenge your stabilisation muscles, and not just through your core muscles but also through your shoulders, lumbo-pelvic–hip complex and all muscles/joints which are required to stabilise to maintain a movement. It is important to understand that while this book has tried to include numerous exercises that involve core stabilisation, not every variation or permutation can be shown. As long as you, the reader, understand the principles of overload and the concepts of instability and proprioception, it is up to you how you vary each exercise relative to your own needs or sporting emphasis.

Later on in the book, Part four identifies alternative training (such as Pilates, or the balance and agility movements that are used in children's fitness) that is akin to core stabilisation with regard to its similar bracing principles. Other forms of exercise and movement (such as the Feldenkrais and Alexander methods) are looked at too; you will see, through the use of such techniques, the outcome of improved or enhanced function and/or enriched life through better movement.

Finally, Part five gives some examples of programme design, both within a class perspective and for individual training. If you are an instructor, this chapter identifies some of the factors to consider when setting up an abdominal class and shows how you can monitor the abilities of your participants and decide which exercises to use.

PART **TWO**

THE EXERCISES

The following chapters demonstrate a number of different abdominal exercises with varying degrees of difficulty. The initial sets of exercises use no equipment and can easily be performed at home. They include both stabilisation and conditioning techniques to train the abdominal muscles. It is important to train the deep stabilisation muscles first as these have greater endurance in comparison with the superficial trunk muscles, which are responsible for movement. In this way your superficial muscles will not fatigue so quickly.

Once you understand the techniques necessary for correct abdominal bracing, you should begin to incorporate specific equipment that requires greater stabilisation to perform a desired movement. As the neuro-muscular system adapts and your stabilisation ability and muscular strength increase, it is a suitable time to introduce greater stabilisation requirements by adding integrated, compound movements with increased resistance. When correct form can be maintained throughout each repetition of the desired movement it will be time to move on to a more advanced exercise.

Remember that the emphasis is not just to complete the required number of repetitions but to achieve perfect form throughout each and every repetition. As with any exercise, an appropriate warm-up and suitable cool down are very important. The stretching exercises within this section are targeted at the muscles likely to have been involved, but they do not represent a comprehensive stretching programme for a total body workout.

When training your abdominals in a supine position or when lying face up, being on your back and lifting the head will require the neck musculature to contract. This can cause a shortening of the muscles at the side of the neck and lead to a forward head posture over time. If you can push your tongue to the roof of your mouth this will activate the deep cervical flexors that stabilise and protect the cervical spine. By remembering to keep your tongue in the roof of your mouth during any exercise in which you

are on your back or face up, you can help to strengthen the deep stabiliser muscles of the neck. This might also be useful if you find your neck begins to hurt during certain postures or movements.

WARMING UP

Before performing any activity it is important to warm up, through graduated movements, those specific muscles and joints that will be involved. For example, if warming up for a 100 m sprint, the warm-up should graduate from mobilisation exercises and dynamic stretching to progressive jogging and running actions. The running movements should increase in intensity, performing sprints of various distances until the body and mind are fully prepared and the muscles ready for such high-intensity sporting action. In top-level athletics it might take up to an hour to warm up for this 10-second event.

When training the abdominals, however, it is unlikely that the intensity of movement will require such elaborate warming-up methods. Consider the movements of the exercises you are about to do – namely various flexion, rotation and bracing movements. The warm-up should replicate these movements but should graduate in intensity and range to mobilise all relevant joints and muscles. In addition, replicating the movements will improve your co-ordination and improve your kinaesthetic awareness. Dynamic movements will increase the blood supply to the muscles and assist enzyme activity in the muscles.

A warm-up should incorporate flexion, extension, lateral and rotational movements of the spine, and should not focus on single-plane activity (e.g. forward and back) but incorporate multi-plane activity: movement in all directions. As the muscles of trunk, hips, shoulder girdle, chest and back (together with, to a lesser extent, the arms and legs) are involved in many of the abdominal exercises, the movements in the warm-up should encourage total body activity.

WARM-UP EXERCISES AND STRETCHES

9

WARM-UP EXERCISES

No equipment is needed to perform these exercises.

Exercise 9.1 Rotations

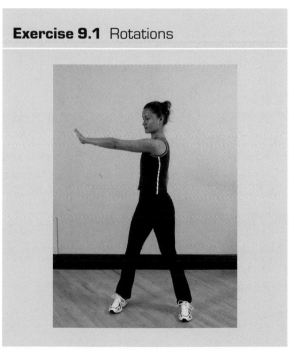

Starting position and action
- Stand with your feet shoulder width apart and legs slightly bent keeping your hips in neutral (see page 5).

- Gently rotate your torso, first to one side then the other, repeating this movement and increasing the range of movement with graduating twists.
- As you increase the range of movement, reach across your torso with your opposite arm. Allow your hips to rotate so that when reaching across to your right with your left hand, the twisting action forces you to come on to the toes of your left foot.
- Increase your arms' involvement, so that you begin to feel a slight stretch across your back and shoulders as you reach.
- Aim for about 15–20 rotations before moving on.

Exercise 9.2 Up and Overs

Exercise 9.3 Lateral Flexion

Starting position and action

- Stand as before, with your feet shoulder width apart and legs slightly bent, arms by your side.
- Flex through your knees and hips, in a squatting action, and bend forwards as if skiing.
- Then stand up slowly, extending your spine and reaching up with your arms.
- Gradually increase your range of movement so that the whole exercise becomes a large swinging and bending action, reaching up, over your head, and bending back slightly at the top phase, while reaching down and behind your legs when squatting.
- Perform 10–15 full movements.

Starting position and action

- Stand with your feet shoulder width apart, legs slightly bent with arms by your side.
- Bending laterally (sideways) at the waist, and being careful not to lean forwards or backwards, reach your right hand down your right leg. Repeat to your left side.
- Gradually increase your range of flexion while being careful to avoid any twisting or forward flexion of the spine.
- Perform 10–15 movements to each side.

Exercise 9.4 Supported Cat Flex

Starting position and action

- Lean forwards, bending your knees, and place your hands on your thighs, just above your knees.
- Push your buttocks away and aim to 'hollow out' your lower back, making a concave shape, to exaggerate the lumbar curve.
- Then, pulling in your abdominals, round the lower back as if to arch it upwards, making a convex shape, like a cat does when it stretches.
- Repeat this arching and rounding movement slowly 5–10 times, gradually increasing the movement where comfortable.

STRETCHING

If you have specific areas or muscles that are tight, either due to over-training, reduced activity or weakness, it is likely that this will have a negative effect on your overall training programme. If this is not addressed through the introduction of corrective exercises to these areas, the problem will be exacerbated and this can have an adverse affect on other muscles due to incorrect alignment or posture and/or a reduced range of movement, causing muscle imbalances.

It is important to encourage flexibility exercises to these tight areas, to return the muscle back to its **normal length**. Having addressed the flexibility or range of movement that a muscle/joint has, the next stage is to train the muscle in correct alignment and in effect to re-educate the muscle on its correct purpose. This is where the stabilisation element of the exercise should be focused, requiring greater balance and joint stability. This will improve the communication between the brain and the muscle, acting together, which will improve neuro-muscular efficiency.

To improve the movement range or flexibility of a specific muscle or joint, static and dynamic stretches can be used, but recent advances in research and training protocol have seen the introduction of a new process to assist flexibility – **self-myofascial release** (SMR). This is an excellent way to target tight muscles and, when used in conjunction with other stretching techniques as mentioned, it can help return a tight muscle to its normal length. SMR works through the use of two neural receptors within the muscles – the **muscle spindle** and the **Golgi tendon organ**.[21]

The muscle spindle identifies changes in muscle fibre length and the rate of change, sending information to the **central nervous system**. This then activates the **myotatic stretch reflex**, which shortens the muscle tissue and can cause pain. The Golgi tendon organ is sensitive to both the change in tension and the rate of the tension change. Stimulation of the Golgi tendon organ inhibits the action of the muscle spindle and decreases muscular tension. This phenomenon is known as **autogenic inhibition**.[21]

Self-myofascial release requires a pressure to follow the line of the muscle.When exercising, this is generally done as part of the warm-up to help release tight muscles in preparation for the workout to follow. Self-myofascial techniques require the use of a **foam roller** or similar. This is a cylindrical tube usually made out of foam that is placed under the part of the body to be stretched. Position yourself so that the desired muscle is resting on a foam roller and, by applying body-weight pressure, you roll over the foam roller so that the entire length of the muscle is rolled. The pressure of the foam roller stimulates the Golgi tendon organ within the muscle and helps to 'iron out' muscle tightness and restore normal muscle length and balance. The movement should be slow and controlled but it can also be quite awkward to get in the correct position to achieve the desired result.

It is worth mentioning though that positioning yourself over certain muscles – the piriformis muscle located above the gluteal muscles for instance – is not always easy. Not only is it easy to fall off the foam roller, it is also quite an effort to support your body weight as you roll across. In addition, if you do suffer from tightness in certain areas the SMR technique can actually be quite painful, despite its positive effect.

If you encounter any tight spots you should just rest at that point for 20–30 seconds. This allows the pressure to stimulate the Golgi tendon organ, which autogenically inhibits the muscle

spindles and thus reduces tension and pain in the muscle. The benefits of self-myofascial release are:

- Neuro-muscular efficiency
- Improved flexibility for specific joints
- Reduction in muscle soreness
- Correction of muscle imbalances.

SMR TECHNIQUES
LATISIMUS
Starting position and action
- Position yourself lying on your right side with the foam roller placed just outside your right armpit.
- Your arm should be outstretched with the thumb pointing upwards.
- Gently roll, remembering that the movement for this exercise is minimal.
- Repeat on other side.

RHOMBOIDS
Starting position and action
- Begin with your arms crossed over your chest and with your fingers touching opposite shoulders.
- Lie face up over the foam roller, keeping your head in neutral.
- Brace your abdominals and lift your hips off the floor.
- Roll the foam roller across your mid-back.

QUADS
Starting position and action
- Begin lying face down over the foam roller, with your arms supporting your body weight.

- Maintain correct alignment by bracing your abdominals, pulling your navel in towards your spine.
- Gently roll across the foam roller so that it travels from your pelvic bone down to your knee.
- Remember to keep the roller towards the outside of your thigh.

HAMSTRINGS
Starting position and action
- Position yourself so that you are sitting on the floor with the foam roller under your right knee.
- Cross your left leg over your right to intensify the stretch for your right leg.
- Support your body weight with your arms and gently move yourself forwards so that the foam roller travels up towards your hip.
- Repeat with the left leg, crossing your right leg over your left and starting again at the knee.

GASTROCNEMIUS
Starting position and action
- Begin sitting on the floor with your left ankle resting on the foam roller.
- Cross your right leg on to your left ankle to increase the pressure.
- Lift your hips up by supporting your body weight on your arms and gently 'walk' yourself down towards the foam roller so that it rolls slowly towards your knee.

IT BAND
Starting position and action
- Position yourself on your side, lying across the foam roller
- The upper leg is used to assist balance and the lower leg is raised with heels off the floor.
- Using your arms to assist, roll the foam roller from the hip joint down to the knee.

TENSOR FASCIA LATAE
Starting position and action
- Position yourself lying face down over the foam roller with your body weight supported on your arms.
- The foam roller is positioned lateral to your pubic bone on your thigh.
- Slowly roll the foam roller down the outside of your thigh towards your knee.

PIRIFORMIS
Starting position and action
- Begin in a seated position on the foam roller, with your left leg crossed over your right knee.
- Support your body weight using your arms.
- Roll the foam roller across the outside of the hip, just above the gluteal area.

For detailed photos of these techniques, please see Appendix on pages 238–241.

STATIC STRETCHES

To assist in returning the muscle to its normal length, a flexibility programme should be developed to work in conjunction with the SMR techniques mentioned previously. Static stretching, such as in the following exercises, should only be done when the muscles are warm. Never stretch when the muscles are cold, unless the action itself is dynamic yet controlled in nature and is combined with other movements that increase body temperature.

While there are many specific stretches and different stretching principles, within this book the emphasis is on improving the core musculature and related muscles of the torso. When incorporating a full body training programme with compound movements, all the muscles will need a sufficient stretching programme to help reduce injuries and maintain correct muscle length. For a fuller explanation of training principles, see *The Complete Guide to Stretching* by Chris Norris.[8] The following stretches will be sufficient in preparation for general training.

THE STRETCHES

Exercise 9.5 Knee Hugs

Starting position and action

- Lie on the floor, face up, with your legs in the air, knees bent.
- Bring your knees towards your chest and hold on to your shins.
- Pull your knees in as tight as is comfortable to round your lower back, stretching the muscles.
- Aim to hold this position for 15–30 seconds and repeat.

Progressions/adaptations

- This stretch can be done with a partner for an increased stretch; however, care must be taken when doing any partner work.
- Lie on your back, bringing your knees in to your chest and have your partner lean forwards so that his/her chest rests against your feet.
- As your partner leans forwards, or puts pressure on your feet, this will force your knees closer to your chest and increase the stretch in your lower back.

Coaching points

- Always talk to your partner while performing any passive stretch so that you are both aware of the intensity or force to apply, and of each other's limitations or flexibility.

Exercise 9.6 Cat Stretch

Starting position and action

- Position yourself on hands and knees, with your weight evenly distributed.
- Suck in your abdominal muscles and draw in your navel towards your spine as you arch your lower back upwards in a cat-like stretch.
- Hold the stretch for 10–15 seconds before relaxing and repeating.

Exercise 9.7 Seated Spinal Twist

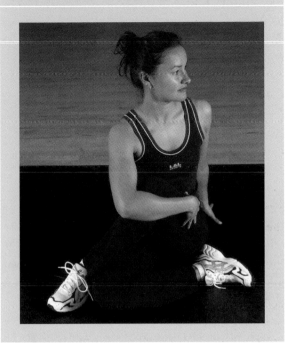

Starting position and action

- Sit on the floor and bring your right knee in towards your chest, keeping your right heel on the floor.
- Twist through your spine, bringing your left elbow towards your right knee, the goal being to twist far enough through your trunk to take your elbow outside (i.e. to the right-hand side of) your right knee.
- Hold this position for 15–20 seconds before repeating the movement, changing legs and twisting to your left.

Coaching points

- Aim to keep an erect spine throughout, without rounding through your lower back.

Exercise 9.8 Bent Leg Crucifix

Starting position and action

- Lie on the floor, face up, with your arms outstretched on the floor in a 'crucifix' position.
- Bend your right knee, bringing the heel in, and lift the knee across your body towards your left side.
- Lower the leg to the floor, allowing gravity to create a stretch through your lower back as you twist.
- Hold for 20–30 seconds before repeating on the other side; this time your left leg crosses your body and pushes towards your right side.

Coaching points

- It is important not to force this stretch but to move slowly and evenly, working with gravity to push the knee further towards the floor. If performing the progression below, allow the pressure of your hand to assist the stretch.

Progressions/adaptations

- To increase the stretch, place your left hand on your right knee (and then vice versa), applying gentle pressure to increase the stretch.

Exercise 9.9 Hip Flexor Stretch

Starting position and action

- Kneel up on the floor (do not rest back on your heels), holding on to a chair by your side for support if needed.
- Extend your right leg forwards so that the thigh is parallel to the floor and the knee is bent at a right angle.
- With your left knee on the floor, lean forwards from the hips so that you sink into a hip flexor stretch of the left leg. Hold for 15–30 seconds.
- Change legs, taking your left leg forwards and kneeling on your right knee to repeat the stretch.
- Repeat each stretch two or three times.

Coaching points

- As you lean forwards, try to tilt the pelvis under to really focus on stretching the hip flexor muscle.

Exercise 9.10 Abdominals

Exercise 9.11 Shoulder Girdle and Chest

Starting position and action

- Lie face down on the floor and place your elbows under your shoulders with forearms on the floor, palms flat and facing down.
- Push up, without lifting too high, so that your elbows and forearms are supporting you.
- Relaxing your torso and legs, try to pull your torso forwards by pulling against the floor with your hands.
- Hold the stretch for 10–15 seconds before relaxing and repeating.

Coaching points

- This is a subtle movement and you should feel the stretch through your abdominals and ribs.
- Avoid pushing yourself too high off the floor.

Starting position and action

- Stand in a doorway or next to a wall and place your right hand and forearm against the wall or doorframe, keeping your arm slightly bent at the elbow.
- Relax your arm and shoulder, and turn slowly towards your left shoulder (i.e. away from your right arm).
- As you turn you should feel a stretch begin in your chest and shoulder.
- Do not turn too far but when you feel the stretch hold your position for 10–20 seconds. Repeat the exercise, this time with your left arm against the wall or doorframe and turning towards your right side.

Coaching points

- Change the height of your hand position to vary the stretch you feel through the muscles in your shoulder girdle.

Exercise 9.12 Upper back

Starting position and action

- Stand upright and hold on to a wall bar or fixed exercise machine with both hands level with your chest. If at home, use a door frame that you can grip on to, or the banister at the bottom of the stairs, provided it is sturdy enough to take your weight safely.
- Holding on tight, lean back so that, by pulling against it, you feel a stretch in your back muscles.
- Hold the stretch for 10–20 seconds.

Coaching points

- Much like the shoulder girdle and chest stretch above, you can vary your hand position (e.g. slide your hands further apart along the bar) to feel the stretch in different areas of your back muscles.
- Use the weight of your body to assist the stretching effect.

STABILISATION EXERCISES

10

No equipment is required to perform these exercises.

THE EXERCISES

Exercise 10.1 Prone abdominal hollowing

Starting position and action
- Lie face down on the floor with your neck straight, chin tucked in and hands loosely together under your forehead.

- Relax the legs, the gluteal and abdominal muscles.
- Slowly contract your abdominal muscles, pulling your navel up away from the floor and in towards your spine.
- Simultaneously tighten your pelvic floor muscles as if you are trying to stop yourself from urinating.
- Maintain your breathing and hold this contraction for 10–30 seconds before relaxing.
- Repeat 5–10 times.

Coaching points
- Only when the correct tension can be achieved and maintained should you move on to the more demanding stabilisation exercises described below.

Exercise 10.3 Four-count Leg Lift

Starting position and action

- Lie on the floor, on your back, with your knees bent and your feet on the floor.
- Keep your hips and spine in neutral alignment and brace your abdominals.
- Place your fingers 3–5 cm above your hips but 5–10 cm from your navel and press down to feel the contraction, or bracing action, of your abdominals.
- Very slowly, and keeping the knee bent, lift your right foot 15–20 cm from the floor and hold it elevated.
- Then, maintaining the contraction through your abdominals, raise your left foot the same distance and bring it adjacent to your right foot.
- Holding the contraction, slowly lower your right leg until the foot just touches the floor.
- Then lower the left leg to the floor.
- Repeat this four-stage movement 5–10 times.

Coaching points

- The important aspect of this exercise is that the pelvis, hips and spine remain still throughout and abdominal tension is constantly present.

Exercise 10.3 Four-count Leg Lowering

Starting position and action
- Lie on the floor as in the previous exercise, this time with both feet raised, your knees over your hips with legs slightly bent.
- Place your fingers as before (3–5 cm above your hip bone and 5–10 cm from your navel) and press down to feel your abdominals brace.
- Maintaining the abdominal tension, lower your right leg slowly to approximately 45 degrees and hold it there.

- Lower your left leg until it is level with the right and hold it, remembering not to hold your breath at the same time.
- Then raise the right leg back to the starting position, followed by the left.
- Perform 10–15 repetitions.

> **Important**
> The emphasis of this exercise is not just to hold the legs off the floor but to do so with correct abdominal bracing and spinal alignment.

Coaching points
- Each leg movement should be slow and controlled, and should take approximately 5 seconds.
- Provided you can maintain the correct alignment through appropriate abdominal tension, start to increase the distance over which the leg is lowered.

Progressions/adaptations
- To decrease the intensity of this exercise, bend your knees more to reduce the relative lever length of the legs and keep the lowering movement small.
- To increase the intensity, only allow a slight bend in the legs, and lower each so that the foot nearly touches the floor.
- Only advanced-level participants should attempt to lower the legs close to the floor as the tension required through the abdominals to maintain the correct alignment is great.

Exercise 10.4 Scissors

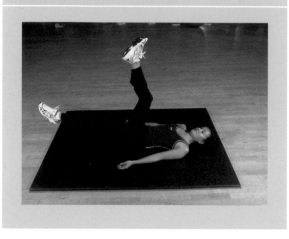

Starting position and action

- Lie on the floor as before, with both legs raised and slightly bent so that the knees are over the hips.
- Keeping your hips and spine in neutral, brace the abdominals to maintain the correct alignment.
- Lower the right leg towards the floor, but hold it at a point that allows you to maintain correct alignment.
- From this position, simultaneously change the positions of your legs in a 'scissors' action.
- Do not hold your breath at any stage during this exercise.
- One complete repetition counts when the leg lowers and then returns to the start position.
- Aim for 15–30 repetitions.

Coaching points

- If you feel that your lower back is moving out of neutral, stop the exercise.

Exercise 10.5 'Superman' Variations

Starting position and action

- Position yourself on all fours (i.e. hands and knees), with your hands under your shoulders and your spine in neutral alignment.
- Contract your abdominals, pulling in the navel towards your spine and squeezing your pelvic floor muscles.
- Slowly raise your right arm in front of you, reaching slightly out to the side at a 45-degree angle to the spine. Aim to keep the arm level with your torso, keeping the thumb up to help engage the shoulder stabilisers.
- Keep your right arm where it is, and extend and raise your left leg behind you, lifting it no higher than your right arm, while maintaining correct abdominal tension and spinal alignment.
- Aim to get your raised arm and leg parallel to the floor.
- Hold for up to 10 seconds and then slowly return to the start position, before repeating with the opposite arm and leg.

Coaching points

- Imagine you are supporting a pole that runs from your extended leg across your back and along your outstretched arm.

Exercise 10.6 Prone Bridging (Plank Work)

Starting position and action

- Lie down on the floor but position your elbows under your shoulders with your forearms on the floor, keeping your eyes looking at the floor.
- Brace your shoulders and abdominals, lifting your hips away from the floor with your body weight supported through your shoulders, forearms and knees.
- Maintain correct spinal alignment throughout, keeping neutral alignment from the neck through to your hips, making sure that your hips do not drop below 15 cm from the floor.
- Hold this position for 15–30 seconds or until you begin to lose abdominal tension, then sit back on your knees to recover. After 10–15 seconds' rest, repeat the exercise.
- Aim to achieve 5–10 bracing positions or 'bridges'.

Coaching points

- Maintain correct alignment throughout this position, keeping your shoulders and abdominals braced.

Progressions/adaptations

- To increase the intensity of the stabilisation required, when in the 'bridge' position on your knees, straighten the legs one at a time so that your weight now balances on your toes.
- Maintain this position for 20–45 seconds.
- When this position can be maintained relatively easily, try raising one foot slightly off the floor for 50 per cent of the time that you intend to hold the bridge, lowering the foot and raising the other foot for the remainder. This can be repeated, again for 5–10 repetitions on each leg.

Exercise 10.7 Lateral Bridging

Exercise 10.8 Two-point Bridge

Starting position and action

- Lie on your right side, resting on your right elbow and forearm, with your knees bent to give you a steady base, heels behind you. Your left arm can lie along your left side. The elbow should be directly underneath the shoulder.
- Bracing the abdominals, push your hips up, towards the ceiling, keeping the knees, hips and torso in line.
- Maintain the tension through the abdominals and hold for 10–20 seconds.
- Lower your hips to the floor for a very brief recovery and repeat, aiming for 10–15 repetitions before lying on your left side and repeating the exercise. Breathe throughout.

Coaching points

- Do not allow the supporting shoulder to lose tension or the torso to 'sag' as this can cause pain in the neck area.

Progressions/adaptations

- To intensify this exercise, straighten the legs, extending them in line with the body, and repeat the movement. Your weight is now supported through your elbow, forearm and the side of your 'underneath' foot.
- It is important not to allow any 'sagging' of the lower back during this movement.

Starting position and action

- Begin as you would if performing a full press-up: with your hands shoulder width apart, legs outstretched behind you and your toes in contact with the floor.
- Brace your abdominals and slowly lift your right arm and left leg simultaneously.
- Aim to keep the knee of the raised leg level with your hips, shoulders and raised arm.
- The raised arm should be out to the side at a 45-degree angle to the spine, no higher than shoulder height, with the thumb up.
- Hold this position for 5–10 seconds before lowering your arm and leg.
- Repeat the exercise with the left arm and right leg, aiming for 15–20 repetitions in total.

Coaching points

- Avoid twisting the spine to maintain balance in this movement.

Progressions/adaptations

- This two-point bridge can be modified as follows. Start as you would if performing a box press-up but, as you push yourself up away from the floor, lift one leg and the opposite arm, as described above, to increase both the intensity and the stabilisation required.

Exercise 10.9 Kneeling Stabilisation

Exercise 10.10 Supine Bridge

Starting position and action

- Start by kneeling on the floor in an upright position (do not rest back on your heels) with your pelvis and spine in neutral.
- Extend your right leg out to the side, keeping it straight. This will tilt your hips to accommodate the position.
- Keeping your left thigh perpendicular to the floor and arms at your sides, brace the abdominals, maintaining alignment of the torso.
- Lean across to your left so that your shoulders are beyond your left thigh aiming to create a straight line from your right leg through your torso to your head.
- Hold this position for 5–10 seconds, remembering to breathe, and return to the upright position.
- Repeat 5–10 times before reversing your leg position and leaning across to your right side.

Coaching points

- Avoid leaning across too far initially.
- Keep your lean slow and controlled throughout.

Progressions/adaptations

- To increase the difficulty level: (i) place your hands by your ears, or (ii) extend your arms over your head to increase the lever length and thus the amount of resistance.

Starting position and action

- Lie on your back, face up, with your arms at your side.
- Keep your knees bent and your feet on the floor.
- Brace your abdominal muscles and slowly push your hips towards the ceiling, lifting your buttocks, lower and mid back off the floor.
- Aim to get your hips in line with your thighs and torso, maintaining the abdominal tension constantly.
- Hold for 10–20 seconds and then lower.
- Repeat 8–12 times.

Coaching points

- Your weight should be through your shoulders, your upper back and feet.
- Avoid pushing your hips up too high as the emphasis is on maintaining neutral alignment of the spine.

Progressions/adaptations

- This bridging movement can be performed with alternate legs in the air to increase the workload of the stabiliser muscles, the hamstrings and the glutes.

Exercise 10.11 'Spiderman'

Starting position and action

- Position yourself on all fours with your weight evenly spread between your toes and your hands.
- Keep your feet and knees 'turned out' slightly to minimise hip flexor involvement.
- Brace your abdominals and keep your torso as rigid as possible, keeping your spine in neutral throughout.
- With small movements of the hands and feet, 'crawl' forwards making sure not to lose the neutral spine position.
- Crawl forwards for up to 30 m without losing form, then rest for 10–20 seconds and repeat 2–3 times. To begin with, you might find a 10 m distance sufficient, remembering that the emphasis is on the technique and contraction as opposed to the distance covered.

Coaching points

- Your torso should maintain a near-horizontal position. In addition, do not allow the buttocks to lift excessively.
- Avoid making large movements with your legs, as this will cause the hips to move out of alignment.

Exercise 10.12 Standing Balance

Starting position and action

- Stand upright with your hips and spine in neutral.
- Brace your abdominals and transfer your weight on to your left leg.
- Lift your right foot 2–5 cm off the floor, maintaining your balance.
- Hold position for 10–20 seconds, before changing legs.
- Achieve 4–5 static holds before progressing to a more advanced progression.

Coaching points

- Before beginning the movement, try to assume a balanced posture and relax.
- Focus on a specific stationary object in front of you as this will help you to maintain your balance, keeping your entire body static.

- Do not lift your leg more than a few centimetres off the floor.

Progressions/adaptations
- To increase the difficulty, close your eyes while raising your leg. This will force you to rely on your sensory proprioceptive skills.

What are sensory proprioceptive skills?
These come into play when there are no visual cues to assist your balance, forcing your brain to rely on sensory feedback from your muscles and the balance receptors in your inner ear.

Exercise 10.13 Horizontal Balance

Starting position and action
- Begin as before, in an upright stance keeping your spine in neutral.
- Transfer your weight on to one leg and lean forwards, bending at the hip; keep your spine in neutral as you continue to lean, extending the raised leg behind you.
- Keep the alignment between your upper body and the extended leg and make sure your supporting leg is bent slightly at the knee.
- Brace your abdominals tightly to maintain your alignment.
- Lean forwards as far as you can go, while maintaining your alignment, until you are in a horizontal position.
- Return to the starting position, change legs and repeat.

Coaching points
- Avoid twisting the spine or tilting the pelvis as you continue the leaning action.
- You might want to work with a partner or use a wall or table to help you balance as you lean further forwards and lower.

Progressions/adaptations
- The emphasis here is on remaining balanced with minimal movement, contracting your abdominals throughout.
- To add to the stabilisation intensity, extend your arms forwards as you lean, to increase your lever length, keeping your arms in line with your torso and extended leg.

CLASSIC ABDOMINAL EXERCISES

11

No equipment is needed to perform these exercises.

THE EXERCISES

Exercise 11.1 Abdominal Curl

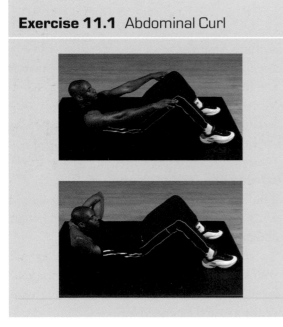

Starting position and action
- Lie down, facing upwards, with your knees bent and your feet on the floor, approximately hip width apart.
- Position your hands so that your palms are resting on top of your thighs.
- Contract your rectus abdominus, slowly curling your ribcage towards your pelvis, lifting your shoulders, upper and mid back off the floor.
- Aim to achieve a 10–15 cm range of movement from the torso so that your palms slide forwards to touch your knees.
- Hold briefly at the top of the range before returning slowly to the start position.

Coaching points
- The emphasis with this exercise is on reducing the distance between your ribcage and your pelvis, rather than lifting off the floor.
- Keep your movements slow and controlled, and do not use momentum.

Progressions/adaptations
- To increase the intensity of the curl: (i) cross your arms across your chest, (ii) position your hands by your ears, (iii) cross your arms behind your head, hands on shoulders, or (iv) outstretch your arms in a V position, thumbs down.
- There are a number of variations based on the classic crunch technique, performed with feet in the air. This has the effect of minimising the involvement of the hip flexors, so greater emphasis is placed on the abdominals.

Exercise 11.2 Oblique Reach

Starting position and action
- Start as before, lying face up on the floor with your knees bent and your feet on the floor.
- Position your hands either together with your arms across your torso, across your chest or by your ears, with your elbows to the sides.
- Curl upwards and then rotate your torso to bring the ribs on your right side over towards your left hip.
- As you curl across, lift your left foot 3–5 cm – but no more – off the floor.
- Hold briefly at the top position before returning to the start.
- Repeat the movement, this time bringing the left side of your ribcage towards your right hip and lifting your right foot 3–5 cm off the floor.

Coaching points
- The total movement range for this exercise should be approximately 10–20 cm.
- Try not to over-reach as this will reduce the benefits of the exercise.

Progressions/adaptations
- As before, moving the arms further back, away from your hips, will increase the lever length of the movement and so the intensity will be increased.

Exercise 11.3 Reverse Curls/Hip Lifts

Starting position and action
- Lie face up on the floor with your legs up in the air, knees bent over your hips and ankles touching or crossed.
- Place your arms by your sides, palms up.
- Contract your abdominals, pulling your navel down towards your spine.
- Tilt the pelvis, lifting your hips towards the ceiling in a controlled manner.
- Pause for 2–5 seconds at the top of the range before slowly lowering your hips back to the floor.

Coaching points
- Your knees will naturally move towards your chest, but focus the movement on lifting your hips rather than swinging your legs over your chest.
- Keep your abdominals contracted throughout the exercise and avoid any jerky movements.

Exercise 11.4 Internal Oblique (Basic Crunch)

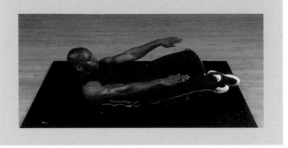

Starting position and action

- Lie on the floor, face up, with your knees bent and your feet on the floor.
- Cross your right leg over your left ankle and rotate your knees to the right so that they are at a 30–45-degree angle to the floor.
- Your arms should be straight, resting lightly on top of your body, hands palms down, with the sides of the thumbs touching and your arms pointing towards your hips.
- Lift your head, shoulders and upper back slightly, and look towards your feet.
- Your chin, left hip and ankles should be in line.
- Squeeze your obliques to curl up over your hips, so that your fingers can almost touch your ankles. Pause briefly at the top phase, before returning to the starting position.
- Aim for 10–20 repetitions before moving on to the other side. This time the left leg crosses over the right ankle and your knees drop down to your left.

Coaching points

- Do not try and come up too far in this exercise as the movement is designed to activate the internal obliques. This means that a total range of movement of no more than 20 cm is necessary.

Exercise 11.5 Internal Oblique (Lateral Crunch)

Starting position and action

- Lie on your right side, with your right arm outstretched and your right hand on the floor, resting your head on your arm to start with.
- Bend slightly at the waist so that your legs are at an angle to your torso of no more than 30 degrees.
- Place your left hand on top of your left thigh, keeping a slight bend in the legs, and brace the abdominals.
- Squeeze your oblique muscles to lift your torso off the floor so that you can reach with your left hand towards your left knee, while simultaneously lifting both legs off the floor.
- Try not to push down with your right hand to assist the lift. Rather, use this hand as a balancing aid.

Coaching points

- Do not allow the hips to drop back as this will encourage the hip flexor to dictate the emphasis of the leg movement.

Exercise 11.6 Slow Eccentric Curl

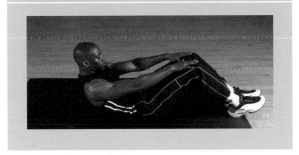

Starting position and action

- Lie on the floor with your legs in the air, knees bent over your hips, and with your hands holding the backs of your thighs.
- Rock yourself forwards, bringing your feet to the floor and almost lifting you into a seated position.
- Extend your arms out in front of you so that your palms are over your knees.
- Contract your abdominals to maintain this position and then slowly roll down through the spine over 15–30 seconds until your shoulders return to the floor. This is one repetition.
- On completion, lift your legs back into the air, hold on to your thighs and roll yourself back to the semi-seated position. Repeat 5–10 times.

Coaching points

- Keep the eccentric curl action controlled throughout, gradually increasing the time taken to perform the lowering part of the movement.

Progressions/adaptations

- To increase difficulty, when in the semi-seated position, place your arms across your chest to increase resistance.
- To increase intensity further, place your hands behind your head.

Exercise 11.7 Super-slow Bicycles

Starting position and action

- Lie on the floor, face up, arms by your sides.
- Raise your shoulders and upper back slightly off the floor, engaging the rectus abdominus.
- Hold on to your right knee; extend the left leg above your hips, then lower it to an angle of approximately 45 degrees. Brace the abdominals and let go of your right knee, keeping it where it is and making sure that there is no movement of the lower back.
- Place your fingers by your temples and rotate the torso slightly to bring your left elbow and shoulder towards your right knee.
- Hold this position briefly before slowly changing legs while rotating the right elbow and shoulder towards the left knee.
- Aim to change the leg position over a 2–5 second count. Each change of legs counts as one repetition, the goal is to aim for 15–30 repetitions in total.

Coaching points

- Maintain the bracing action of the abdominals, preserving a neutral spine throughout.
- **Important:** The lower back should not move from the start position. If it does, it is likely that the hip flexors have overcome the tension required by the abdominals to maintain the original position of the lower back.

THE INTRODUCTION OF UNSTABLE BASES

12

Core stability can be enhanced dramatically by the use of equipment that has an unstable base, requiring you to stabilise various muscles to assist your balance. This not only helps to improve posture in daily activities but can also increase confidence, technique and power in many sports. If you perform movements on an unstable base like a stability ball, your muscles and senses have to respond to stop you falling off. Equipment such as the Reebok Core Board™, BOSU™, wobble boards and other equivalents all work on a similar principle (see Chapter 5). Each have an unstable base and as such require added stabilisation from your muscles to assist balance.

The use of an unstable base can encourage the core stabilisation muscles, and the muscles surrounding the joints involved, to contract effectively to maintain a balanced posture. This can be useful in many sporting disciplines and has a functional use in day-to-day activities as well.

STABILITY BALLS

Stability balls have been used for many years by osteopaths, physiotherapists and other rehabilitation specialists, both to aid neurological improvements in muscle contraction and in corrective postural therapy. In the 1980s stability ball exercises were introduced into performance training for athletes, initially in a rehabilitation role, but because of the gains achieved in core strength and balance, which enhanced athletic performance on the field of play, they have become an excellent tool for sports coaches and trainers. Today, they are commonplace in most gyms and an invaluable tool for personal trainers working on a one-to-one level with their clients. Stability balls offer a very effective way to increase abdominal strength and core stability for three main reasons.

1 They are round and, like any ball, have minimal stability compared to, say, a bench, which is obviously stable. Consequently, when performing movements on a stability ball you have to engage your stabiliser and neutraliser muscles to maintain correct form throughout the exercise. The stabiliser muscles are those that surround the joints and protect them from injury; the neutraliser muscles act alongside other muscles to counteract any external force that could disrupt your balance, helping to maintain a smooth movement. Even just sitting on a ball requires a minimal amount of stabilisation from the trunk muscles.

2 As you lie on, or rest over, the ball you have a greater movement range than you would have on the floor. This means that you can train the muscle through a greater range than before. Take an abdominal curl, for example: when lying face up on the floor your movement range is restricted by the floor itself, as the spine cannot extend any further. However, when lying face up on a stability ball performing the same exercise, your back can extend further back over the ball so that you begin to feel a stretch through your abdominals. As you perform the curl you are contracting your abdominals through their full range of movement and for most people this will mean working the muscle through a range it has never experienced before.

3 Because of the new balancing skills that need to be learned, a stability ball class can be a lot of fun. Everyone will have their own limitations with certain exercises, but the opportunity to increase dynamic core strength while 'rolling around on an inflated ball' is one too good to miss. For many of us, if exercise can be disguised as 'play', and we enjoy ourselves during a class, it is likely that we will want to come back, and so our ability will progress.

Due to the advances in gym machine design, many fixed-weight exercises require little or no stabilisation control, so the muscles responsible for posture and spinal alignment are not being trained. Exercises performed on an unstable base such as a stability ball encourage the recruitment of the stabiliser and neutraliser muscles. The more unstable your training environment the greater the activation required from your stabiliser and neutraliser muscles to maintain both correct balance and correct form.

Another advantage of stability ball exercises is that they are very easy to graduate and, often, each exercise will be open to a vast array of modifications to either increase or decrease the intensity or skill factor required. This is always an advantage both on a one-to-one level and in a class environment. As with any activity, there may occasionally be certain exercises that should not be performed by some people – if they have specific injuries, say, certain medical conditions or skeletal problems. However, there will usually be a slight modification, adjustment or even alternative exercise available, which can be used to train the muscles in a similar, but safe, way.

When choosing your stability ball it should be large enough so that when seated on it with your feet together, your thighs are parallel to the floor and your knees at a 90-degree angle or slightly higher. The ball should be relatively firm. However, it must be remembered that the firmer the ball the more difficult the exercises will be. A guide to correct sizes is shown in Table 12.1.

Most balls come with a foot pump (however, if you are an instructor and are using a number of balls in a class environment, it is worth purchasing a motorised air pump). Remember not to over-inflate the ball and always buy from a reputable dealer. Not all stability balls are of the

Table 12.1	Stability ball size guide
Your height	Ball size
Under 5'2"	45 cm ball
5'3" to 5'8"	55 cm ball
5'9" to 6'3"	65 cm ball
Over 6'3"	75 cm ball

same quality and it is advisable to choose a ball that is anti-burst. Prices vary, but a good anti-burst ball can usually be purchased for £15 to £20.

Before you begin your workout, make sure that the area on which you will be exercising is flat and free from any sharp objects that could puncture the ball (pins, staples or even small stones or bits of grit). If necessary, use a mat under the ball; this will also reduce any slipping that may occur if you are exercising on a polished wooden floor.

As with any exercise regime, warming up is very important. The warm-up should be related to the activity that follows it and should consist of some mobilisation exercises, followed by single sets of some of the stability ball exercises. These sets should be performed at a lower intensity than the exercises 'proper' and with a reduced movement range; you should increase the range of movement as you work through the set.

WARM-UP EXERCISES

Exercise 12.1 Seated Pelvic Tilting/Rotation/Figure of Eight

Starting position and action

- Sit upright on a stability ball with your knees bent and your feet shoulder width apart, keeping your spine in neutral.
- Then rock forwards and back by tilting your pelvis (very small movements). Gradually increase the range of these movements.
- Repeat this rocking effect laterally (from side to side).
- Link the movements (alternating the action forwards, to one side, backwards, to the other side), until you are performing a 'figure of eight' action using small movements of your pelvis.
- Once again, graduate these movements, increasing their size to a much larger movement range, where the whole ball is moving and you are having to focus on abdominal bracing to maintain your balance.

Exercise 12.2 Rotations

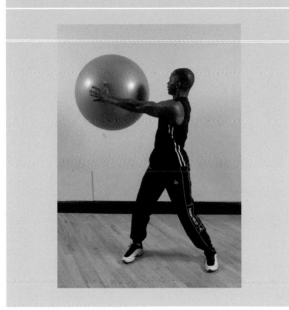

Exercise 12.3 Squat and Press

Starting position and action

- Stand upright, holding the ball with both hands and keeping you knees slightly bent.
- Keep your hips still and begin with small rotations of the torso, to either side.
- Gradually increase the range of movement and allow your hips to move as well, encouraging functional muscular activity and joint mobilisation.
- Increase the range of movement, modifying the action so that you are performing dynamic swings across the body, with your arms reaching to either side.

Starting position and action

- Hold the ball and squat down, placing the ball on the floor, then extend your hips and legs to stand up, lifting the ball above your head.
- Gradually increase the range of trunk movement and activity so that you are lifting the ball overhead and leaning back slightly to increase the dynamic stretch of the torso.

STABILITY BALL EXERCISES: BEGINNERS

Exercise 12.4 Seated Pelvic Tilting

Starting position and action
- Sit on a stability ball with your arms by your sides, and your knees and feet together.
- Brace your abdominals by pulling your navel in towards your spine.
- Sit upright and tilt your pelvis forwards and back to increase the curve in your lower spine and then 'flatten' it.
- Keep your body still but aim to 'rock' backwards and forwards on the ball through small movements from your pelvis, repeating the tilting action 10–15 times.

Coaching points
- Unlike in the warm-up, where mobility is the primary factor, aim to keep your upper body relatively still as you perform this movement.

Exercise 12.5 Seated Leg Lift

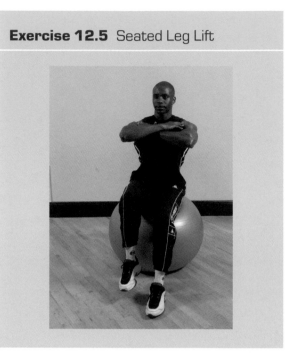

Starting position and action
- Sit on the stability ball with arms by your sides, your pelvis in a neutral position with abdominals braced, and knees and feet together.
- Lift the right foot off the floor about 10 cm and hold for 10–20 seconds without tilting the hips.
- Return the right foot to the floor and repeat with your left leg.
- Complete 3–5 lifts with each leg.

Coaching points
- Maintain your balance, trying not to adjust your torso position or move out of alignment.

Progressions/adaptations
- After lifting your right foot, straighten the leg so that it is parallel to the floor, hold for 10–20 seconds then return to the start. Repeat with your left leg.

- An advanced alternative is to start as before, with feet together and pelvis in neutral; however, this time lift both feet off the floor at the same time, holding for up to 20 seconds before lowering them to the floor.
- Take care in this movement not to lose your neutral spine or tip the pelvis forwards or back.

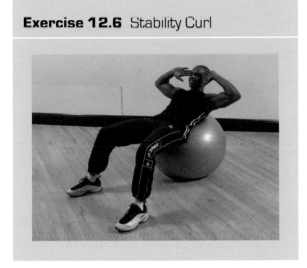

Exercise 12.6 Stability Curl

Starting position and action
- Lie facing upwards so that your lumbar and mid spine is supported by the stability ball.
- Position your arms across your chest, with hands on shoulders.

- Keeping feet on the floor, approximately hip width apart, lower yourself backwards over the ball so your lower back forms a curve and a slight stretch is felt through the abdominals.
- Curl upwards and forwards, bringing your ribcage towards your pelvis.
- Aim to achieve a 10–15 cm range of movement from the torso.
- Hold briefly at the top of the range before returning slowly to the start position. Repeat 10–15 times.

Coaching points
- It might feel uncomfortable at first going through a fuller range of movement when lying back over the stability ball, so initially go only as far as is comfortable, remembering to brace your abdominals prior to all movements.

Progressions/adaptations
- To increase the intensity of the curl: (i) position hands across your chest, (ii) position hands by your ears, (iii) cross arms behind your head, hands on shoulders, or (iv) have your arms outstretched in a V position, thumbs down.
- Bringing your feet close together will increase the stabilisation control required.

Exercise 12.7 Oblique Curl

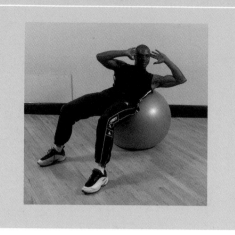

Exercise 12.8 AB Curl Using Ball as Resistance

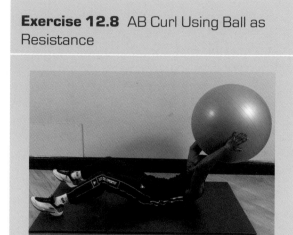

Starting position and action

- Lie face up on a stability ball with your lower back supported.
- Position your hands by your ears, with your elbows pointing out to the sides.
- Curl upwards and rotate your torso to bring your right shoulder towards your left hip.
- The movement range for this exercise should be approximately 10–20 cm.
- Hold briefly at peak position before returning to the start.
- Repeat the movement, this time bringing your left shoulder towards your right hip. Continue for 8–10 repetitions each side.

Coaching points

- Keep the movement controlled throughout and avoid twisting across too far.

Progressions/adaptations

- By moving your feet and knees together the stabilisation factor is increased.

Starting position and action

- Lie on the floor, face up, holding the stability ball above your head (and pressed close against the top of your head).
- Contract your rectus abdominus, slowly curling your ribcage towards your pelvis, lifting your shoulders, upper and mid back off the floor.
- Aim to keep your hips still so that only your abdominals are involved.
- Even though the ball has minimal weight, as the arms are holding it tight to your head the lever length is increased and so the exercise will feel harder.
- Keep your movements controlled and smooth throughout but always keep the ball in a fixed position above your head.
- Aim for 10–20 controlled repetitions.

Coaching points

- If this exercise feels too difficult initially, hold the stability ball to your forehead or even your chest to shorten the lever.

Exercise 12.9 Lateral Flexion/Crunch

Starting position and action

- Begin by kneeling on the floor with the stability ball to your right-hand side.
- Reach out with your closest arm (the right one) and lift yourself up so that your body weight is over the ball and you are lying across it on your right side.
- Extend both your legs and separate them to give you better stability.
- Keeping your feet on the floor, place your fingers against your temples and increase your stretch over the ball.
- Then, before losing your balance, brace your abdominals, emphasising your oblique muscles to lift your upper torso laterally, aiming to squeeze the leading side of your ribcage towards your hips.
- Pause at the top position briefly before returning to the start.
- Aim for 10–15 repetitions before adjusting your position to repeat the whole thing on your left side.

Coaching points

- Initially, as you perform this movement it might be easier to secure your feet on a wall for increased stability.

Exercise 12.10 Back Extension

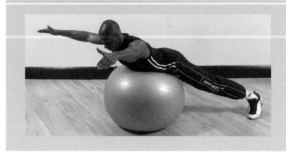

Starting position and action

- Lie face down over the stability ball with your torso and hips resting on it.
- Have your arms by your sides but with your hands holding the stability ball loosely.
- Keep your legs separated to assist balance. Brace your abdominals.
- Extend through your back to lift your chest off the ball, keeping your head in neutral alignment.
- As you raise up, bring your spine into a neutral position and pause briefly, then lower to return to the start position.
- Repeat 8–10 times, keeping the movement slow and controlled.

Coaching points

- Tense your abdominals before initiating any movement and keep them braced throughout.
- Avoid lifting too far and arching your back.
- Be careful not to twist the spine to maintain your balance.

Progressions/adaptations

- By bringing your legs and feet together and coming on to your toes, you can maximise the stabilisation required.
- Increase the intensity by bringing your hands up to your ears or reaching forwards, extending arms in front, in line with your torso.

Exercise 12.11 Prone Press-ups (Hips/Knees/Feet on Ball)

Starting position and action

- Lie face down over the stability ball with your hips and upper thighs on the ball and your hands on the floor in front of you.
- Your hands should be slightly wider than shoulder width apart in a press-up position.
- Brace your abdominals and keep your body rigid throughout the movement.
- Perform a press-up, lowering your head and chest to the floor.
- As your chin or chest nears the floor, push against the floor with your arms to lift yourself back to the start position.
- Exhale as you push yourself back to the starting position. Repeat 10–15 times (try to increase this number as you become more proficient at the exercise).

Coaching points

- Depending on your strength and stabilisation ability, begin this exercise with your hips and thighs on the stability ball to reduce the lever effect with a wide hand position.

Progressions/adaptations

- When you can comfortably perform 15–20 repetitions, position the stability ball further

down your legs so that it lies under your (i) knees, (ii) shins, (iii) ankles or (iv) toes.
- The stabilisation aspect can be made harder too, by bringing your hands closer together under your shoulders. This not only narrows your base, increasing the stabilisation required, but also places greater emphasis on the shoulders and triceps.

Exercise 12.12 Prone Roll-in

Starting position and action

- Start in a prone position, face down, as if to perform a press-up, with the stability ball near your feet.

- Place one leg followed by the other on the top of the stability ball so that your shins and ankles are in contact with it.
- Keep your hips in line with your shoulders and your arms extended, hands shoulder width apart.
- Simultaneously bend both knees and lift your hips to roll the stability ball towards your arms. This movement should cause the stability ball to move approximately 1 m.
- Pause briefly before extending your legs (still in contact with the stability ball) and roll it back to the start position.
- Repeat the movement for 10–15 complete rolls.

Coaching points
- Keep your abdominals braced throughout the movement.

Progressions/adaptations
- This exercise can be performed using alternating legs, so that you roll the ball forwards with one leg and then back with the other.
- Alternatively, roll the ball forwards and back using your right leg; when the ball is back to the start position, change legs and roll it forwards and back using your left leg.

Exercise 12.13 Lying Torso Rotation, Arm Extended

Starting position and action
- Position yourself lying face up on a stability ball with your arms extended overhead.
- Only your shoulders and upper back should be in contact with the ball.
- Clasp your hands together loosely, keeping your arms slightly bent.
- Push your hips upwards so your torso and thighs are parallel to the floor, keeping your hips in neutral and your feet shoulder width apart.
- Brace your abdominals and rotate your torso so that your shoulders roll across the stability ball and both arms point to the right, finishing almost parallel with the floor.
- Pause briefly and return to the start position.
- Repeat the rotation to the left, aiming for 10–15 rotations to each side.
- It is important that, throughout this exercise, you do not allow the hips to drop.

Coaching points

- To begin with, keep your rotational movement small until your confidence improves, then increase your movement range.

Progressions/adaptations

- To increase the difficulty level, bring your feet and knees closer together.

STABILITY BALL EXERCISES: INTERMEDIATE

Exercise 12.14 Supine Bridge Ball Rolls

Starting position and action

- Lie on the floor, face up, with your feet outstretched and resting on the stability ball.

- With your arms at your sides, lift your hips and buttocks off the floor to create a 'bridge'.
- Keep your abdominals braced throughout and maintain neutral alignment of your spine.
- Keeping your feet on the ball, bend your knees, drawing the stability ball in towards your buttocks.
- Keep your hips in line with your shoulders and knees.
- Hold briefly, then return to the start position.
- Aim for 15–20 repetitions.

Coaching points

- Keep your arms wide initially to assist your balance, and avoid letting your hips drop.

Progressions/adaptations

- To make this harder, cross your arms over your chest to increase the stabilisation required from the abdominals.
- This exercise can be made harder by rolling the ball in and then out using one leg, before changing and rolling the ball in and then out using the other leg.

Exercise 12.15 Stability Ball Roll-out

Starting position and action
- Kneel behind the stability ball with your forearms resting on top of it.
- Brace your abdominals and lean forwards on to the ball.
- Your body weight should now be through your arms and shoulders, not your knees.
- Keeping the abdominals braced, roll the ball forwards only as far as you can while maintaining the tension throughout the trunk.
- Repeat 10–15 times.
- Hold briefly in the final position, remembering not to hold your breath, and exhaling as you return to the start position.

Coaching points
- Do not allow your head or lower back to drop.
- Stop if you feel any discomfort or pain in your lower back.

Progressions/adaptations
- An advanced version of this exercise can be performed from a standing position.

Exercise 12.16 Prone Extension with Leg Rotation, Gripping Ball

Starting position and action
- Begin face down in a prone position but with the stability ball near your feet.
- Place one leg, followed by the other, on top of the stability ball and separate the legs slightly so that your shins and ankles are gripping the stability ball in a 'ten to two' position.
- Keep your hips in line with your shoulders and your arms extended, hands shoulder width apart.
- Maintain torso tension and rotate the ball so that your legs roll towards the left, then return to the start position before repeating to your right side.
- Aim to achieve 8–12 rotations to each side.

Coaching points
- Try to keep your shoulders and upper back parallel to the floor.
- Begin with small movements and gradually increase them to create a rotation of 60–80 degrees.

Progressions/adaptations
- Perform the same movement but with your hands closer together and your feet 10–15 cm apart on the ball.

Exercise 12.17 Prone Hip Extension

Starting position and action

- Lie face down over a stability ball with your hands on the floor.
- Brace your abdominals to maintain your balance and raise your legs off the floor.
- Increase the height to which you lift your legs so that your weight is balanced on the stability ball with your hands in contact with the floor to assist stabilisation.
- Aim to lift your legs to a horizontal position, and maintain your balance.
- Hold this position for 10–15 seconds, remembering not to hold your breath, then lower and repeat 8–10 times.

Coaching points

- Initially you may find that you need to hold on to a fixed object, like a secure bench or wall bar, to lift your legs sufficiently.

Progressions/adaptations

- This movement can be developed into the 'dive' extension position as described in the advanced section (see page 87).

Exercise 12.18 Supine Lateral Ball Roll

Starting position and action

- Lie back on a stability ball with your shoulders and upper back supported by the ball.
- Lift your hips upwards so that your torso and upper thighs are parallel to the floor.
- Brace your abdominals and hold your arms out sideways in a 'crucifix' position, palms up.
- With feet shoulder width apart, take small steps laterally to the right, to 'walk' your entire body to the side, rolling across the ball.
- Aim for a 10–20 cm movement, pausing briefly at the end position, before returning to the start and repeating to the left.
- Continue moving across the ball, aiming for 8–10 movements to each side.

Coaching points

- Keep your hips, shoulders and arms parallel to the floor, maintaining this 'rigid' position and avoiding any twisting.
- If you can move far enough so that your head comes off the ball, leaving just your shoulders in contact, do not allow the head to drop down, but maintain a neutral spine.

Progressions/adaptations

- Increase your movement range so that you can roll across the ball leaving just one shoulder in contact while you maintain correct alignment, keeping your hips pushed up.

Exercise 12.19 Supine Ball Rotation

Starting position and action

- Lie on the floor as before, face up, with your feet and ankles gripping the stability ball in a 'ten to two' position.
- With your arms by your sides, lift your hips and buttocks off the floor to create a 'bridge'.
- Keep your abdominals braced throughout.
- Gradually rotate the stability ball to the right, pausing momentarily before returning to the start position.
- Repeat, rotating to the left side, aiming for 8–10 rotations to each side.

Coaching points

- It is important not to over-rotate initially as the intensity might prove too great and your legs are likely to fall off the ball.

Progressions/adaptations

- By placing your arms across your chest you can increase the stabilisation requirement.

Exercise 12.20 Two-ball Prone Balance

Starting position and action

- You will need two stability balls.
- Kneel down on the floor with the balls in front of you and one hand on each ball.
- Bend your arms to form a right angle at the elbow, leaning forwards to bring your forearms into contact with the balls.

- Keeping the balls level, apply pressure to them with your arms and lift your knees off the floor. Your weight is now on your toes.
- Maintain a straight body, bracing the abdominals throughout, and hold for 10–20 seconds.
- Gradually lower your knees to return to the start position. Recover before repeating. Aim to complete 5–8 static holds.

Coaching points

- Do not allow your back to sag in this movement and do not hold your breath.

Progressions/adaptations

- To increase the difficulty, when on your toes in the 'raised' position try to move both balls by pulling your right arm back and in towards your ribs and moving your left arm forwards and away.
- Pause briefly before returning to the position where the balls are level, then repeat, this time drawing your left arm back and in and pushing your right arm forwards and away.

Exercise 12.21 Two-ball Supine Balance

Starting position and action

- Again you will need two stability balls, as in the previous exercise.
- Lie backwards over the stability balls with your forearms on one ball each, by your sides.
- Keep your arms bent to form a right angle at the elbow and lean back, applying pressure to the balls with your arms, to allow your legs to 'walk' forwards.
- In this position, bend your knees to form a bridge position and brace your abdominals to maintain a line between your shoulders, hips and thighs.
- Keeping your abdominals braced, hold this position for 10–30 seconds.
- Gradually relax the tension and lower your hips to the floor, back to the start position, before repeating. Aim to complete 5–8 static holds.

Coaching points

- Maintain a strong shoulder bracing action and keep the abdominals contracted throughout the holding phase of the movement, maintaining correct alignment.

Progressions/adaptations

- To increase the difficulty, when in the raised position try to move both balls by pulling your right arm back and in towards your ribs and moving your left arm forwards and away.
- Pause briefly before returning to the raised position, so that the balls are level, then repeat, this time drawing your left arm back and in and pushing your right arm forwards and away.

Exercise 12.22 Two-ball Prone Pec Dec

- Kneel behind the stability balls, and place your hands and forearms on one ball each.
- Lean onto the balls so that your body weight is supported through your arms and your knees.
- Extend your legs so that your weight is now on your toes and arms, and brace your abdominals to keep your torso rigid.
- Keeping your abdominals braced, allow the balls to separate slightly by moving your arms out sideways – this will lower your torso slightly and move it in line with your forearms.
- Contract your chest muscles, drawing your forearms and elbows together to lift your body upwards as the balls move together again, and back to the start position – your elbows should be below your chest.
- Aim to complete 10–12 repetitions.

Coaching points
- If the intensity is too great, keep your knees on the floor.
- Do not allow your torso to drop too low as this will put strain on your shoulders.

Progressions/adaptations
- This exercise can be made harder by elevating your feet onto a bench, wobble board, medicine board or similar.

Starting position and action
- Again you will need two stability balls, as in the previous exercise.

STABILITY BALL EXERCISES: ADVANCED

Exercise 12.23 Prone Arm Extension, Gripping Ball

Exercise 12.24 Stability Ball Power Drive

Starting position and action

- Begin in a prone position, as if to perform a press-up but with the stability ball near your feet.
- Place one leg followed by the other on top of the stability ball and separate them slightly, so that your shins and ankles are gripping the stability ball in a 'ten to two' position.
- Brace your abdominals and keep your torso in line with your legs.
- Slowly extend one arm, pointing forwards, aiming to keep it at an angle of 45 degrees to the torso (with the arm raised no higher than shoulder height and with the thumb up).
- Hold briefly, remembering to breathe constantly, before returning your hand to the floor.
- Pause for a few seconds and repeat with your other arm.
- Aim for 10–12 repetitions with alternate arms.

Coaching points

- Keep your hips in line with your shoulders, your arms extended, and your hands shoulder width apart.

Starting position and action

- Lie face up on a stability ball with your knees bent and your hips in neutral alignment.
- Position yourself so that your upper left arm and left shoulder are in contact with the ball, but your right shoulder is slightly off the ball with your right forearm supporting you on the floor.
- In a dynamic movement, brace your abdominals and drive your right arm upwards to bring your elbow towards the ceiling and your right forearm parallel to the floor.

- As you do this your right hip will follow the line of movement and raise up slightly while your left arm and shoulder will be supporting your body weight on the ball.
- Hold the top position briefly, then return to the start position, being careful not to drop the hips or move beyond neutral alignment as you lower your right forearm to the floor.
- Repeat this movement 5–10 times before repeating on the other side, leading the movement with your left arm.

Coaching points
- Your torso is twisted but your hips should remain in neutral alignment.

Progressions/adaptations
- This movement should be performed dynamically and the intensity can be increased with the use of a dumbbell.

Exercise 12.25 'Dive' Hip Extension

Starting position and action
- Lie face down over a stability ball with your hands on the floor.
- Brace your abdominals to maintain your balance and raise your legs off the floor.
- Increase the height you lift your legs so that your weight is through your arms and the ball, and your thighs have lifted off in line with your torso so that your legs are nearly vertical to the floor.
- Maintain form for a few seconds and then gradually lower your legs to the floor to recover. Repeat 5–10 times.

Coaching points
- Be careful when performing the movement not to over-extend your back and lose your balance.
- You might find this position easier to maintain with your forearms on the floor and elbows bent.

Exercise 12.26 Stability Ball 'Superman'

Starting position and action
- Lie face down over a stability ball, so that your toes and fingers can just touch the floor.
- Brace your abdominals and raise your right arm and left leg off the floor simultaneously.
- Keep the arm at a 45-degree angle to the spine, with the thumb up, and aim to get the arm and leg parallel to the floor.
- Hold this position for up to 10 seconds before returning to the start position.
- Repeat with the opposite arm (left) and leg (right) alternating to complete 10–15 repetitions with each opposing limb.

Coaching points
- Keep your movement as slow as possible as faster movements can be harder to control and may cause you to lose your balance.
- Keep the head in neutral alignment throughout and avoid any arching of the lower back.

Progressions/adaptations
- To increase difficulty, as you return your right arm and left leg to the floor, simultaneously lift the opposing limbs. In this way your entire body is balanced on the ball for a few seconds.
- To increase the difficulty further, try to balance with your arms and legs off the floor for periods of up to one minute, maintaining correct form and alignment throughout.

Exercise 12.27 Kneeling Balance

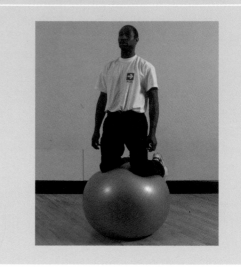

Starting position and action
- Position yourself near a wall (facing it), standing behind a stability ball, and gently place your right knee and shin on the ball.
- Hold the wall for balance with one or both hands and place your left leg on to the ball too, so that you are kneeling with the ball under your shins, sitting back on your heels.
- Brace your abdominals to help stabilise yourself.
- As you gain your balance, lift yourself up so that your spine and hips are in neutral, still holding on to the wall.
- Gradually take your hands away from the wall to balance unaided.
- Aim to increase the time you can balance until this movement becomes relatively easy.

Coaching points
- Try to work with a partner or have something to hold on to nearby such as a wall, post or secure gym machine.

Exercise 12.28 Kneeling 'Superman'

Starting position and action

- This advanced exercise takes the previous 'Superman' positions to another level.
- As your balance will be very advanced by now it should be relatively easy to start this exercise simply by standing behind the stability ball and kneeling straight on to it.
- This time, bend forwards to bring both hands on to the ball, next to the knees.
- Bracing your abdominals, raise your right arm forwards and extend your left leg behind you, lifting them off the stability ball.
- Keep your arm at a 45-degree angle to the spine, with the thumb up, and aim to get the arm and leg parallel to the floor.
- Hold this position for 2–10 seconds before returning to the start position.
- Repeat with your opposite arm (left) and leg (right).
- Keep your head in neutral throughout and avoid any arching of the lower back.

Important

This is a very advanced technique and should only be attempted when maintaining balance in the previous exercises becomes relatively easy.

Exercise 12.29 Standing Balance

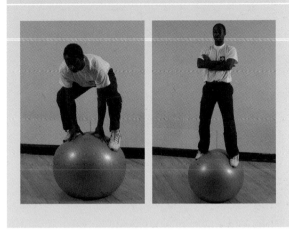

Starting position and action

- This exercise is by far the most difficult and should only be attempted by highly competent stability ball enthusiasts.
- Begin by standing behind the stability ball and facing a wall.
- Place one foot on the stability ball, gripping the wall for balance, then step on to the ball with your other foot.
- Stand upright, holding the wall, with your legs slightly bent and your abdominals braced.
- Having adjusted your body position as necessary, gradually reduce your grip on the wall until you can stand unaided.
- Increase the time you can stand upright.

Important

Again, this is a very advanced technique, yet once mastered it opens up many more stabilisation possibilities using additional resistance machines and equipment.

ALTERNATIVE UNSTABLE BASE EXERCISES 13

The principle behind unstable base training in sport has two perspectives. Certain sports (such as skiing, surfing and skateboarding) are performed on unstable surfaces, so for training to be sports-specific you need to replicate the movements that closely match the sport itself. Wobble boards, Bongo Boards™, and so on, create the required unstable base and are ideal for sports-specific training. The other perspective is that if you replicate a movement from a sport but impose greater difficulties, such as slightly increased resistance or an unstable base, the muscles will be trained to overcome the relevant difficulty. When you then perform these movements on a flat playing field or sports court, your movement and technique will have improved. The theory is that with the instability factor removed, the execution of the movements or strokes will be easier and so your body will be able to apply greater force or control to the stroke.

REEBOK CORE BOARD™

The Reebok Core Board™ is the brainchild of Alex McKechnie, a physical therapist and consultant for various sports teams in Canada and the USA. Initially the board was created as a tool to assist rehabilitation after injury for athletes. However, McKechnie linked up with Reebok in 1999 and, through collaboration with some of the Reebok master trainers, helped create the Core Training Programme. This piece of equipment has since been bought by various gym chains and has become a valuable tool in helping to develop core stability in a group exercise environment.

The Reebok Core Board™ differs from other 'unstable' devices in that it has a multi-directional tilt based over a single vertical axis. In addition, it has a self-righting, or reactive, nature; this enables it to spring back to its original position. So if you were to position your weight on one side of the board, the board's recoil effect would exert a force to try and push you back. Lastly, the board can be twisted about its axis; again, its inbuilt torque effects would try to resist the twist, attempting to return the board to its original position. This multi-dimensional tool allows you to work through three planes of movement simultaneously, whether standing, sitting or lying on, or holding on to the board.

This board is of use for both athletes and novices as it has three grading levels. The board can be set at varying amounts of instability. Level 1 is relatively rigid, so the extent of stabilisation required is less. Level 3 offers the least stability, so all exercises will require a high level of abdominal muscle firing to maintain balance. The novice can perform simple movements, such as stepping or lunging on and off the board, at varying levels of difficulty. The trunk muscles have to engage rapidly to assist stability and aid balance. Athletes, on the other hand, can 'shadow' or 'mimic' sports-specific movements or shots. In addition, many exercises can be performed together with a medicine ball, in throwing and catching routines with a partner. Due to the instability of the base, the proprioceptive muscles have to work overtime just to maintain balance.

You can vary the difficulty factor simply by adjusting your stance when on the board. For example, a narrower stance will make the exercise much harder. The dynamic nature of the board's movement makes it an excellent training aid for surfers, snowboarders and skateboarders.

CORE BOARD EXERCISES

Exercise 13.1 Rotations/Tilts

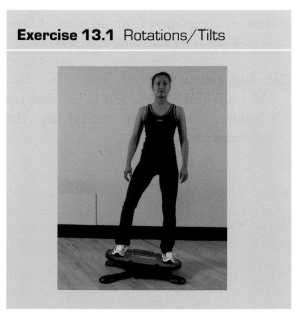

Starting position and action

- Stand on a Core Board with your feet shoulder width apart.
- Maintain a balanced posture so that the board is level, your knees are slightly bent and your hips and spine in neutral alignment.
- Brace your abdominals, pulling your navel in towards your spine.
- Begin by tilting the board to the left, then to the right, in small movements.
- Gradually increase the movements, keeping your torso relatively still.

Coaching points

- As the exercise becomes easier, place your feet closer together.
- Make sure that, as you tilt, you maintain your neutral spine position.

Progressions/adaptations

- Alternative movements are to tilt the board backwards and forwards, then to introduce diagonal and rotational movement.

Exercise 13.2 Alternate Squat Thrusts

Exercise 13.3 Press-up

Starting position and action

- Begin face down, with both hands on the edges of the Core Board in a press-up position.
- Extend both legs back behind you, with hips in line with your shoulders, torso and knees.
- Step forwards with your right leg to bend at the knee, with your knee adjacent to your right elbow.
- Brace your abdominals and rapidly change your leg position.
- Continue changing your leg position for 15–30 repetitions.

Coaching points

- Where possible, try to minimise any movement from your torso.

Starting position and action

- Hold on to the side edges of the board, face down, with your feet extended behind you.
- Maintain a neutral spine position, with your abdominals braced.
- Slowly bend your arms at the elbows to lower your chest towards the board.
- At the lowest point, hold briefly and then extend your arms to push yourself back to the start position.
- Aim to complete 15–20 press-ups before progressing to the following modifications.

Coaching points

- Make sure that the hips stay in line with the shoulders throughout, preserving the abdominal tension.

Exercise 13.4 Press-up with Rotation/Twist (Press-up adaptation i)

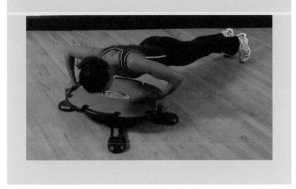

Starting position and action

- Begin in the same starting position as before, face down, with legs extended behind you and your hips in line with your shoulders.
- Maintaining a neutral spine, bend at the elbows to lower your chest towards the board, while simultaneously twisting the board clockwise approximately 10–45 degrees.
- Pause briefly at the bottom phase of this movement before extending your arms, pushing yourself back to the start position and allowing the recoil of the board to rotate your arms anti-clockwise back to the original start position.
- Repeat, this time rotating the board anti-clockwise, completing 8–12 repetitions to each side.

Coaching points

- As you rotate the board, and throughout the exercise, maintain correct neutral alignment and abdominal bracing.

PRESS-UP WITH ROTATION AND KNEE PULL

Starting position and action (Press-up adaptation ii)

- Begin as before, with your hands holding the edges of the Core Board and your legs outstretched behind you. Brace your abdominals, and keep the hips in line with the shoulders.
- As you lower your chest towards the board, rotate the board clockwise at the same time, and bring your right knee towards your elbow, maintaining a braced position but squeezing your oblique muscles.
- Hold briefly with the knee in then slowly return to the start position, extending your arms and placing both feet together. Avoid tilting your hips or pelvis as you draw the knee in.
- Aim to complete 8–12 repetitions to each side.

Exercise 13.5 Incline/Decline Squats

Exercise 13.6 Squats with Leg Lift/Raise

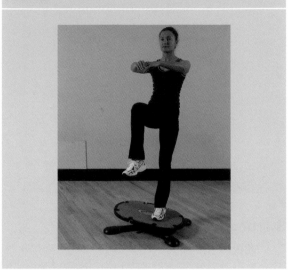

Starting position and action

- Basic squat movements can be performed on the board, starting in a balanced, level position. They can also be performed off-centre so that your body weight is slightly forward or back from centre. In addition, the exercises can be performed off-centre laterally, to the right or left.
- Begin by bracing the abdominals to assist your balance and squat down, bringing your thighs nearly parallel to the floor. Hold briefly, maintaining your balance, before returning back to the start position.
- You should be able to perform 10–20 quality repetitions, advancing to the modifications described below.

Coaching points

- Maintain neutral spine and do not allow your pelvis to tilt as you squat down.

Starting position and action

- Perform a squat as before with your body weight either central and balanced or beginning in an off-centre position as above.
- Squat down, bracing your abdominals throughout, but during the lifting phase of the movement lift your right leg up either to the front by driving the knee forwards and upwards or laterally, raising the leg to the side.
- On completing the squat movement, maintain the raised-leg position, holding this briefly (2–5 seconds) before lowering the leg and repeating.
- Aim to achieve 10–15 squat/lifts on one leg before adjusting the start position as necessary and repeating with the other leg.

Coaching points

- As you raise the knee, maintain your balance and focus on your abdominal bracing action to assist your balance.

Exercise 13.7 Lateral Squat with Leg Lift

Exercise 13.8 Lunges

Starting position and action

- Start with one foot on the board and the other to the side on the floor.
- The foot that is on the board should be at the centre for greatest stability. Positioning it at either side of centre will cause the foot to laterally, or medially, invert as you perform the squat and lift.
- Brace your abdominals and squat down.
- As you stand up, take your weight on to the foot on the board and raise your other leg out to the side.
- Complete 10–15 repetitions before changing your supporting leg. Repeat, lifting the other leg.

Coaching points

- Do not have a stance that is too wide as this will cause your spine and pelvis to lose alignment when you raise your leg, compromising the movement.

Starting position and action

- Stand a stride length behind the board, in an upright position with abdominals braced.
- Take a step forwards and plant your right leg firmly on the board.
- As your foot strikes the board, increase the brace through your abdominals to assist your balance.
- Bend your leading leg so that you lower your torso down, then push yourself back up, returning to the start position.
- Repeat, this time leading with your other leg, until you have completed 10–15 repetitions with each leg.

Coaching points

- Do not stand too close to or too far away from the board as your technique will be compromised.

Progressions/adaptations

- To increase the difficulty factor, as you place your foot on the board, place it off-centre to the left or right. This places greater demands on your stability: as you step on to the board, forcing it to tilt in one direction, so your foot, knee, hip and abdominals have to work harder to maintain balance.

- The further you step either side of centre, the greater the stabilisation required.

Exercise 13.9 Reverse Lunge/Lift/Jump

Starting position and action

- Repeat the lunge action as described above, but this time start by standing centrally on the board.
- Take a step back off the board, lunging backwards with your right foot landing on the floor.
- Brace your abdominals to assist your balance, and contract your left thigh and buttock muscles to bring you back to the start position.
- Repeat, leading with your left leg.

- You should be able to complete 15–20 lunges with each leg before introducing any of the power movements described below.

Coaching points

- You might find that you need to use a pole or have a partner nearby as you learn the power movements in this drill.

Progressions/adaptations

- The intensity of the lunge can be increased by driving forwards with your rear leg, bringing it to a raised position to the front with your thigh parallel to the floor at hip height. Maintain this balanced position for a few seconds.
- The next intensity variation is to perform the same movement but apply more force from the leg and buttock muscles of the leg on the board, to drive you into the air in a leaping action.
- Make sure your abdominals remain braced to help assist stabilisation as you land back on the board.
- To increase your stabilisation requirement, stand slightly off-centre on the board.

Exercise 13.10 Bicycles

Starting position and action

- Lie down, face up, on the Core Board with your fingers touching your ears.
- Take both legs up to a vertical position, then lower your right leg to 45 degrees, keeping it extended. Bend your left leg and rotate your torso to bring your right elbow toward your left knee.
- Hold this position, keeping the abdominals braced and then slowly change your arm and leg position, mimicking a cycling movement.
- Keep the abdominals braced throughout the movement, as the board will be unstable as you change position.
- Complete 15–20 cycles with each leg.

Coaching points

- Keep your movement slow as momentum could affect your balance.

Progressions/adaptations

- Lowering your legs will put greater stress on your back and require greater stabilisation to maintain a neutral spine position.

WOBBLE BOARDS, BONGO BOARDS™, STABILITY DISCS AND BOSU™

Wobble boards, Bongo Boards™, BOSU™ and even stability discs – not to mention countless other new pieces of equipment – have recently become available from numerous suppliers, with the focus of stabilisation in mind. All of these pieces of equipment require varying amounts of stabilisation, depending on the specific movement required. Such items can be very effective tools in sports conditioning as sports-specific movements can be performed with an increased stabilisation requirement.

In the past, **wobble boards** were circular-shaped wooden boards with a hard spherical ball at the centre. They were, and are, designed so that they tip in any direction when you stand on them if your weight is not perfectly central. Many producers have made them more exciting by manufacturing them in plastic and incorporating games where, for example, you have to get balls into holes. Such game-based activities can make some balancing skills more interesting; however, wobble boards are best used (apart from in a rehabilitation setting) when working with additional equipment (such as tennis balls or medicine balls) to help train co-ordination, balance, stability and power.

Stability discs can be placed under both feet so that your stance is not compromised. They have the advantage of increasing this stabilisation requirement because each foot is challenged independently. In addition, when replicating a specific movement from sport, it is sometimes necessary to have a wider stance than is possible on a single wobble board. Consider a tennis forehand stroke: the stroke itself is played with legs slightly wider than shoulder width apart; training on a wobble board would not directly replicate this sporting action, but using a stability disc might offer a solution.

Stability discs can also be used in conjunction with other unstable equipment. For example, when sitting on a stability ball you can place your feet on the stability disc to increase the stabilisation required. Dynamic power and trunk strength can be achieved when the disc is used with medicine balls.

A Bongo Board™ is essentially a skateboard with one big wheel the board balances on (the wheel is moveable, which is the source of its balance-testing capabilities). The board allows predominantly lateral movement and is a training aid specific to snowboarding, skateboarding and surfing.

The piece of equipment called a BOSU™ gets its name from the phrase 'BOth Sides Utilized' and was created by David Week. It is 25 inches in diameter and half of it can be inflated to create a 'half dome' on one side and a flat base on the other.

As the BOSU™ is filled with air, it is dynamic in nature and will require constant stabilisation. If you stand on it dome side up, it has an ever-changing surface. Any tiny adjustments to your body position will affect your centre of gravity and will result in variations to the air pressure in the BOSU™ in the area immediately beneath your feet. This makes it a great tool for training your stabilisation muscles. Its constantly changing surface area requires continual adjustment from your muscles to maintain correct body position or movement and, when it is turned the other way up, the inherent instability of the BOSU™ becomes all too clear!

The BOSU™ does not have a self-righting effect like the Reebok Core Board™, but its instability means that any movement will require both balance and stabilisation control from the muscles. Like the Reebok Core Board™, it is a great tool for fitness enthusiasts at all levels, and is excellent for athletes and sports teams.

It is important to remember that stabilisation and core stability exercises can be carried out with several different pieces of equipment. There is no optimum one – it really depends on your fitness and the level of core stability sought in relation to function and/or sport-specific application. Much like cardio machines in the gym, each piece of unstable equipment has its strengths and weaknesses.

The focus, as with all core stability exercises, is to continually challenge your muscles and motor skills through constant progressions and intensity variations, and to work on different aspects of fitness, both at a functional level and by applying the various principles of fitness that are directly relative to your own sport. Provided that you understand the principles of core stability, and choose your equipment accordingly, then imagination is the key to continued success.

BOSU™ EXERCISES

Exercise 13.11 Squats

Starting position and action
- Stand with your feet on the BOSU™ in a balanced position, keeping abdominals braced.
- Slowly bend down, keeping your head and spine in neutral alignment, to sit back into a squat position.
- Hold the squat position briefly before returning back to the standing position, maintaining your balance throughout.

Progressions/adaptations
- This exercise can be modified by twisting your torso, so that you reach down to one side as you squat. To intensify this exercise further, hold on to a medicine ball with both hands as you twist.
- Holding the medicine ball, reach down with the ball towards your right ankle and then, as you stand back up, reach above your head to the opposite side.
- Repeat 6–8 times to one side before repeating to the other.

Exercise 13.12 One Leg Stance

Starting position and action
- Stand on the BOSU™ with your weight balanced and feet together.
- Brace your abdominals and gradually transfer your weight onto your right leg, allowing you to slowly lift the left leg approximately 10–20 cm off the floor.
- Hold this position for 10–20 seconds, keeping the tension in your abdominals before changing legs.
- Repeat each stance 3–5 times.

Progressions/adaptations
- As this single leg balance becomes easier, try to maintain the balance with your eyes closed.

Exercise 13.13 Alternating Jumps (across)

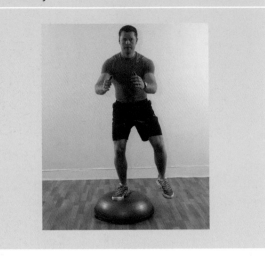

have to reach and touch cones positioned perhaps 2 m from the BOSU™ to both the left and the right.
- For added variety, and to add multi-directional movement, you could place the cones in different positions.

Exercise 13.14 Kneeling 'Superman'

Starting position and action
- Stand upright, with your right leg bent at the knee and your right foot on the BOSU™.
- Brace your abdominals and push down on the BOSU™ with your right leg to propel yourself into the air and across the BOSU™.
- Use your left foot to land first on the BOSU™, followed by your right foot on the floor.
- Make sure to keep your abdominals braced as you push off the BOSU™, and also when landing, to maintain your posture and assist stabilisation.

Progressions/adaptations
- Perform this movement but add a half-turn. You step on with your right foot but, as you push yourself into the air, you turn so that you land on your right foot but facing the opposite direction.
- To intensify further, you could add greater distances to start from – for example, you might

Starting position and action
- Kneel on to the BOSU™ and place both hands near your knees.
- Brace the abdominals, raise your right arm forwards and extend your left leg behind you, lifting them off the BOSU™.
- Keep the arm at an angle of 45 degrees to the spine with the thumb up, and aim to get the arm and leg parallel to the floor.
- Hold this position for 2–10 seconds before returning to the start position.
- Repeat with opposite arm (left) and leg (right).
- Keep the head in neutral throughout and avoid any arching of the lower back.

Exercise 13.15 Lateral Crunch

Starting position and action

- Lie over the BOSU™, reaching out with your closest arm (right) so that you are lying across it on your right side.
- Keeping your knees slightly bent, with your legs separated to give you better stability, place your fingers against your temples and increase your stretch over the BOSU™.
- Bracing your abdominals, contract your oblique muscles to lift your upper torso laterally, aiming to squeeze the sides of your ribcage towards your hips.
- Pause at the top position briefly before returning to the start.
- Aim for 10–15 repetitions before adjusting your position to lie on your left side and repeat.

Exercise 13.16 Abdominal Curl

Starting position and action

- Lie facing upwards over the BOSU™ so that your lumbar and mid spine is supported, your lower back forms a curve, and a slight stretch is felt through the abdominals.
- Position arms across the chest, with hands on shoulders and brace your abdominals.
- Curl up and forwards, bringing your ribcage towards your pelvis.
- Aim to achieve 10–15 cm range of movement from the torso.
- Hold briefly at top range before returning slowly to the start position.

Progressions/adaptations

- To increase intensity of curl, either: (i) position hands across chest; (ii) position hands by ears; (iii) cross arms behind head with hands on shoulders; or (iv) stretch out arms in a V position, thumbs down.

Exercise 13.17 Press-ups One Leg Raised

Starting position and action

- Begin in a press-up position with hands shoulder width apart on the BOSU™.
- Lower yourself down as in a press-up action, keeping your abdominals braced. But as you push back up, keep your right leg in line with your hips, torso and shoulders, approximately horizontal to the floor.
- Hold this position for 5–10 seconds before performing another press-up in which you lower yourself to the floor and raise your left leg as you push back up.

Exercise 13.18 Prone Cobra

Starting position and action

- Lie face down over a BOSU™ with your legs apart and toes on the floor. The BOSU™ should be under your abdominals.
- Place hands by your shoulders to give you stability and then, bracing your abdominals and squeezing your shoulder blades together, lift your back into an extended position with your hands off the floor. Keep your head in its natural alignment looking down.
- As you lift, bring your arm around to your side in a modified crucifix position. Keep your thumbs up and arms pulled back towards your torso.
- Maintain this position for 3–5 seconds before slowly lowering yourself back down to the floor and repeat 8–10 times.
- Try not to over-extend the spine by lifting up too high.

Progressions/adaptations

- To increase the intensity of the exercise, begin with your arm reaching forwards and holding on to light dumbbells to add resistance as you lift and retract the shoulder blades.
- To increase the stabilisation required, bring your legs and feet together, with toes touching the floor.

STABILISATION EXERCISES WITHIN CONVENTIONAL TRAINING

14

All too often, gym enthusiasts use fixed weight apparatus as part of their conditioning programme. It has to be said that, while fixed apparatus machines are beneficial, they minimise the stabilisation required and restrict the functional strength gains possible when using other resistance formats.

When you first join a gym and have never trained with weights before, the most important thing to learn when using resistance equipment is the technique of the exercise. Depending on your time available and fitness goals, it is likely that you will be given between six and ten resistance exercises working the major muscles. Most of these exercises should focus on compound movements rather than isolation exercises.

The nature of exercise for many newcomers is daunting enough. There is often so much to remember with regard to arm movements, body positions, seat heights, grips, repetitions, not to mention breathing, that all too often something is forgotten. The training should emphasise the technique and smoothness of the movement in both the lifting and lowering phase. Breathing is important, but should not be focused on to the detriment of the movement. As long as sufficient oxygen is being taken in, absorbed, utilised and then expired, when you breathe is largely irrelevant

when using light weights. Obviously, as technique improves and strength increases, the breathing and abdominal bracing will become far more relevant.

It should be remembered that fixed machines only allow movement through a specific plane. Because the machine is fixed, there is no requirement for your stabiliser and neutraliser muscles to be used. It is unlikely that the base is unstable as it is probably screwed to the floor. So it is very easy for the brain to relax and not engage all the muscles necessary to keep correct tension and body position when lifting the resistance.

Consequently, if training were only ever carried out on fixed weight machinery, very little functional strength gains would be achieved. In other words, while muscular strength and endurance would be achieved, the strength and stabilisation around the joints would not carry over to normal life movements.

Once the technique has been learned, it is important to introduce functional training techniques and incorporate exercises where your brain has to work to maintain the position and load.

Exercises performed in a standing position, or using a stability ball or similar device requiring stabilisation control, will train the brain to incorporate the neuro-transmitters responsible for firing the stabiliser and neutraliser muscles. As the brain identifies its self-righting mechanisms and stabilisation control, it can allow greater recruitment of muscle fibres from the prime mover. This allows for greater strength and power because, now that stabilisation control has been learned, the brain can focus its efforts on movement.

The greater the instability in your training environment, the greater the involvement of the joint stabilisers and neutralisers. This leads to better stability and, as a result, the more stable the joints, the greater the force that can be applied from the prime movers.

In a sports environment, athletes are constantly challenged from forces in three dimensions. This multi-plane approach should be identified within the training protocol. The closer training is to the sporting action, the better the results.

Prior to the introduction of adjustable cable pulley machines, now commonplace in most gyms, it was very difficult to apply rotational or linear movements unless these were against gravity. This meant that only certain muscles could be trained, and often the functional nature of an exercise had to be modified or restricted in some way.

When using an adjustable cable pulley machine it is important that you move smoothly throughout the exercise. Initially, this movement should be slow and controlled, but depending on the specificity of your training and the relative sports emphasis, this movement should progress to become more dynamic in nature. This means that although there are greater forces of inertia to overcome on the initial movement, this movement, while dynamic, should be totally under control, pausing at the end stage before making the return movement in a controlled way.

If an adjustable cable pulley machine is not available (if you are exercising at home, for example), many of the following exercises can be performed using a resistance tube. However, care must be taken when attaching or fastening the tube, as whatever you attach it to must be completely solid and secure. If in the gym, depending on the height required, a solid bench, wall bar or even the upright of a secure machine is ideal.

Using a resistance tube differs from using an adjustable cable pulley machine in that it offers variable resistance and this means the greater the stretch, the greater the resistance felt. At the initial phase of the movement there is minimal resistance yet the resistance increases throughout the movement range.

Resistance tubes come in varying resistance levels and, as with the cable pulley machine, you might find that certain exercises require more resistance than others for them to be effective.

CHEST EXERCISES

Exercise 14.1 Chest Press on Stability Ball

Starting position and action
- Sit on a stability ball holding the dumbbells by your side at arm's length.

- Carefully swing the dumbbells up towards your chest as you lie back, moving down the ball so that your back is now being supported.
- Brace your torso and press the dumbbells to arm's length above your chest and complete the movement by adjusting your position so that your middle and upper back are being supported.
- Brace the abdominals and press the dumbbells above your head.
- Lower slowly on a count of four and repeat, pushing the dumbbells up above your head.
- Aim for 8–12 repetitions.

Coaching points
- It is important not to lower the dumbbells too far as this can cause unnecessary stress to the joint.

Progressions/adaptations
- Initially, keep feet on floor, approximately shoulder width apart, to assist stability As you progress, move feet closer together.
- To intensify further, extend one leg in line with your hips so that only one foot is on the floor.

Exercise 14.2 Dumbbell Flye

Starting position and action

- Lie back over the stability ball as before and press the dumbbells over your head, with palms facing each other.
- Keep your abdominals braced and arms slightly bent.
- Lower the dumbbells out to your side in an arc movement.
- When you feel a slight stretch, return the dumbbells to the start position, remembering to exhale on the return phase.
- Keep the movement slow and controlled throughout.
- Aim for 10–12 repetitions.

Progressions/adaptations

- As in the previous exercise, this exercise can be made more difficult by bringing the feet together or by extending one leg so that only one foot is on the floor.

Exercise 14.3 Cable Flye

Starting position and action

- Position yourself holding the grips of the cable crossover machine and lie back over the stability ball, face up.
- Push your hips upwards, with your shoulders and upper back in contact with the ball, keeping hips and spine in neutral. Brace your abdominals.
- Maintain a slight flexion in your arms but keep them fixed.
- Contracting through your chest muscles, pull the grips across your chest at arm's length in an arc movement.
- Aim to pull the grips across each other so that the arms just cross at the elbows.

Progressions/adaptations

- Try working unilaterally, pulling one cable in and then returning it, followed by the other arm, maintaining your balance and avoiding leaning to one side.
- Vary your feet position, taking one foot off the floor.

Exercise 14.4 Stability Ball Press-up

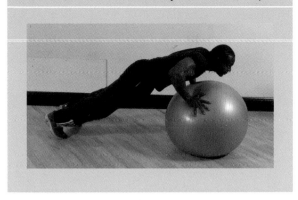

Exercise 14.5 Stability Ball Pull-over

Starting position and action

- Stand behind a stability ball, placing your hands on the ball in a 'ten to two' or 'five to one' position, and grip the ball.
- Extend each leg behind you so that your weight is through your arms and shoulders on to the ball, keeping your feet shoulder width apart.
- Brace your abdominals and keep your body rigid in the neutral spine position.
- Bend your elbows and lower your chest towards the ball.
- Extend your arms, pushing yourself back up to the start position.
- Repeat for 8–12 repetitions.

Coaching points

- This is an advanced exercise so, to assist movement, only lower yourself halfway or three-quarters through the movement range until your assisting muscles can overcome the stabilisation required by the ball.
- Increase the range of movement over time until you can perform the full movement, bringing your chest to touch the ball.

Starting position and action

- Lie back over a stability ball so that your upper back is supported and your hips are pushed upwards, keeping your pelvis and spine in neutral.
- Hold on to a light dumbbell or bar with both hands and extend your arms over your head, keeping your arms slightly bent.
- Bracing your abdominals and keeping your feet on the floor, slowly lower the bar over your head.
- Do not take the bar too far, but far enough to feel your ribcage expand and a slight pull on your abdominals and the muscles at the sides of your chest.
- Return the bar back overhead to the start position, repeating 10–15 times.

Coaching points

- As you lower the bar, breathe in to expand your ribcage and then exhale as you raise the bar back to the start. Preserve the abdominal tension throughout.

Exercise 14.6 Cable Chest Press

Starting position and action

- Stand in front of a multi-cable machine, facing away from the machine and holding the cable grips at chest height.
- Maintain a neutral stance (feet parallel, hip distance apart) and brace your abdominals.
- Slowly press the cables forwards so that your hands meet together, with arms extended in front of you at chest height.
- Slowly return the cable grips back to the start position, level with your chest.
- It is important not to lean back during this exercise as this reduces the stabilisation effect.
- Maintain a solid torso and, if necessary, reduce the amount of resistance used.
- Focus on a controlled movement, with minimal torso movement throughout.
- Repeat for 8–12 repetitions.

Progressions/adaptations

- Once control of this movement is achieved, increase the resistance accordingly.
- An alternative to increased resistance is to perform the exercise from a kneeling position.
- Alternatively, perform the exercise from a standing position while standing on a Reebok Core Board™, stability discs or a BOSU™.
- Another variation is to be in a seated position on a stability ball.
- To intensify this exercise, try performing the press seated on a stability ball with one leg extended off the floor or even standing on a BOSU™ or stability disc on a single leg. Alternatively, perform the movement from a kneeling position, with hips in neutral alignment.

Exercise 14.7 Cable Press/Single Arm Press

Starting position and action

- Stand in front of the cable pulley machine, facing away from it and holding the cable grips at chest height.
- Keep your hips in neutral and square to the machine in either a neutral or staggered stance.
- Hold the pulley handle in your right hand at shoulder height, with your elbow bent and at the same height.
- Your left hand can be outstretched in front of you to assist your movement and act as a guide or marker.
- Brace your abdominals and rotate through your torso, pressing the pulley handle forwards.
- As your body rotates, draw your left arm back and 'punch' through with your right hand, transferring the arm position.
- Do not try to 'over-reach' with your right arm.
- Gradually return to start position and repeat.
- Aim for 10–15 repetitions before changing arms and repeating with the left arm.

Progressions/adaptations

- To increase the stability factor, this exercise can be performed standing on one leg or standing on a stability disc, BOSU™ or Core Board.

BACK EXERCISES

Exercise 14.8 Lateral Pull-down

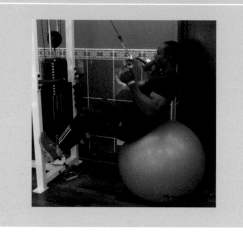

Starting position and action

- Position yourself under a high pulley machine, sitting on a stability ball.
- Aim to keep your pelvis in neutral but lean back while holding the pulley bar, arching slightly to keep your chest uppermost.
- Squeezing your shoulder blades together and downwards, pull down on the bar, bringing it towards your chest.
- It is important to aim for a smooth, controlled movement throughout and not to pull the bar any lower than nipple level.
- Aim for 10–12 repetitions.

Coaching points

- It is also possible to place the feet actually on the supports of the equipment for an alternative stance.

Progressions/adaptations

- Perform a seated row, by lowering the adjustable pulley to chest height or below.

Exercise 14.9 Seated Single-arm Row (cable)

Starting position and action

- Sit on a stability ball next to a low or adjustable pulley machine.
- Take hold of the pulley handle in one hand and ease yourself back so that you are holding a manageable weight off the stack.
- Keeping your legs slightly bent, lean back slightly.
- Keeping your abdominals braced and retracting your shoulder blades, pull the cable handle back towards your chest, leading with the elbow. Allow a small rotation of the torso to assist with the movement.
- At full contraction, pause momentarily before gradually returning the cable handle to the start position.
- Aim for 10–12 repetitions.

Progressions/adaptations

- A variation to the previous exercise is to hold onto a fixed bar with both hands and place both feet on the machine, while sitting on the ball.
- Brace your abdominals and lean back slightly to take the weight, keeping your spine in a neutral position.

- Squeeze your shoulder blades together and pull the bar towards your chest.
- Pause briefly as it touches your chest, and return to the start position.

Exercise 14.10 Kneeling Stability Ball One-arm Row

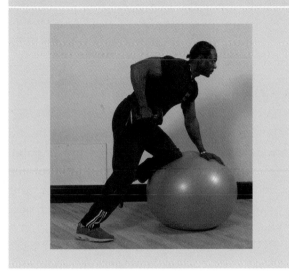

Starting position and action

- Kneel on a stability ball with your right knee and hold the ball still with your right hand so that your weight is balanced.
- Maintain a neutral posture, keeping your torso approximately parallel to the floor.
- Hold a dumbbell in your left hand with your arm extended and your palm facing the ball.
- Brace your abdominals and, leading with the left elbow, pull the dumbbell towards your ribcage.
- Pause briefly at the top range, maintaining a neutral posture and avoiding any twisting of the torso.
- Perform 10–12 repetitions in a slow and controlled manner, then repeat with the opposite arm.

Exercise 14.11 Reverse Cable Press

Starting position and action

- Stand facing the cable pulley machine with feet shoulder width apart.
- Hold the cable grips in both hands with palms facing inwards at chest height.
- Brace your abdominals and retract your shoulder blades.
- Keep both legs slightly bent and lean back slightly to take the weight of the resistance.
- Pull back with both arms, leading with the elbows to bring the cable grips towards your ribs.
- Pause briefly and then return the cables to the start position.

Progressions/adaptations

- The height of the pulleys can be adjusted up and down to vary the pulling angle.
- To intensify the movement, perform the exercise standing on one leg or alternately on a BOSU™ or stability disc.

Exercise 14.12 Standing Single-arm Row

Starting position and action

- Stand facing the cable pulley machine, with your feet shoulder width apart.
- Hold the cable in your right hand so that it is at chest height with your right arm extended and your torso slightly rotated to your left and left elbow retracted.
- Brace your abdominals and retract your shoulder blades.

- Leading with your right elbow, pull the cable back, rotating your torso slightly to the right.
- Pause briefly at the retracted position before returning back to the start position.
- Repeat 10–15 times before changing hands and repeating with the left hand.

Coaching points

- Try to avoid using too much resistance that affects your posture and control. Avoid leaning to one side when pulling on the cable.

Progressions/adaptations

- Perform the exercise while balanced on one leg. Before you lift your leg, ensure you have braced your abdominals and your posture is good. Then slowly lift one leg a few inches from the floor. Ensure you do not compromise your posture by leaning forwards or to either side. To increase the difficulty, try standing on a BOSU™ or stability disc.
- Perform a partial single-leg squat by bending the supporting knee. This is a very advanced technique and should only be performed by experienced trainers. Start as before, holding the cable in your right hand, but bend the supporting knee to lower yourself down towards the cable resistance, keeping your abdominals braced throughout. At the lowest point, retract your shoulders and pull the cable towards your ribcage, pausing at full contraction before returning to the start position and standing up. Repeat for 8–12 repetitions using your right hand before changing hands and repeating with the left, this time standing on your other leg. It is possible to vary your hand and leg options, i.e. using your right hand and standing on your right leg or using your opposite hand and supporting leg.

SHOULDER EXERCISES

Exercise 14.13 Seated Shoulder Press

Starting position and action
- Sit on the stability ball holding a dumbbell in each hand at shoulder height.
- Keep your spine in neutral, being very careful not to lean backwards.
- Brace your torso and press the dumbbells overhead, remembering not to lock your elbows on extension.
- Gradually lower the dumbbells back to the start position at the shoulders, keeping spinal alignment and maintaining form throughout.
- Keeping the feet together will increase the stabilisation required and make the exercise more difficult.
- Perform 8–12 repetitions with good form.

Progressions/adaptations
- An alternative, yet similar, exercise is the Alternate Dumbbell Press. In this exercise the weights are pressed alternately. This increases the stabilisation effect once again.

Exercise 14.14 Seated Lateral Raise

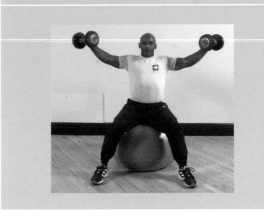

Starting position and action
- Sit on a stability ball holding a dumbbell in each hand, with your arms by your sides, the dumbbells resting lightly on the ball.
- Keep your pelvis and spine in neutral and your abdominals braced.
- Keeping your arms slightly bent at the elbow, raise both dumbbells in an arc movement until they are almost level with your shoulders.
- Pause momentarily before slowly lowering the dumbbells to the start position.
- It is important not to swing the dumbbells and to maintain the correct sitting position during this exercise.
- Aim for 10–12 repetitions.

Coaching points
- Avoid locking out your arms. Allow sufficient bend at the elbows to maintain correct form, remembering that slight flexion at the elbow will mean a longer lever and thus greater resistance to work against, whereas greater flexion will reduce the intensity as the lever length is shortened.
- Keep the head still throughout, keeping your eye level fixed.

Exercise 14.15 Prone Frontal Extension

Exercise 14.16 Prone Bent-Over Laterals (on Stability Ball)

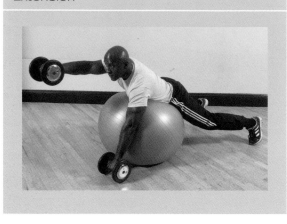

Starting position and action

- Lie face down on a stability ball, holding a pair of dumbbells in each hand.
- Keep your legs slightly bent but separated, with your toes on the floor to assist balance.
- Your ribcage should rest on top of the ball, but keeping your spine extended. Your chest should be just off the ball to allow free movement of the arms.
- Brace your abdominals and retract your shoulder blades.
- Keeping your arms slightly flexed and holding the dumbbells with your palms facing inwards and thumbs up, lift the dumbbells, one hand at a time, so that your arms stay parallel to the floor, before returning.
- Aim for 8–10 repetitions with each arm.

Starting position and action

- Lie face down on a stability ball holding a pair of dumbbells in each hand.
- Your legs should be slightly bent and separated, with your toes on the floor to assist balance.
- Your ribcage should rest on top of the ball, but keep your spine extended. Your chest should be just off the ball to allow free movement of the arms.
- Keeping your spine extended and with your abdominals braced, retract your shoulders and allow the dumbbells to rest against the stability ball.
- Raise the dumbbells laterally so that your elbows and hands are approximately level with your shoulders.
- Perform 10–12 repetitions.

Coaching points

- Maintain a slightly flexed arm position throughout to avoid putting any stress on your elbow joint.
- It is important to minimise any movement of the torso when lifting the dumbbells.

LEG EXERCISES

Exercise 14.17 Wall Squat

Starting position and action

- Stand next to a wall, facing away from it. Place the stability ball between yourself and the wall so that, by leaning back slightly, you press the stability ball into your lower back and against the wall.
- Keep your feet shoulder width apart and your feet in line with your knees.
- Make sure that the stability ball is not too high up your back before you begin to squat.
- Keeping the pressure against the stability ball by leaning against it and the wall, bend both knees to lower your body.
- The stability ball will begin to roll up, towards your mid and upper back.
- Make sure that your feet are far enough forwards so that your knees are always above or slightly behind your toes.
- Only lower as far as is comfortable, but aim to get your thighs almost parallel to the floor.
- Reaching this point, push yourself back to the upright position using your legs and buttocks.
- Aim for 12–20 repetitions.

Exercise 14.18 Single-leg Wall Squat

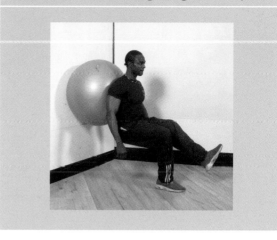

Starting position and action

- To increase the intensity level of the previous exercise dramatically, perform a single-leg squat.
- This is an advanced exercise and should only be attempted by regular gym-goers.
- As with the previous exercise, stand next to a wall, facing away from it. Place the stability ball between yourself and the wall so that, by leaning back slightly, you press the stability ball into your lower back and against the wall.
- Position your feet together to start with and then lift your left foot off the floor with your toes pointing up.
- Adjust your body position so that you are balanced on your right leg and ready to perform the exercise.
- Bend your right leg at the knee to gradually lower yourself.
- Keep your raised leg forwards so as not to hinder your movement.
- Aim to get your thigh parallel to the floor, but go no lower than this. Push down to return to the upright position.
- Aim to complete 5–10 repetitions with each leg.

Coaching points

- This is an advanced movement so, to start with, aim for partial flexion of the knee and thus a partial squat.
- As your strength increases, extend your range of movement, but don't allow your thigh to drop below horizontal.

Exercise 14.19 Lunge (Foot on Stability Ball)

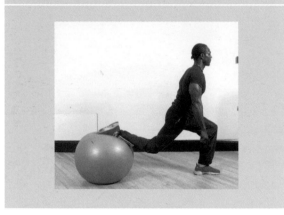

Starting position and action

- Stand in front of a stability ball. Place one leg behind you on the ball, keeping the leg bent.
- Your front leg should be maintaining your balance and supporting your body weight.
- Brace your abdominals to help you keep your balance during this exercise.
- Bend your front leg at the knee to lower yourself towards the floor.
- Aim for a near 90-degree flexion at the knee before extending your leg, returning to a standing position.
- Aim for 8–10 repetitions with one leg before changing to the other one.

BICEP EXERCISES

Exercise 14.20 Seated Bicep Curl

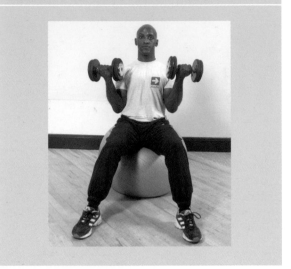

Starting position and action

- Position yourself sitting on a stability ball holding a dumbbell in each hand.
- Keep your pelvis and spine in neutral and your abdominals braced.
- Curl the dumbbells towards your chest, squeezing the biceps at the top of the movement before lowering to return to the start position.
- Aim for 10–12 repetitions.

Progressions/adaptations

- Alternate the curling action so that you curl the dumbbell up with your right arm as you lower the other dumbbell with your left, aiming for 10–12 repetitions on each arm.

Exercise 14.21 Lying Cable Curl

Progressions/adaptations

- To increase the level of stabilisation required, bring your feet and knees together. Alternatively, lift one leg, raising your foot off the floor.

Exercise 14.22 Prone Stability Ball Concentration Curl

Starting position and action

- Lie face up on a stability ball, holding the pulley cable bar of a high pulley machine.
- Push your hips upwards, keeping your thighs in line with your hips and shoulders, and your spine in neutral.
- Your grip on the cable bar should be underhand (with your palms facing your head).
- Allow the weight of the resistance to pull the arms to full extension above your head.
- Keep your feet shoulder width apart.
- Contract your biceps to curl the bar towards your forehead, squeezing at the point of peak contraction before returning the bar to the start position.
- Complete 8–12 reps slowly and under control.

Starting position and action

- Lie face down over a stability ball with your chest resting on the ball and your arms forwards, holding a dumbbell in each hand.
- Keeping your spine in neutral, brace your abdominals and keep your feet on the floor.
- Keeping your palms up, contract your biceps, bending at the elbows to lift the dumbbells towards your shoulders.
- At the top point, squeeze your biceps and then lower the dumbbells to return to the start position.
- Repeat 8–12 times.

Exercise 14.23 Tricep Dips

Starting position and action
- Sit on the edge of a bench with your legs outstretched but slightly bent, and your feet on the stability ball.
- Keep your fingers pointing forwards and your hands slightly wider than shoulder width apart.
- Brace your abdominals to assist with your balance, and lift yourself so that your body weight is supported through your arms.
- Bend your arms, lowering your body towards the floor to achieve a 90-degree angle at the elbows.
- Straighten your arms to return to the start position, repeating 8–15 times.

Progressions/adaptations
- To make this exercise easier, increase the flexion at the knee, bringing the ball closer towards you, or rest your calves and the backs of your knees on the ball, so that the legs support more of your body weight.
- To make this exercise more difficult, take one foot off the stability ball to increase the level of stabilisation required.

Exercise 14.24 Lying Tricep Extension

Starting position and action
- Lie face up on a stability ball, holding the pulley cable bar of a low pulley machine.
- Allow your mid and lower back to be supported by the ball so that your body is at an angle of approximately 30 degrees to the floor.
- Grasp the cable bar or pulley rope with your elbows above your head at full flexion.
- Keeping your elbows and upper arms fixed, contract your triceps to straighten your arms (do not lock them), pulling the rope/bar to the end position above your head.
- Squeeze your triceps when your arms are straight and then return the rope/bar to the start position with your hands just behind your head.

Exercise 14.25 Kneeling Tricep Kickbacks

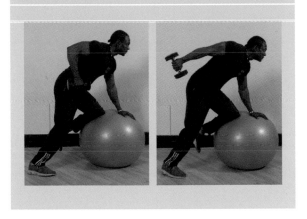

Starting position and action

- Kneel on top of a stability ball with your right knee, keeping your right hand on the ball to aid your balance.
- Hold a dumbbell in your left hand, but flex your arm at the elbow to lift the weight back so that your upper arm is parallel to the floor with your forearm vertical.
- Brace your abdominals and keep your torso in alignment without any twisting of the torso.
- Extend your arm to move the weight back in an arc to finish with the arm almost straight and approximately parallel to the floor.
- Pause briefly at the top position before returning to the start.
- Repeat 10–15 times before changing hands.

Coaching points

- It is important to return the weight so that the forearm rests in a vertical position. An incorrect action can lead to unnecessary swinging (use of momentum) and 'cheating'.

ABDOMINAL EXERCISES

Exercise 14.26 Overhead Lateral Flexion

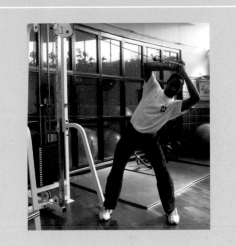

Starting position and action

- Stand next to the high pulley cable with your hands clasped together, holding the pulley handle above your head.
- You should be side on to the pulley machine, with your feet shoulder width apart and your knees slightly bent.
- Brace your abdominals, keeping your spine in neutral.
- Bend sideways, holding the pulley cable above your head.
- Pause momentarily at the end stage and return to the start position.
- Repeat 10–15 times before adjusting your position and repeating on other side.

Coaching points

- Do not bend forwards at any stage.
- Use a light weight that will allow you to bend sideways.

Exercise 14.27 Cable Crunch (Kneeling)

Starting position and action

- Start in a kneeling-up position, holding a pulley rope above your head.
- Brace your abdominals prior to movement.
- Emphasise your rectus abdominus by slowly curling your ribcage towards your pelvis.
- Aim to keep your hips still so that only your abdominal muscles are involved.
- Focus on controlled movement and remember that the goal is not to bring your nose to the floor, but to shorten the distance between your ribcage and your pelvis.

Exercise 14.28 Cable Crunch on Stability Ball

Starting position and action

- Lie facing upwards over a stability ball so that your lumbar and mid spine is supported by the ball.
- Hold on to the cable handle or rope with both hands.
- Keeping your feet on the floor approximately hip width apart, lower yourself backwards over the ball so that your lower back forms a curve and a slight stretch is felt through the abdominals.
- Make sure there is sufficient tension in the pulley cable before you begin to lift.
- Curl up and forwards, contracting your rectus abdominus to bring your ribcage towards your pelvis, keeping your head in natural alignment throughout the movement. Keep your tongue pressed to the roof of your mouth to reduce neck strain.
- Aim to achieve a 10–15 cm range of movement from the torso.
- Hold briefly at the top of the range before returning slowly to the start position.
- Repeat for 8–12 repetitions and build up to 20.

Progressions/adaptations

- Bringing your feet closer together will increase the stabilisation control required.
- Increase the weight lifted only when you can perform 20 repetitions under control.

Exercise 14.29 Stability Ball Oblique Curl

Starting position and action

- Start as before, lying face up on a stability ball with your lower back supported on the ball, and holding on to a cable rope in both hands with your elbows forwards.
- Keeping your knees bent and your feet on the floor, curl upwards and rotate your torso to bring your right shoulder towards your left hip.
- The movement range for this exercise should be about 10–20 cm.
- Hold briefly at peak position before returning to the start.
- Repeat the movement, this time bringing your left shoulder towards your right hip.
- Do not hold your breath during this movement and do not use too much resistance.
- Complete 8–15 repetitions to each side.

Exercise 14.30 Cable Machine Wood Chop

Starting position and action

- Stand sideways on to a cable pulley machine, holding the cable pulley with both hands at shoulder height or slightly above, making sure you are twisted towards the cable pulley.
- Your abdominals should be fully braced and your pelvis in neutral alignment. Your legs will need to be slightly bent for balance.
- Twist from your waist, turning the torso so that the cable pulley is pulled from over your right shoulder, across the torso and down towards your left shin in a smooth action.
- It is important not to 'over-twist' in this movement and not to use excessive resistance.
- Try 10–15 repetitions before changing sides.

Progressions/adaptations

- This exercise can be performed from a kneeling position to minimise hip and leg involvement.
- Variations for this exercise are to change the start and finish point of the movement by varying the height of where you are pulling from, and the angle and direction of pull.

Exercise 14.31 Reverse Wood Chop

Exercise 14.32 Reverse Golf Swing

Starting position and action

- Stand as before, holding the cable pulley with both hands, making sure you are twisted to one side. This time, start with your hands towards the base of the machine.
- Your abdominals should be fully braced and your pelvis in neutral alignment.
- Your legs will need to be slightly bent for balance.
- Twist from your waist, turning the torso so that the cable pulley is pulled from near your right shin, across the torso and over the left shoulder in a smooth action.
- It is important not to 'over-twist' in this movement and not to use excessive resistance.
- Try 10–15 repetitions before changing sides.

Progressions/adaptations

- This exercise can be performed from a kneeling position to minimise hip and leg involvement.

Starting position and action

- Begin in an upright kneeling position, with your hips in alignment with your thighs and shoulders, keeping your pelvis in neutral.
- Hold on to the cable grip with both hands, facing the machine, keeping your hands in the low position and your arms slightly bent.
- Brace your abdominals, thighs and lower back, keeping your shoulder blades retracted.
- Rotate your torso to the left, pulling your arms and the cable upwards in an arc to finish with your arms at shoulder height and at a 90-degree angle to the cable machine, facing left.
- Pause briefly at the end point and then return to the start position.
- Repeat, this time rotating to your right.

Exercise 14.33 Cable Crunch (Supine)

Exercise 14.34 Cable Resisted Oblique Reach

Starting position and action

- Lie down on the floor, with your head near the pulley machine, holding the cable pulley handle behind your head.
- Keep your knees bent and your feet on the floor.
- Make sure there is sufficient tension in the pulley cable before you begin to lift.
- Curl upwards, using the abdominal curl technique (see page 101), contracting your abdominals to bring your ribcage towards your pelvis.
- Keep your head in natural alignment throughout the movement.
- Do not hold your breath during this movement and do not try to lift too much resistance.

Starting position and action

- Start as before, lying face up on the floor with your head towards the low pulley machine.
- Position your hands by your ears, holding the pulley rope with your elbows above your head.
- Curl upwards and rotate your torso to bring your ribs on your right side towards your left hip.
- The movement range for this exercise should be approximately 10–20 cm.
- Hold briefly at the end point before returning to the start position.
- Repeat the movement, this time bringing the left side of your ribcage towards your right hip.

HANDS-ON PARTNER WORK

15

One aspect of resistance training that is often forgotten is partner work. This is where, instead of working against a fixed resistance, such as a medicine ball or dumbbell, you work against the resistance that your partner is placing on you. This can be very effective in certain exercises as it means that the resistance does not have to rely on gravity to create the load.

For example, if you were to play a tennis forehand stroke, as the movement goes 'across' gravity and not against it, gravity does not provide a resistance to the stroke itself but is applying downward pressure to your body. Your skeletal muscles and trunk muscles are stabilising your body to maintain an upright posture, yet the only resistance to the stroke itself is the weight of the tennis racquet and the relative weight of the tennis ball as you hit it. It is possible to add resistance to the stroke itself, albeit by modifying it slightly, by using a variable resistance tube or working with a partner holding a towel. This creates a new resistance to challenge the muscles – both in relation to performing the 'stroke' and maintaining correct body alignment and form throughout.

It has to be said that partner work is a learned skill and clear communication is very important. You should talk to each other and work together so that you learn how much resistance is the correct amount for certain exercises and each other's strength. Certain movements will require minimal resistance; others will require a lot more. It is important to remember that when applying a hands-on technique you can create the resistance from any angle and this can be very useful. You need to be aware of the range of movement possible in relation to the muscles you want to train, and how much resistance to apply to recruit these muscles optimally.

When applying resistance to someone else, or working against resistance placed on you, it is imperative that any movements are performed in a controlled manner. Correct resistance cannot be applied if the movements are jerky. In addition, when performing an exercise, you might find that, during the movement, the intensity varies at different points. Bear this in mind when your partner applies resistance, otherwise your movement might be restricted too much and you will not be able to train your muscles effectively. Similarly, when you are resisting your partner while maintaining a static position, if he or she does not apply enough resistance, you will not be stimulating the muscles sufficiently.

As you progress with hands-on work you will begin to get a feel for how much resistance to apply during the various exercises, as you will be aware of how hard your partner is working and will know when and whether to increase or decrease the resistance.

Some exercises in this section require movement; these are classed as isotonic exercises, where there is either muscle shortening and/or lengthening as you perform the exercise. Other exercises require you to work your muscles against a resistance that involves little or no movement. These static exercises can be classed as isometric.

As in any resistance exercise, correct breathing is important. This is especially so during high-intensity movement and isometric exercises when there is a risk of raising your blood pressure. You should never hold your breath during isometric exercises, but should take short, sharp breaths, keeping constant tension in your abdominal muscles throughout.

Before you begin to apply partner resistance, practise a few normal movements for each exercise without any resistance. Or, if it is a static contraction, focus on firing the appropriate muscle fibres as this will help to prepare you for the exercise to come. This mental and physical preparation is useful as the visualisation and rehearsed movement help to stimulate the nerves to focus on the desired movement to follow. Many athletes will perform similar tasks when preparing for a specific shot or stroke (for example, when putting in golf).

When you are both comfortable with the movement and muscle contraction required, get into position and focus on the initial contraction with your partner applying minimal resistance. Then, depending on the nature of the exercise, gradually increase the resistance by applying a greater contraction and focused movement accordingly. Always work with each other and after each repetition talk to each other to decide whether the resistance applied was sufficient, too great or too little.

THE EXERCISES

Exercise 15.1 Partner Twist (Statues)

Starting position and action
- Stand upright in a balanced position with neutral spine, feet apart and with abdominals braced.
- Your partner then tries to move you out of this position by applying force and twisting you.
- Don't hold your breath.
- You should try to resist for 3–10 seconds repeatedly over periods of up to a minute before swapping over.

Coaching points
- Remember that the focus is to move the position of the torso rather than just try to push your partner around the room.

Exercise 15.2 Kneeling Oblique Twist

Starting position and action

- Begin by kneeling opposite your partner, facing each other and in an upright position with pelvis and spine in neutral.
- Keep your knees shoulder width apart but bring your heels together to give you more stability with a triangular base.
- Have your partner place their right hand directly in front of them and on to your left shoulder; they should place their left hand around the back of your right shoulder as if they were going to twist your torso.
- Both of you need to brace your abdominal muscles in preparation for what is to come.
- You will now try to resist against your partner by turning to your right, against the pressure of your partner.
- Your partner simply resists your movement by increasing the pressure against you.
- Make sure you emphasise your abdominal bracing throughout, aiming to resist for 5–10 seconds before changing sides.

- This time, your partner places their left hand on your right shoulder and their right hand around the back of your left shoulder, and you aim to twist to your left, remembering not to hold your breath.
- Aim for 3–5 twists each side before swapping so that your partner tries to twist with you resisting.

Coaching points

- It is important to maintain the focus on your abdominals throughout this movement, otherwise it is possible other muscles (such as hamstrings, glutes and shoulders) will try to assist.

Exercise 15.3 Resisted Ab Curl

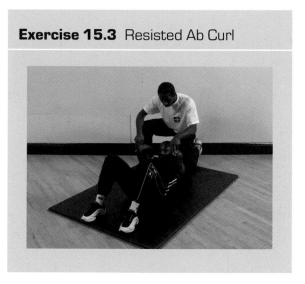

Starting position and action

- Lie down on the floor, face up, with your knees bent, feet on the floor.
- Position your arms across your chest, with your hands resting on your shoulders.
- Your partner should kneel down behind your head so that they can rest their hands on your elbows.

- Brace your abdominals and begin to curl up, with your partner providing resistance against your elbows.
- Your movement range will be limited but aim to get your shoulders and upper back off the floor as in a normal curl movement.
- Your partner has to adjust the resistance they apply to allow you to move but it is important that you keep your movement constant and controlled, avoiding any jerking actions as these would make it difficult for your partner to provide constant and effective resistance.

Exercise 15.4 Resisted Standing Flexion (Vertical)

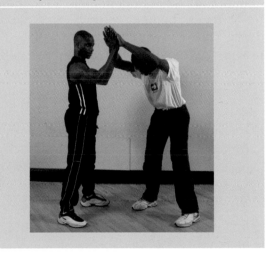

Starting position and action
- Stand upright, with your knees slightly bent in a balanced, or 'sporting', stance. Keep your abdominals braced.
- Place your hands together, palms down, with your arms out in front of you at an angle of approximately 45 degrees to the floor, slightly above your head.
- Your partner should stand to your side with one hand resting against your lower back (to prevent flexing at the waist – this hand can be removed as you master the technique) and the other underneath your hands.
- Focusing on your abdominal muscles, aim to curl your torso, bringing your ribcage towards your hips.
- You should aim to keep your arms at the same angle to your body throughout.
- Your partner provides resistance with the hand they are holding under your palms but should allow a 15–30 cm movement of the arms, which translates to a 5–10 cm movement of the torso.
- It is important that you focus on contraction of the abdominals to create the movement rather than flexion of the hips.
- It is also important that your partner allows you some movement but provides adequate resistance so that you are really having to work the abdominals hard to initiate movement.

Exercise 15.5 Resisted Standing Flexion (Vertical)

Starting position and action

- Stand as before in an upright, 'sporting', stance with your knees slightly bent and your abdominals braced.
- Clasp your hands together, outstretched in front of you at shoulder height.
- Keep your arms slightly bent but firm and tense your abdominals, keeping your torso rigid.
- Your partner should stand in front of you, with their hands on your hands or forearms.
- Your partner applies pressure to your arms, trying to 'move' them laterally by pushing against you.
- You must resist this pressure, trying to maintain neutral.
- Remember to breathe constantly throughout the exercise.
- Your partner should only apply resistance for periods up to but not exceeding 10 seconds.

Exercise 15.6 Resisted Tennis Shots (Forehand/Backhand)

Starting position and action

- Begin by holding a towel, or something similar, in your preferred playing hand.
- Get into a 'sporting', or 'ready', stance, as if to play a tennis stroke (forehand or backhand).
- Your partner should stand behind you, holding the other end of the towel, but should not hinder your movement.
- As you perform the tennis stroke, try to visualise actually hitting an imaginary ball. Focus on contracting your abdominals throughout but placing greater emphasis on the point of 'imaginary contact'.
- Your partner should allow enough resistance to keep the towel taut while not restricting any movement.
- As you perform the movement, your partner should gradually increase the resistance by restricting the movement of the towel – but only at the final stage (the point of 'imaginary contact').
- At this point, really focus on your technique, placing emphasis on both your abdominal contraction and correct stroke form.

Exercise 15.7 Back Extension Off Banch (Feet Held)

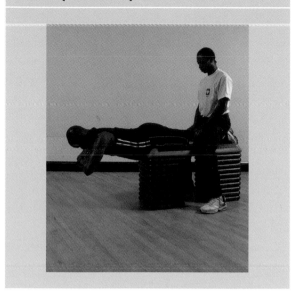

Exercise 15.8 Back Extension Off Banch with Rotation (Feet Held)

Starting position and action

- Lie face down over a bench with your hips on the edge to allow unrestricted flexion of the torso.
- Get your partner to hold your legs securely at the ankles or calves.
- Place your arms across your chest and flex forwards so that your upper torso is lowered towards the floor.
- Brace your abdominals and, contracting through your lower back, raise up to a horizontal position, pausing briefly before repeating.

Starting position and action

- Lie face down over a bench with your hips on the edge to allow unrestricted flexion of the torso.
- Get your partner to hold your legs securely at the ankles or calves.
- Place your arms across your chest and flex forwards so that your upper torso is lowered towards the floor.
- Brace your abdominals and, contracting through your lower back, raise up to a horizontal position.
- As you lift, twist your torso so that you lead the raise from your right shoulder, pausing briefly before lowering to the floor.
- Repeat, this time twisting the left shoulder uppermost.

Exercise 15.9 Resisted Stability Ball Abdominal Curl

Starting position and action

- Lie back over the stability ball, face up, so that your lower and mid back is supported over the ball.
- Position your arms across your chest, with your hands resting on your shoulders.
- Your partner should stand behind you so that they can rest their hands on your elbows.
- Brace your abdominals and begin to curl up, with your partner providing resistance against your elbows. Keep your tongue pressed to the roof of your mouth to reduce neck strain.
- Your movement range will be limited but aim to curl your shoulders and upper back off the ball and towards your hips.
- Your partner will have to adjust the resistance they apply to allow you to move, but it is important that you keep your movement constant and controlled, avoiding any jerking actions, as these will cause difficulty for your partner and he or she will be unable to provide constant and effective resistance.
- Repeat 5–10 times.

Progressions/adaptations

- This movement can be repeated with your arms extended over your head, keeping them in line with your torso. In this position, your partner would just need to rest their hands on your arms, as the resistance is already quite strong.

Exercise 15.10 Resisted Flexion (Lateral)

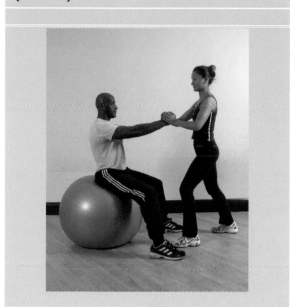

Starting position and action

- Sit on a stability ball with your feet shoulder width apart and your knees bent, keeping your abdominals braced and your spine in neutral.

- Clasp your hands together, outstretched in front of you at shoulder height.
- Keep your arms slightly bent, but firm, and tense your abdominals, keeping your torso rigid.
- Your partner should stand in front of you, with their hands on your hands or forearms.
- Your partner then applies pressure to your arms, trying to 'move' them laterally by pushing against you. This pressure should be to the left and then right for 1–3 seconds each.
- Vary both the duration and the intensity for a total time of not more than 15 seconds.
- You should resist this pressure, trying to maintain neutral. Try not to lean against the direction of pressure, rather focus on maintaining neutral and overcoming any external force from your partner.
- It is very important to breathe constantly throughout this exercise.
- Your partner should only apply the resistance for periods up to but not exceeding 15 seconds.
- Do 3–5 complete repetitions, allowing 10–20 seconds recovery between each.

MEDICINE BALL TRAINING

16

A medicine ball is a weighted ball, weighing between 1 and 10 kg. Medicine balls can vary in size and used to be made of brown leather; these days they are graded in different colours according to size and are made out of soft plastic. The main principle with medicine ball training is that, in order to throw or catch it, one has to tense many abdominal muscles. This creates a solid or stable base to work from. In much the same way as the foundations are laid when building a house, the stronger the foundations the greater the forces that can be applied. Another advantage is that, unlike weights, which you invariably have to lift upwards against gravity, medicine balls can be thrown 'across' gravity, or in any direction relative to the sporting activity or muscle group you are training. You can be working against both the inertia of the ball when throwing and the momentum of the ball when catching. That's why those athletes and sportspeople that require upper body power use medicine balls in their workouts.

Different sports have varying amounts of fluidity, rhythm, focus and applied power. You might think that the type of abdominal training used in each discipline is very different and to a certain extent it is (for example, bracing and stabilisation are very important parts of dance training and yoga as there are many positions/stances that require exceptional balance). Different sport-specific movements incorporate relative proprioceptive stabilisation techniques in order to maintain balance.

Power depends on a strong base. In fact, much of the appropriate training in sports and martial arts comes from indirect training (for example, when taking or throwing a punch in, say, boxing, you need to brace or tense in order to minimise any pain felt or to create optimum power).

Think about a tennis serve, volleyball spike or chest pass. Without optimal bracing or contraction of the transverse abdominus, with a small rapid contraction of the rectus abdominus, there would be no power. We often think of the transverse abdominus as the muscle responsible for intra-abdominal pressure and breathing out (consider the grunts and groans you might hear during a game of tennis, for example).

Medicine ball exercises are an excellent way of training the core muscles to help achieve power. They can also be used to train for specific sports: the movements of a sporting action can be replicated and appropriate resistance applied in a controlled manner to train the muscles effectively.

Medicine ball training is great fun and can

make boring exercises dynamic and interesting while still having the desired conditioning effect. Compare these: performing 20–30 oblique twists on the floor on your own or throwing a 4 or 5 kg medicine ball with all your force at a moving target (i.e. your partner) for them to catch and throw back. Not only is the latter a more interesting option, but training the muscles in this way is much closer to the sporting movement required.

If abdominal training is made to relate to sport through partner interaction, functional objectivity and above all fun, sports teams and athletes are likely to spend more time on the principles of core conditioning. The resulting improvements in balance, power and general game-play achieved by the athletes should then be sufficient motivation for them to continue and develop this area of dynamic power training. The weight of the medicine ball used will be dependent on your initial strength and specific goal. However, it should be remembered that, unlike weight training, the goal isn't necessarily to use the heaviest ball, rather to perform the desired movement with adequate resistance to achieve sufficient strength or power gains. With a sporting application, the resistance of the ball used should never impair or compromise the sporting movement.

Specific sporting movements that benefit from the main medicine ball exercises are:
- flexion and rotation
- power and speed
- dynamic stabilisation and balance.

It is important to remember that while I have listed a number of progressions and/or adaptations for the following exercises, there are likely to be many more specific alternatives directly related to each specific sport; unfortunately, I do not have the space to go into such specific detail here.

FLEXION AND ROTATION

Exercise 16.1 Basic Curl

Starting position and action

- Lie down, face up, with your pelvis in neutral, knees bent and your feet on the floor.
- Hold on to the medicine ball so that it rests comfortably on your chest.
- Brace or tense your abdominals and lift your head away from the floor, partially bringing your chin towards your chest.
- Contract the abdominal muscles to lift your shoulders and upper back off the floor, bringing your ribcage towards your pelvis.
- Lift as far as is comfortable but do not allow your lower back to come off the floor.
- Return slowly to the start position.
- As you are using the ball as a resistance tool aim for 10–15 repetitions before increasing the size/weight of the ball.
- A 1 kg or 2 kg ball should be suitable for the general-level exerciser and 4–6 kg might suit the more advanced.

Coaching points

- An approximate upper range of movement would be when the chin is at the same level as the knee (i.e. you can just see over the tops of the knees).

- Don't tense your neck – keep it relaxed but with the eyes looking forwards.
- Keep all movements slow and controlled; never opt for increased weight if this would mean loss of control.

Progressions/adaptations

- To increase the resistance, place the medicine ball (i) on your forehead, (ii) on the top of your head, or (iii) held 10–15 cm above your head (the hardest progression).
- It is important to remember not to initiate the movement with your arms and to make sure that the medicine ball's position in relation to the body stays fixed throughout the exercise.

Exercise 16.2 Russian Twist

Starting position and action

- Sit on the floor with your knees bent and your feet on the floor.
- Lean back so that your torso is at an angle of 30–45 degrees to the floor.
- Hold a medicine ball at arm's length in front of your chest.
- Brace your abdominals.
- Rotate your torso to bring the ball towards the floor on your left side, pause momentarily, then rotate to bring the medicine ball to your right side.
- Complete 15–20 twists to either side.

Coaching points

- Keep the movement controlled, remembering to focus on the abdominal bracing throughout.
- Make sure the torso angle does not drop or lift beyond the desired range.
- Ideally, touch the ball to either side (this may be difficult at first).

Progressions/adaptations

- Gradually increase the weight of the medicine ball used.
- Keeping your abdominals braced, increase the speed and/or range of movement, maintaining correct form.
- To increase intensity, keep your arms nearly straight as the further away from your torso the ball is, the harder the exercise will feel.

Exercise 16.3 Give and Receive

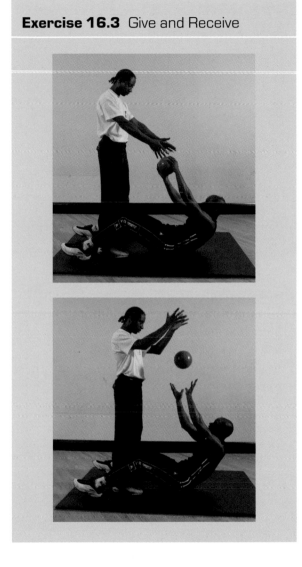

Starting position and action
- Lie down with your knees bent and your abdominals braced.
- Get your partner to stand over you holding the ball above your hips.
- Curl up so that at peak contraction you can reach the ball held by your partner. Pause momentarily to grasp and take the ball with arms outstretched and then return to the floor, holding the medicine ball under control.
- On reaching the floor, curl up again, to return the ball to your partner, who retrieves it, then return to the floor as before but without the ball.
- Repeat this two-stage movement until failure; this should take no longer than one minute and no less than 20 seconds, otherwise you need to change the weight of ball accordingly.

Coaching points
- Try not to rush through this exercise, as unnecessary speed will allow 'cheating' to occur and detract from the effectiveness.
- Don't use a ball that is too heavy for you or you will not be able to perform the correct movement.
- Do not attempt to move on to the following progressions until you can perform at least 15–10 full repetitions of the basic exercise.

Progressions/adaptations
- Level 2 is similar except that the ball is dropped by your partner and you catch it in the curl position, remaining static momentarily (utilising the stabilisation muscles of the trunk) before returning to the floor with the ball.
- Level 3 is as Level 2 but, after catching the ball, returning to floor and curling up again with ball, you tense your abdominals and throw the ball up for your partner to catch it, before returning to floor.

Important
The Level 3 option is a very tough exercise and useful in all racquet sports, as well as sports that involve throwing or passing a ball.

Exercise 16.4 Goalkeeper Drill

Starting position and action

- Lie down on the floor with your partner 1–2 m away in front of you, holding a medicine ball.
- Begin performing an abdominal curl but at the top phase (head, shoulders and upper back off the floor) your partner should throw you the ball to one side.
- Catch the ball and throw it straight back to your partner before lowering yourself back to the floor, then repeat.
- Your partner should throw the ball so that you have to reach to either side alternately.
- Repeat the throwing and catching movements for 30–60 seconds.

Coaching points

- At the point of catching the ball, brace your abdominals and keep them tensed as you absorb the momentum of the ball before throwing it back to your partner.

Progressions/adaptations

- Initially, it might be wise to begin with a lighter ball, such as a football or basketball, progressing to a medicine ball when you are ready.

DYNAMIC STABILISATION AND BALANCE

Exercise 16.5 Dynamic Plank/Bridge

Starting position and action

- Get into a press-up position (prone/face down) but with your weight resting on your forearms and elbows rather than your hands.
- Pull in your abdominals, bracing through the torso.
- Position your feet carefully so that they are balanced on the medicine ball.
- Keep your body in a straight line from shoulders to ankles.
- Hold for 15 seconds initially and build up to a minute.

Coaching points

- Keep your body rigid throughout the exercise.

Progressions/adaptations

- To increase the difficulty, (i) try to draw a circle with your toes while they are resting on the medicine ball, (ii) have alternate legs resting on the medicine ball, (iii) have one leg on the medicine ball and **abduct** the other leg approximately 1–2 feet.

Exercise 16.6 Press-ups on a Medicine Ball

Starting position and action

- Begin in a press-up position (prone/face down), with one hand on the medicine ball and the other on the floor, arms at least shoulder width apart.
- Keep your abdominals braced throughout the movement.
- Lower your chest to the floor by performing a press-up movement, then return to the start position.
- Repeat to complete 10–20 full press-ups.

Coaching points

- Maintain correct form and body alignment throughout the exercise.

Progressions/adaptations

- Level 2 is as Level 1, but after each press-up swap the ball to the other hand by rolling it across.
- Level 3 is similar but involves 'power swapping', which means that the ball stays still while in the dynamic power press-ups you have first one hand then the other on the ball. This is similar to a clap press-up, but it adjusts the body position too.
- This is a very tough exercise and trains all your stabilisation muscles, arms, shoulders and chest, as well as testing your co-ordination.

Exercise 16.7 Dynamic Medicine Ball Press-up

Starting position and action

- Position yourself in a press-up position (prone/face down), with your arms extended.
- Position your feet carefully so that they are balanced on the medicine ball.
- Keep your body in a straight line from shoulders to ankles.
- Brace your abdominals throughout the exercise.
- Lower your chest towards the floor, bending at the elbows as you perform the press-up, then extend your arms to push back to the start position.
- Repeat 10–20 times, maintaining correct form throughout.

Coaching points

- Try not to lock the arms in the top phase.
- The emphasis again is on maintaining rigidity throughout the torso. Do not let the torso sag.
- Keep the movement slow to begin with, gradually speeding up. Maintain control throughout.

Progressions/adaptations

- Level 2 is to perform push-ups with both feet on the ball. You have to focus on your stabilisation muscles to avoid falling off the ball.
- Level 3 is to perform the press-up but, as you lift upwards, extend one arm to reach forwards so that the arm is parallel to the floor.

Exercise 16.8 Interactive Passing Drill

Starting position and action

- Stand on one leg, maintaining a balanced position and holding a medicine ball.
- Tense your abdominals throughout the exercise to help you balance.
- Throw the medicine ball to your partner repeatedly at various heights.
- Keep throwing and catching the ball until someone is forced to put their foot down for balance; when this happens they have 'lost' the game. Keep 'playing' for up to three minutes at a time.

Coaching points

- Try to make your partner lose their balance by throwing the ball at different heights and speeds.

Progressions/adaptations

- If you need to, begin with a lighter ball, such as a basketball, and first work on speed before progressing gradually to heavier medicine balls (up to 5 kg).

POWER AND SPEED

One of the main advantages of using a medicine ball in core training is that it enables you to introduce power exercises and throws while standing – allowing you to perform sport-specific movements. The following exercises will teach you to apply sufficient abdominal tension in order to create a solid base, allowing you to generate greater force on each throw or pass.

As your technique improves, and you begin to generate more power during the throws, try introducing elements of instability – such as standing on one leg – or performing the exercise while standing on a wobble board or Reebok Core Board™.

Exercise 16.9 Chest Pass

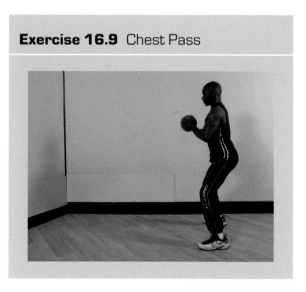

Starting position and action

- Stand opposite a partner or in front of a wall, holding the medicine ball at chest height.
- The chest pass can be performed in a neutral or split stance (with either leg forwards) position.

- Tense the abdominals as you push the ball away from your chest before releasing it.
- Either pass the ball to your partner or pass it to strike against a wall about 5–10 m away.
- Perform 10–20 passes, focusing on correct stance and technique throughout.

Coaching points
- Keep your abdominals braced and your torso movement minimal.
- Focus on speed, power and direction, with minimal 'sway' or backward movement.

Progressions/adaptations
- When confident about the power and accuracy of your pass, take a step back to increase the throwing distance.
- This drill can also be performed as a bounce pass to a partner.
- Another option is to increase your distance from the wall or your partner, and to substitute the medicine ball for a lighter basketball for increased sport-specific action.
- When you feel that you have good control and power, try standing on a wobble board or Core Board to increase the level of stabilisation required.

Who benefits?
Chest pass drills are great for basketball and netball players.

Exercise 16.10 Stability Ball Chest Pass

Starting position and action
- Begin in an upright kneeling position on a stability ball, opposite a partner or a wall, and holding the medicine ball at chest height.
- Tense your abdominals as you push the ball away from your chest before releasing it.
- Either pass the ball to your partner or throw it against a wall approximately 2–5 m away.
- If throwing to a wall, make sure you are bracing as you catch the ball so that you absorb the momentum.
- Complete 15–20 powerful pass movements.

Coaching points
- As you pass the ball, contract your abdominals tight and preserve the tension through your hips and legs, keeping everything braced to assist your balance.

Progressions/adaptations
- For the very advanced athlete, this exercise can be performed while standing on the stability ball.

Exercise 16.11 Kneeling Oblique Throw

Starting position and action

- Kneel down facing a wall, approximately 2–3 m away from it.
- Keep your hips in neutral and brace your abdominals.
- Holding the medicine ball at arm's length, rotate through your waist and throw the ball diagonally and hard at the wall.
- Aim to catch the ball as it rebounds towards your opposite side.
- Repeat the throws against the wall to complete 10–15 throws from each side.

Coaching points

- Don't allow unnecessary hip involvement or excessive arm action as these will detract from the benefits to the abdominal muscles.
- Allow for a functional rotation without losing form.
- Keep your arms fixed but do not lock out your elbows.
- Focus on achieving power with each throw and don't use a ball that is too heavy.

Progressions/adaptations

- This drill can be carried out with a partner instead of a wall – they should mirror the movements accordingly.
- Alternatively, both versions can be performed standing up.
- Stand opposite your partner, with your knees soft and your arms fairly straight. Throw the ball to each other, twisting from your waists, with minimal arm movement to emphasise the obliques.
- Further variations include a 'reverse oblique throw', where the ball is thrown behind you to a wall or partner.
- Try standing on a wobble board or Core Board to increase the level of stabilisation required.

Exercise 16.12 Stability Ball Oblique Throw

Starting position and action

- Sit on a stability ball with your feet shoulder width apart, facing a partner or wall approximately 3–5 m away.
- Keeping your hips in neutral and holding the medicine ball at arm's length, brace your abdominals, maintaining your balance.
- Rotate through your waist and throw the ball diagonally and hard at the wall or your partner.
- Aim to catch the ball as it rebounds from the wall on your opposite side, or have your partner throw the ball hard for you to catch on your opposite side.

Coaching points

- Don't allow unnecessary hip involvement or excessive arm action as these will detract from the benefits to the abdominal muscles.

Progressions/adaptations

- To increase the difficulty, try kneeling on the stability ball.
- Your partner can either throw the ball back for you to catch it, or pass it back, according to your ability.
- Another variation is the 'reverse oblique throw', where the ball is thrown behind you to a wall or partner.

Who benefits?

Oblique throw drills are great for those who play tennis, rugby and golf.

Exercise 16.13 Overhead Throw to Floor

Starting position and action

- Stand up, holding the medicine ball with both hands above your head.
- Your knees should be bent slightly in a 'sports stance', or 'ready' position, with your abdominals braced.
- Rapidly contract your transverse abdominus, followed immediately by your rectus abdominus to initiate partial flexion.
- Continue the movement by throwing the medicine ball to the floor with a powerful arm action so that the ball bounces approximately 1 m away from your feet.
- This exercise is about maximum power and rapid abdominal contraction. Aim for only 6–10 quality throws with perfect form.

Coaching points

- This is a rapid action and requires appropriate bracing to apply the necessary force.
- The power behind this movement comes from the trunk, not the arms.

- It is possible to complete this movement without the appropriate abdominal contraction, but this defeats the object of the exercise.
- This rapid bracing is a learned technique and often takes time to master.

Progressions/adaptations

- This drill can be performed by modifying the throwing angle slightly, still aiming downwards but targeting a point approximately 2–3 m away so that the ball bounces upwards to a partner or off a wall.
- Try performing this exercise standing on one leg, on a wobble board or on a BOSU™.

Exercise 16.14 Overhead Flat Throw

Starting position and action

- Begin as before, holding the medicine ball above and slightly behind your head.
- Keep in a **sports stance** (neutral) or a **split stance** (with either leg forwards).
- Rapidly contract your abdominals to initiate the movement and then powerfully follow

through with the arm action, throwing the ball forwards in a flat trajectory.

- Aim at a wall or partner positioned approximately 10–15 m away.
- Aim to complete 10–15 powerful throws, focusing on the quality of each throw.

Coaching points

- It is fine to lean back slightly prior to making the throwing action, but avoid excessive hyper-extension.
- Remember to change your leading leg if you are throwing from a split stance position.
- Use a lighter medicine ball (1–2 kg), or even a basketball or football to start with.
- The emphasis of this movement is speed and accuracy.

Progressions/adaptations

- By applying a greater reverse lean (hyper-extension), this movement can be modified into a full throw technique.
- In the full throw technique, the emphasis is on the distance the ball travels.
- The trajectory will obviously be more parabolic than in the basic exercise, so make sure your partner is far enough away.
- It is possible to restrict leg involvement in both full and flat throw options by throwing from a kneeling position, or by standing on an unstable base such as a Core Board or BOSU™.
- Alternatively, the exercise can be executed with a one- or two-step approach, to relate it more closely to a specific sport that involves a similar throwing action.

Exercise 16.15 Reverse Overhead Throw

Starting position and action

- Start in a neutral stance with your abdominals braced.
- Hold the medicine ball at waist height.
- Bend your knees and back as you swing the ball towards your legs, keeping it under control all the time.
- Then extend your back and legs to help swing the ball upwards, using your arms to throw the ball vertically into the air.
- When the ball returns to the ground, retrieve it and repeat.
- Complete 10–15 throws.

Coaching points

- Gradually build up to a heavier medicine ball over time.
- Make the movement dynamic, but always keep it under control.

Progressions/adaptations

- Instead of a vertical throw, aim the ball over your head but behind you.
- Aim to increase the height and distance for which the ball travels.
- Introduce a wobble board to stand on when you are ready.

Who benefits?

This movement is essential to generating upper-body power. It is also great for football and rugby players.

Exercise 16.16 Single-arm Throw/Pass

Starting position and action

- Stand in either a split or sports stance position, holding a medicine ball over your head with one hand.

- Brace your abdominals throughout the movement.
- Rapidly contract your transverse abdominus prior to any upper body movement.
- Initiate a downward throwing action with your arm, aiming the medicine ball at the floor approximately 3–5 m away.
- Repeat 6–10 times with each arm.

Coaching points

- Keep your torso static and ensure that there is minimal movement.
- Use a lighter medicine ball (1–3 kg).

Progressions/adaptations

- This drill can be performed with either a bent or straight arm for variation.
- The direction and angle of the throw can also be varied but the emphasis should be on power and execution of technique.
- When you feel able to generate sufficient power with good core control, try standing on an unstable base, such as a wobble board.

Who benefits?

This is an excellent drill for volleyball and tennis players.

Exercise 16.17 Interactive Chest Pass with Movement

- On releasing the ball, move out of the way so that the ball rebounds off the wall and is caught by your partner. You should now be standing slightly further back than your partner.
- Having caught the ball, your partner repeats the chest-pass action, throwing the ball hard against the wall, before moving out of the way so that you can catch the ball.
- Repeat for 20–40 seconds and build up to no more than one minute.

Coaching points

- The focus throughout this drill is on dynamic power and agility.
- Emphasis is placed on fast footwork and good reactions.
- The flight of the ball needs to be high enough to allow sufficient time for it to be caught by your partner.

Progressions/adaptations

- As you improve, vary not only your distance from the wall, but also the flight of the ball.
- It is possible to use two balls (starting with one each), but accuracy and concentration is vital.

Starting position and action

- Begin by standing in front of your partner, with both of you facing a wall.
- With your abdominals braced and in a sports stance, throw the medicine ball hard against the wall (using the chest pass technique).

Who benefits?

This is a great drill for basketball, netball, rugby and handball players.

PART **THREE**

THE WAY FORWARD

Now you have developed a sound understanding of the requirements of core stability training – including the relevant intensities, balancing positions and contractions that occur in various exercises – the next stage is to increase the stabilisation required as suggested in some of the previous exercises. This will take core stability to another level, yet it must be remembered that the following multi-level exercises are designed for the confident core stability exerciser who has taken the necessary time to understand the principles involved and is proficient in many of the exercises covered in Part Two.

MULTI-JOINT AND PLANE MOVEMENTS

17

THE EXERCISES

Exercise 17.1 Step Up to Balance with Overhead Press

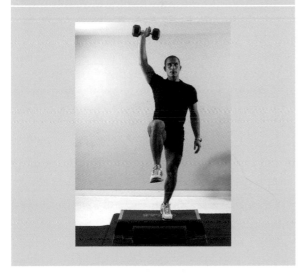

Starting position and action

- Stand behind a step bench or a platform approximately 12–16 in high.
- Hold a dumbbell in your right hand with your arms by your side.
- Brace your abdominals and step up on to the platform, leading with your right leg and following with your left leg. Stand on the platform with your feet hip distance apart.
- As your left leg reaches the platform, curl the dumbbell in your right hand towards your right shoulder and then press it overhead.
- Pause briefly at the 'upper' position before lowering the dumbbell back to shoulder height and then to your hips.
- As the dumbbell returns, step back with your left leg to lower yourself back to the floor and then step down with your right leg to return to the start position.
- Repeat 6–10 times, leading with your right leg before transferring the dumbbell to your left hand and repeating the movement, this time leading with the left leg.

Coaching points

- Do not use a weight that is too heavy until you have mastered the technique.
- Avoid leaning to either side or 'swinging' the dumbbell as you lift it.

Progressions/adaptations

- As you perform the step up, bring the trailing leg (the one on the floor) up to a raised position, with the thigh parallel to the floor. In this position you are balanced on one leg with one arm holding a dumbbell overhead.

- It is possible to vary the hand you use to hold the dumbbell in relation to your lead leg. You could either step up with your right leg while holding the dumbbell in your right hand, or you could hold the dumbbell in the opposite hand to your lead leg. This will affect both your co-ordination and balance.

Exercise 17.2 Single Leg Touchdown with Overhead Press

Starting position and action

- Sometimes referred to as a 'Romanian dead lift', this is an advanced exercise and requires excellent balance and muscle bracing.
- Stand holding a dumbbell in your right hand with the dumbbell by your side.
- Brace your abdominals and slowly lift your right leg off the floor while maintaining your balance.

- Keeping your abdominals braced, bend down. Reach across your body with your right hand towards your left shin, bending at the knee and the waist.
- Keep your head in neutral, your body aligned and avoid leaning to either side to compensate as you perform the movement.
- Pause briefly at the lowest point and then return back to the start position by straightening your leg and extending your back into an upright posture.
- As you become upright, curl the dumbbell in your right hand towards your right shoulder and then press it above your head with your arm fully extended.
- Pause briefly at this 'upper' position before returning back to the start position.
- Repeat this exercise 8–10 times before transferring the weight into your left hand and repeating, this time bending and reaching down across your body to your right shin on the lowering phase.

Coaching points

- This is a complex movement and the technique should be mastered with no resistance at first.
- Once mastered, begin with a relatively light weight (3–5 kg) before increasing.
- If necessary, this movement can be broken down so that you perform only the first phase of the movement without the need for the overhead press.

Progressions/adaptations

- For the adventurous, this exercise can be performed on an unstable base such as a Core Board, stability disc or a BOSU™.

Exercise 17.3 Cable Press with Part Lunge

Exercise 17.4 Wood Chop with Side Lunge

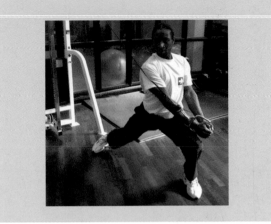

Starting position and action

- Stand in front of the cable pulley machine, facing away from it.
- Keep your hips in neutral and square to the machine, with your torso twisted slightly to your right.
- Hold the pulley handle in your right hand, at shoulder height, with your elbow bent and at the same height.
- Your left hand can be outstretched in front of you to assist your movement and act as a guide or marker.
- Brace your abdominals and rotate through your torso, pressing the pulley handle forwards.
- As your body rotates, draw your left arm back and 'punch' through with your right hand, transferring the arm position. As you do this, step forwards into a lunge position. This movement can be performed stepping with either leg.
- Gradually return to the start position and repeat.
- Aim for 10–15 repetitions before changing arms and repeating with the left arm.

Starting position and action

- Stand sideways on to the cable pulley machine, holding the pulley with both hands and making sure you are twisted towards the cable pulley.
- Your abdominals should be fully braced and your pelvis in neutral alignment.
- Your legs should be bent slightly for balance.
- Twist from your waist, turning the torso so that the cable pulley is pulled from over your right shoulder, across the torso and down towards your left shin in a smooth action. As you rotate, step away from the machine and lunge outwards into a side lunge position.
- Try 8–10 repetitions before swapping to the other side.

Progressions/adaptations

- Vary the direction of lunge, remembering to ensure that you press the cables against the angle of resistance created from the machine.
- Only increase the resistance when you have comfortably mastered the technique through the repetition range.

Exercise 17.5 Stability Ball Wood Chop

Starting position and action

- Sit on a stability ball, sideways on to a cable pulley machine, holding the cable pulley with both hands, and making sure you are twisted towards it.
- Your abdominals should be fully braced and your pelvis in neutral alignment.
- Keep your knees bent and your feet firmly on the floor.
- Twist from your waist, turning the torso so that the cable pulley is pulled from over your right shoulder in an arc movement, across the torso and down towards your left shin in a smooth action.
- It is important not to 'over-twist' in this movement or to use excessive resistance.
- Try 10–15 repetitions before changing sides.

Progressions/adaptations

- Variations on this exercise include changing the start and finish point of the movement by varying the height of where you are pulling from, and the angle and direction of pull.
- This exercise can be performed from a kneeling position on the ball, but the amount of resistance used will need to be reduced.
- For the very advanced athlete, this movement can be performed while standing on the ball.

Exercise 17.6 Kneeling Clock Drill with Medicine Ball

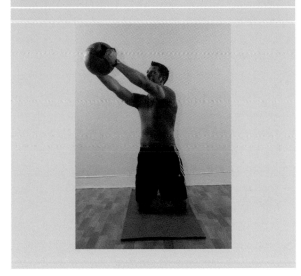

Starting position and action

- Begin in an upright kneeling position. Make sure you are not 'sitting back' on your heels.
- Hold a medicine ball at arm's length, but initially with the ball resting on the floor beside you.
- Brace your abdominal muscles and then lift the ball to a position in front of you with your arms outstretched. Imagine a clock face and position the ball at an imaginary 4 o'clock position.
- Hold this position briefly (for 1–5 seconds) and then return to the start position with the medicine ball resting on the floor.

- Repeat, but lift the medicine ball to another position – for example an imaginary 10 o'clock position – with your arms outstretched and abdominals braced.
- Begin with a light resistance, such as a 1–2 kg medicine ball.
- Aim to achieve a clock face (1–12), holding each position for 1–5 seconds.
- It is important when performing this exercise that you maintain the initial start position with correct muscle bracing and do not lean back to maintain balance.
- This exercise grows more difficult the further the ball moves away from your torso. The resistance is greater as the ball moves further away from your centre of gravity.

Progressions/adaptations

- Increase the resistance of the medicine ball, moving up to 5 kg and potentially 10 kg.
- To add greater instability, perform the exercise on a Reebok Core Board™ or, for the very advanced, a BOSU™ or even a stability ball.
- If you have a partner, instead of holding the ball at various positions you could take the ball to the 'clock face' position and hold briefly before throwing the ball from that position to your partner, who would then catch and pass the ball back to you. Again this action could be performed on a Reebok Core Board™, BOSU™ or stability ball.

Exercise 17.7 Ball Cobra – Interactive Catch on Stability Ball

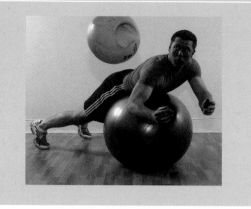

Starting position and action

- Start by lying face down over a stability ball.
- Position your legs shoulder width apart with your toes acting as an anchor on the floor. The stability ball should be positioned under your waist.
- Brace your abdominals and tense your gluteal muscles. Extend the torso to raise up into an extended position.
- Have a partner stand a couple of metres to your left side with a medicine ball.
- Fully brace your abdominals and position your hands in front of your chest in a catching position.

- Have your partner throw a light medicine ball for you to catch in the extended position and then throw the medicine ball back for your partner to catch.

Coaching points

- This is an advanced exercise and so should only be undertaken by fully competent athletes with an advanced level of core strength.
- Do not try to hyper-extend by raising up too far, as this will put extra stress on the spine.
- Make sure that you start with a medicine ball that is relatively light, perhaps 1–3 kg, before increasing the resistance.
- At the point of catching and throwing the forces are increased, so ensure your abdominals are fully braced throughout.

Progressions/adaptations

- Moving your feet closer together will dramatically increase the stabilisation required.
- Vary the distance and direction that your partner is from you. A greater distance will intensify the power (and thus stabilisation) needed.

Exercise 17.8 Cable Dead Lift and Row

Starting position and action

- Begin by standing in front of a low pulley cable machine, facing the machine.
- Standing with your feet hip distance apart, and with toes pointing forwards, squat down and grasp the low pulley bar with both hands.
- Bracing your abdominals, and keeping the spine in neutral alignment, contract through your leg and gluteal muscles to return to a standing position, lifting the bar as you stand.
- As you reach a near standing position, continue to pull the bar upwards by contracting through your upper back and biceps muscles to pull the bar to your ribcage.
- As you pull the bar to your ribcage, ensure you keep your upper back muscles retracted throughout.
- Hold the bar briefly at the fully contracted position (with the bar pulled to your ribcage), before gradually lowering the bar and squatting back down to the start position.
- Remember to keep correct alignment throughout the movement and keep your abdominal muscles braced throughout.
- Repeat the exercise 8–12 times, ensuring the movement quality is correct throughout.

Progressions/adaptations

- To increase the stabilisation factor for this exercise, perform the entire movement standing on one leg with your supporting leg slightly bent.
- To increase the stabilisation effect further, try standing on a stability disc, Reebok Core Board™ or even a BOSU™.
- If using a single leg stance, aim for 4–8 repetitions with each leg.

Exercise 17.9 Cable Lat Pull Down with Squat/Lunge

Exercise 17.10 Multi-direction Lunges

Starting position and action

- Stand in front of a multi-cable pulley machine, facing the machine with the pulleys set at high level.
- Hold on to both pulley cables and pull down, drawing your elbows towards your ribcage. As you pull the cables down, ensure your abdominals are braced throughout.
- As you pull both cables down, sit down in a squatting action so that your knees achieve a near right angle and both thighs are almost parallel to the floor.
- At this point your elbows should be fully drawn in towards your ribcage. Keep your rhomboids retracted.
- Hold this contraction briefly (1–4 seconds) before returning slowly to the start position.
- Repeat the exercise for 8–12 repetitions.

Progressions/adaptations

- A variation of this movement is to perform alternating reverse lunges instead of squats.

Starting position and action

- Begin standing with your feet shoulder width apart. Hold a barbell with both hands, with the barbell resting on your shoulders.
- Take a lunge, stepping with your left leg diagonally forwards and to the left at approximately 45 degrees.
- As your left leg touches the floor, bend both knees and lunge down. Lower your torso towards the floor until your left thigh is almost parallel to the floor.
- Remember to maintain correct postural alignment throughout the exercise and brace your abdominals throughout the movement.
- Pause briefly at the lower part of the lunge and then return back to the start position.

- Repeat, this time with the right leg lunging diagonally towards the right. Change the direction slightly though by lunging at approximately 60 degrees.
- Repeat lunges, alternating legs and varying the direction of the lunge from directly forwards to lunging at 90 degrees to either side.
- Repeat alternate lunges to either side. Make sure you do not lean forwards when lunging with the barbell on your shoulders.

Progressions/adaptations
- Once you have confidently mastered alternate lunges diagonally forwards, try incorporating lunges that go beyond 90 degrees and are thus reverse lunges, stepping diagonally backwards at angles of up to 180 degrees.
- To increase the stabilisation and intensity when in the lunge position, perform an overhead press with the barbell while maintaining correct form throughout the torso.
- As a further progression, add a knee lift on the return phase – that is, as you return to the start position, lift the leg that has initially lunged diagonally forwards. As such, it is raised to a knee lift position, holding your thigh almost parallel to the floor on the return phase.
- Instead of using a barbell, you could use a single dumbbell held in one hand at hip height.
- As you lower into the lunge position, curl the dumbbell towards your shoulder and then, in the lowest part of the lunge, maintain the position and press the dumbbell overhead.
- Pause briefly at the top position and then lower the dumbbell back to your shoulder. As you push back to the upright position, lower the dumbbell back to your hips.
- Repeat 6–10 times before changing the dumbbell to your opposite hand and leading with your opposite leg.

Exercise 17.11 Lunge to Side with Medicine Ball Overhead Press

Starting position and action
- Begin with a medicine ball positioned approximately 1.5–2 m to your left.
- Take a sideways lunge to your left so that you can reach the medicine ball.
- Brace your abdominals and bend your left leg at the knee so that you can reach the ball. Push off your left leg by contracting your quads, hamstrings and gluteal muscles to return to the start position.

- Remember to keep your abdominals braced while holding on to the medicine ball, maintaining correct posture and alignment throughout.
- When you have returned to the start position, keep your abdominals braced and press the medicine ball with both hands while still holding it above your head. Remember to maintain correct form as you press the medicine ball overhead.
- Lower the medicine ball to chest height and take a lateral lunge back to your left. Maintain tension through your abdominals and torso and place the medicine ball back where it was.
- Release the ball and return to the start position.
- Repeat the entire exercise to the left 6–10 times. Position the medicine ball to your right.
- Repeat the exercise to your right side, picking up and replacing the medicine ball 6–10 times.
- Ensure that you don't begin to lose core control and begin bending forwards and/or twisting unnecessarily as you begin to fatigue.

Progressions/adaptations

- This is a complex movement and there are a number of ways to add intensity or progression.
- As you press the ball overhead, you could raise the leg you have just lunged with so your thigh becomes parallel to the floor, thus increasing the balancing/stabilisation requirement.
- You could position the medicine ball in different places. This will force you to reach further for the ball.
- By adding speed to the movement, you increase the intensity but also increase the risk of injury if your abdominals are not fully braced.

Exercise 17.12 Walking Lunge with Twist

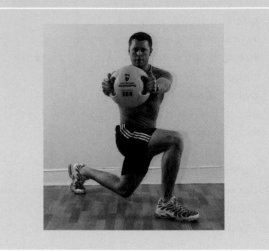

Starting position and action

- Stand upright, with your arms relaxed and by your sides.
- Take a large step forwards with your right leg ready to perform a forward lunge.
- As your right foot touches the floor, bend both your front and rear legs at the knee so that you lower your body towards the ground until the front thigh is almost parallel to the floor. Remember not to allow your knee to go in front of the toes.
- Your rear knee should lower towards, but not touch, the floor.
- As you begin lowering, clasp your hands together in front of you and start to twist at the waist to your right side. Keep your arms together and parallel to the floor.
- Continue to rotate your torso so that your arms and torso are fully rotated and pointing to the right at approximately 90 degrees to your right thigh.

- Remember to maintain correct posture by bracing your abdominals throughout the movement. Do not hold your breath at any point.
- Begin rotating back to the centre as you start to lift your left leg from the floor. Contract the glutes, hamstrings and quad muscles of your right leg and buttocks to lift yourself back to a standing position.
- In a continuous action, take a large step forwards with your left leg.
- As your left foot touches the floor, bend both knees and begin rotating your torso to the left with arms outstretched and hands together, arms parallel to the floor.
- Lower until your left thigh is almost parallel to the floor and your torso is fully rotated with your arms outstretched and pointing to the left.
- Continue to lunge forwards with alternate legs while alternately rotating to each side with your arms outstretched and parallel to the floor.
- Always remember to keep your torso upright and as relaxed as possible throughout the movement and remember to maintain balance.

- Initially aim to achieve 8–12 walking lunges with a twist before increasing to 15, then 20.

Progressions/Adaptations

- It is important to maintain correct form throughout the movements while keeping your core muscles braced.
- This exercise can be made harder by increasing the speed with which you perform each lunge movement and transition. Remember that increased speed will put greater demands on your balance skills and posture throughout the movement phases.
- In addition, a medicine ball or light dumbbell can be held to increase the difficulty of this exercise.
- It is important to place the emphasis on control and alignment rather than speed of execution or even resistance of medicine ball/dumbbell.
- When proficient, begin with a medicine ball not exceeding 5 kg. Resistance exceeding 10 kg detracts from the objective of this exercise except in the case of sport-specific training.

Exercise 17.13 Walking Lunge with Interactive Catch

Starting position and action

- A modification of the previous exercise involves a walking lunge technique as before but starting off without the medicine ball.
- Begin with a walking lunge technique, but don't twist your torso to either side.
- Your arms should remain in a 'ready' position in preparation for catching a medicine ball.
- Your partner is positioned approximately 2 metres away to your left side, holding a medicine ball.

- Begin lunging forwards, remembering to keep correct form and maintain tension through your core muscles. Keep your abdominals braced.
- As you enter into a lunge position with your left leg, your partner throws the medicine ball for you to catch in the lower position.
- Having caught the ball, immediately rotate to your right. Hold the ball at arm's length, still in the lunge position.
- Rotate to your left and throw the medicine ball back to your partner as you come up from the lower position of the lunge to a standing stance.
- Repeat this walking lunge technique for 10–15 lunges, but throw and catch the ball only as your left leg lunges down.
- Repeat with your partner throwing on your right side as you lunge forwards with your right leg.

Coaching points

- This is a very advanced drill and should not be attempted until you are competent with both the walking lunge technique and with appropriate muscle bracing.

KETTLEBELL TRAINING

18

A kettlebell looks much like a cannonball but it has a handle. It has been a favoured piece of equipment for the Russian army and special forces. Kettlebells date back to the 1900s and many of the strong men from this period would have used them as a major part of their training.

Similar objects have been reportedly used by the Shaolin monks to assist power development in martial arts. Long a favourite for Russian athletes, kettlebell training is becoming more and more fashionable within Western training and has even been used by the US Marines and some US police forces.

Traditional Russian kettlebells or *girya* come in specific weights called *poods* and are available in 1, 1.5 and 2 poods. A typical pood weighs approximately 36 lb or nearly 16 kg and is generally suitable for the average man. However, the demand from the West has been so strong that various weights are now available.

The use of kettlebells requires explosive force and power to swing, lift and press the balls repeatedly. In order to apply this explosive force, you need excellent core stabilisation to brace the torso effectively without the risk of injury.

Kettlebell training is dynamic in nature and so the user has to deal with varying resistances,

inertia and momentum throughout the movement. These exercises can be effective in strengthening the connective tissues (tendons and ligaments) around a joint, provided control and stabilisation are not lost.

Kettlebell exercises tend to involve higher repetitions (more than 20) and incorporate total body movements, thus involving many different muscles all struggling to overcome the increased forces caused by the swinging of the kettlebell. For this reason, and the power and effort required, it is an excellent training method for increased core and total body strength. Because of the energy expended during a workout, it is also an excellent way to burn calories. But in all honesty there is no magic here: any high intensity total body workout using resistance will have a similar effect in burning calories.

Whilst kettlebells can be used in a very similar way to dumbbells, as in classic exercises such as Biceps Curls or Triceps Extensions, they really come into their own with dynamic movements such as Swings, Cleans and Snatches. These form the basis of a kettlebell workout and within each of these movements there are a number of modifications/alternatives to intensify the movement itself. Such modifications might be changing from a single hand grip to a double hand grip, using two kettlebells together or alternating the arm movements.

THE EXERCISES
KETTLEBELL SWINGS

The kettlebell swing exercise really highlights the dynamic and potentially ballistic nature of movements that can be explored with kettlebell training. It is an excellent whole body exercise, as to allow for a correct and safe swinging action, the core muscles, shoulder and lumbo-pelvic hip complex of muscles all work in unison. It is also an excellent posterior chain exercise, in that it works the muscles of the lower back, glutes, hamstrings and calves. Lastly, the nature of repeated dynamic swinging with a relatively heavy resistance puts huge demands on the cardiovascular system, training both muscular endurance and power.

Exercise 18.1 Double-arm Kettlebell Swing

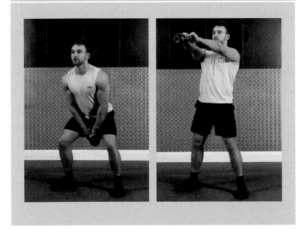

Starting position and action

- Begin standing over the kettlebell and keeping correct spinal alignment with abdominals braced, bend your knees to pick up the kettlebell with both hands on the handle.
- Lift the kettlebell to waist height using a 'dead lift' technique, keeping your arms straight, shoulders retracted but relaxed and down, with your glutes tight.
- Using your hips, push the kettlebell away from the body, propelling it forward, allowing the arms to rise.
- As you lower the kettlebell, bend at your knees and hips and lean forwards, pushing your backside backwards but keeping your core muscles braced throughout to ensure correct spinal alignment as the kettlebell swings down and between your legs.
- Then drive your hips forwards contracting your glutes to propel the kettlebell upwards to approximately chest height, ensuring your abdominals are braced throughout with shoulders relaxed as you return to a standing position.
- Repeat 'swinging' action 15–20 times before slowing the movement so that the kettlebell is under control and you can slowly lower it to the floor by bending your knees. You should then be able to advance to the following modifications.

Coaching points

- Remember not to hold your breath during these swings: try to breathe in as you lower the kettlebell through your legs and breathe out as you apply the force through your hips and glutes to propel it upwards.

Exercise 18.2 Single-arm Kettlebell Swing

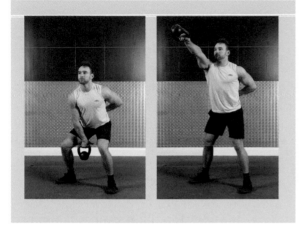

Starting position and action

- All principles remain the same as for the Double-arm Swing, but this time hold the kettlebell in your right hand and perform 8–15 swings before changing hands and repeating for another 8–15 swings.

Coaching points

- There are two differences in technique for this exercise. Firstly, you rotate the kettlebell 90 degrees, pronating your forearm so that your thumb points downwards and inwards as you swing the kettlebell between your legs.
- Secondly, you will have a 'free' arm during the swinging actions. You can hold your arm at various positions to suit, such as a natural position in front of you to assist balance, placed behind you in the small of your lower back or even above your head, as all will have different stabilisation requirements for your core muscles.

Exercise 18.3 Alternating Single-arm Kettlebell Swing

Starting position and action

- All principles for the Single-arm Swing apply but this time at the 'top' point of the movement, where you have 'swung' the kettlebell to approximately chest height, very quickly change hands from right to left before applying the 90-degree inward rotation so that your left hand passes the kettlebell thumb-down between your legs.
- As it passes between your legs with your hips flexed and knees bent, forcefully extend the hips and legs to drive the kettlebell back up to the top position, moving it back into your right hand. Repeating 15–20 times.

KETTLEBELL CLEAN AND RACK

The Kettlebell Clean and Rack is a great total body exercise on its own, but at the same time it is the technique that should be utilised to bring the kettlebell to the shoulders for all pressing movements or exercises in which you are holding the kettlebell overhead.

Exercise 18.4 Single-arm Kettlebell Clean and Rack

Starting position and action

- Stand over the kettlebell, which is on the floor between your legs, with your feet shoulder width apart.

- Brace your abdominals and reach down with one hand to take hold of the kettlebell.
- Using your legs and hips, swing the kettlebell between your legs, with your thumb inwards before extending through your hips and legs to powerfully drive the kettlebell upwards, lifting it in an arc movement.
- As the kettlebell reaches shoulder height, 'sink' slightly by bending your legs as you drop your elbow and 'flip' your wrist underneath the kettlebell, as it rotates over to 'land' mid-way between your elbow and shoulder on your upper arm with your elbow tucked in. This end position is called the 'Rack' position and is the start position for all pressing movement overhead.
- Pause briefly in the 'Rack' position before rotating the kettlebell and lowering down in a swinging action, again leading through your legs thumb first.
- Repeat the complete action 10–15 times before lowering the kettlebell and changing hands to repeat as before with your opposite hand.

Coaching points

- Ensure you keep your core muscles activated and maintain correct spinal alignment throughout, especially during the swinging movements.
- It is important that your grip on the kettlebell is not primarily supported through your fingers, but by holding your palm next to your thumb as this will take greater weight and force and allow for the pressing movements which follow.

Exercise 18.5 Double Kettlebell Clean and Rack

Starting position and action

- Begin as before, standing over two kettlebells with your feet shoulder width apart. Bend down and brace your abdominals before grasping the handles of the kettlebells.
- Then lift as before, using your legs and hips, and swing the kettlebell between your legs with both thumbs pointing inwards before extending through your hips and legs to powerfully drive the kettlebells upwards, lifting them in an arc movement.
- Then 'sink' slightly by bending your legs as you drop your elbows and 'flip' your wrists underneath the kettlebells, which will rotate over to 'land' midway between your elbow and shoulder on your upper arms. Keep your elbows tucked in.
- Pause briefly in the 'Rack' position before rotating the kettlebells and lowering down together in a swinging action, again leading through your legs thumbs first.

- Repeat the complete action 10–20 times before lowering the kettlebells back to the floor.

Progressions/adaptations

- Modify this exercise by using an alternate arm action in two different ways.
- Firstly, the left arm remains down as the right arm performs the complete Clean and Rack movement.
- When the right kettlebell has lowered to the start position, the left arm begins the movement to clean the kettlebell, held in the left hand, up to the 'Rack' position before being lowered.
- As the left arm completes the movement and lowers the kettlebell to the start position, the right arm begins the complete Clean and Rack movement again with the kettlebell held in the right hand.
- Repeat alternating arm movements 10–20 times.
- Another more intense variation of the alternating action described in this exercise is to keep the kettlebells moving continuously with both arms.
- Perform the Clean and Rack movement with your right arm, but at the top of the movement when the kettlebell has rested on the upper arm ('Rack' position), initiate the movement lifting with the left arm to the 'Rack' position as you simultaneously lower the kettlebell in your right hand.
- This is a very dynamic and advanced movement and should only be attempted by experienced kettlebell users.

KETTLEBELL CLEAN AND PRESS

The Clean and Press is one of the best total body exercises when using kettlebells and requires full muscle integration to execute correctly. This can be performed with a single kettlebell as in the Single-arm Clean and Press or with two kettlebells as in the Double-arm Clean and Press.

Exercise 18.6 Single-arm Clean and Press

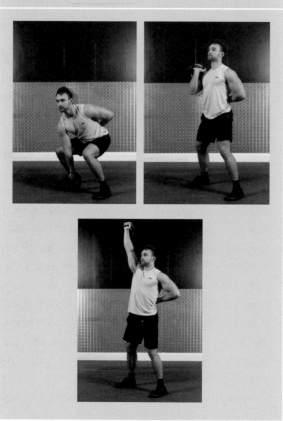

Starting position and action

- Stand over the kettlebell, which is on the floor between your legs, with your feet shoulder width apart.

- Brace your abdominals and reach down with one hand to take hold of the kettlebell.
- Then lift as before, using your legs and hips, and swing the kettlebell between your legs with both thumbs pointing inwards before extending through your hips and legs to powerfully drive the kettlebells upwards, lifting them in an arc movement.
- Then 'sink' slightly by bending your legs as you drop your elbows and 'flip' your wrists underneath the kettlebells, which will rotate over to 'land' midway between your elbow and shoulder on your upper arms. Keep your elbows tucked in.
- From the 'Rack' position, keeping your abdominals braced, push the kettlebell overhead by extending your arm, keeping the forearm vertical with your elbow facing forward.
- Pause briefly at the top position with the kettlebell held overhead and then carefully lower the kettlebell back to the 'Rack' position, before rotating the kettlebell and lowering it down in a swinging action, again leading through your legs thumb first.
- Repeat complete movement of Clean, Rack, Press, Lower and Swing 10–15 times before lowering the kettlebell and changing hands to repeat as before with your opposite hand.

Coaching points

- Ensure you keep your core muscles activated and maintain correct spinal alignment throughout, especially during the swinging movements.
- It is important that your grip on the kettlebell is not primarily supported through your fingers but by keeping your palm next to your thumb as

this will take greater weight and force and allow for the pressing movements which follow.

- Remember to keep breathing during this movement and don't hold your breath.
- It is often a good idea to breathe in during the downward lowering elements and exhale during the upward clean movement overhead press, but until the weight of the kettlebell and number of repetitions dictate when and how you should breathe, just maintain regular breathing throughout.

THE SNATCH

The Snatch is a fantastic total body exercise that helps develop strength, power and endurance. Due to its movement range and dynamic nature it involves many different muscle groups working together including the core muscles, shoulder complex, lumbo-pelvic hip complex and also the posterior chain muscles. The Snatch is an advanced kettlebell exercise and as such should only be attempted when you are confident with the Swing and Clean and Rack exercises.

Exercise 18.7 The Snatch

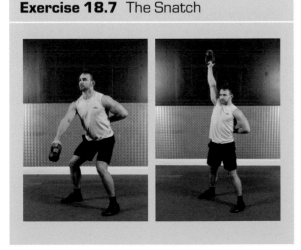

Starting position and action

- Stand over the kettlebell with feet shoulder width apart.
- Bend down and brace your abdominals before grasping the kettlebell, then drive up through your legs and hips to push the kettlebell outwards.
- As it swings back between your legs with thumbs pointing inwards, keeping neutral spine, bend your legs and at the hips lean forwards before dynamically extending your legs and hips to swing the kettlebell upwards in a forceful arc.
- As the kettlebell reaches shoulder height, 'punch' through the kettlebell or rotate the arm slightly so that the kettlebell settles on your forearm.
- Continue the swing movement so that you finish with your right arm locked and with the kettlebell held overhead.
- Maintaining correct form and with your abdominals braced, begin the down swing, rotating the kettlebell back around the wrist, keeping your thumb upwards and the kettlebell close to your body so as not to overload the shoulders.
- Ensure you have control of the kettlebell in the downward swing movement but keep the swing active as you will need to use the momentum when it travels through your legs to assist the next repetition.
- Repeat 10–15 times before changing hands and repeating with your left hand holding the kettlebell.

OVERHEAD LUNGE

This exercise builds lower body strength in the quads, glutes and core, while improving balance and proprioception.

Exercise 18.8 Overhead Lunge

Starting position and action

- After picking the kettlebell up using a deadlift technique with the kettlebell in your right hand, extend through your legs and hips to come up to a standing position.
- Brace your abdominals and perform the Clean and Rack movement and then press the kettlebell up above your head with your arm locked out at the elbow.
- With your right arm extended over your head holding the kettlebell, lunge backwards with your right leg, bending at the knee and lower towards the ground.
- Keep your weight over your front leg and maintain correct spinal alignment throughout.
- Push through your left glutes and leg to return yourself back to a standing position.
- Repeat 8–15 times and lower the weight and transfer the kettlebell to your left hand before repeating the sequence, cleaning and pressing overhead this time with your left arm, keeping elbows locked.
- Repeat the reverse lunge movement, this time stepping back with your left leg and lowering towards the ground.
- Push through your right leg, contracting the glutes and quads to come back to a standing position.
- Repeat 8–15 times before lowering to floor.

Exercise 18.9 Overhead Squat

Exercise 8.10 Figure Eights

Starting position and action

- Begin with the kettlebells on the floor in front of you. Take hold of the handles and lift them above your head by performing a Clean and Press action.
- With the kettlebells above your head and both elbows locked, brace your abdominals and squat down, sitting back but remembering to keep your back in neutral alignment.
- Keeping your core muscles activated, push through your heels to return to a standing position with arms still extended and both kettlebells over your head.
- Repeat 12–15 times and after the final repetition lower the kettlebells back to the 'Rack' position, before lowering again to the floor. To modify, repeat this exercise using a single kettlebell in one hand and performing a number of squats before lowering the weight to the floor and repeating the same number of repetitions, this time with the kettlebell in the other hand.

Starting position and action

- Begin with feet slightly wider than shoulder width apart. Squat down, keeping neutral spinal alignment, with the kettlebell on the floor in front of you. Brace your abdominals and lift the kettlebell from the floor.
- Then, keeping your abdominals braced, 'feed' the kettlebell through your legs passing it from your right hand to your left hand which takes the kettlebell from the rear. Then move the kettlebell around the outside of your left leg to the front to 'feed' between your legs back to your right hand. Then take the kettlebell from the rear, around the outside of your right leg and back again to the front, completing the 'figure eight' pattern.
- Continue this movement for 6–10 complete 'figure eights' feeding from the front, before reversing the direction and feeding from the rear for another 6–10 complete 'figure eight'.
- Ensure that correct spinal alignment is maintained and your core muscles are braced throughout. Remember not to hold your breath but to breathe freely throughout the exercise.

Exercise 18.11 Windmills

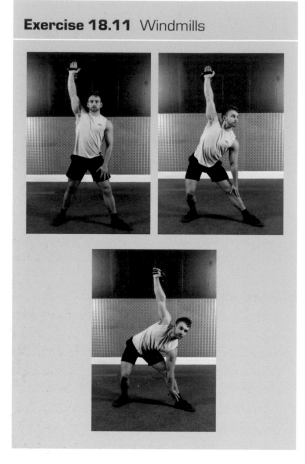

Starting position and action

- This is an excellent exercise to strengthen core muscles, lumbo-pelvic hip complex and shoulders.

- With feet shoulder width apart, holding the kettlebell in your right hand, perform a Clean and Rack and then press the kettlebell above your head. Turn your feet slightly to the left and keep your abdominals pulled in.

- Keep your arm locked at the elbow and then sit back pushing your hips to the side as you bend forward. Keeping your left hand on your leg, run your hand down your leg bending slightly at the knees while maintaining the kettlebell over your shoulders with elbow still locked.

- Reach down until you can touch the floor with your left hand, all the time maintaining control of the extended right arm that is holding the kettlebell.

- Then, maintaining a strong core with abdominals pulled in, drive up through your heel to return to a standing position with your right arm extended.

- Repeat for your desired number of repetitions and then lower the kettlebell to the 'Rack' position before returning to the floor.

- Repeat entire process again using your left hand for desired number of repetitions. This time your feet will turn slightly to the right as you perform the 'windmill' movement.

- Complete 12–15 times and return kettlebell to floor.

THE TURKISH GET-UP

This is a great total body exercise that requires stabilisation of the core muscles and shoulder complex. It is a very demanding exercise that helps strengthen your hips, glutes and legs, but also challenges your balance and proprioception skills.

Exercise 18.12 The Turkish Get-up

Starting position and action

- Begin lying on your back holding a kettlebell in your right hand above your chest with your elbow locked.
- Bend your right knee to bring your right foot towards your glutes – so that your knee is bent at 90 degrees – and place your left arm out to the side, perpendicular to your torso.
- Brace your abdominals and push the kettlebell into the air by pushing your right heel into the floor and lifting the chest forwards, leaning on your left forearm, which acts as support.
- Continue this driving movement, keeping your core muscles engaged so you lift up to support yourself on your left hand.
- Then lift your hips off the floor, pushing through your right heel, and draw your outstretched left leg underneath and behind you so that you come up to a kneeling position on your left knee, maintaining the kettlebell in an overhead position with your elbow locked.
- When you are balanced, breathe in and maintain your core tension as you take your left hand off the floor, maintaining a kneeling lunge position.
- Drive up pushing through your glutes and quads, while still holding the kettlebell above your head. As you stand up your 'free' left arm should be out to the side to assist your balance.
- To return back to the floor, repeat entire process in reverse ensuring you are bracing the abdominals throughout.
- This is a very challenging exercise so aim for 5–10 repetitions before swapping kettlebell to other hand and repeating from the floor position.

ViPR
TRAINING

19

ViPR Training (an acronym for Vitality, Performance and Reconditioning) is one of the newest trends in the industry. It has been created by Michol Dalcourt, a Canadian Strength and Conditioning Coach, who wanted to create a way of evolving fitness training by fusing strength training with functional movement, a term Dalcourt quotes as 'purposeful movement'. Having worked with Canadian ice hockey teams, Dalcourt struggled to understand why the players with backgrounds of working on farms were always the strongest and most powerful. He concluded that even though other players might 'lift' more in the gym during training, this 'strength' did not transfer to the ice during a game. His understanding for this was that the 'farm kids' had better transferable strength and that their strength was due to integrated function as a consequence of 'natural movements' – lifting, dragging, crouching, shovelling, pushing, pulling, lunging, etc. By integrating function through movement the muscles respond to the demands of the ViPR by working in unison to overcome the momentum forces of acceleration and deceleration. Consequently the demands to the core musculature are potentially huge, subject to the weight of the ViPR and the speed of movement.

The ViPR is unlike any previous resistance training tool for a number of reasons, but primarily because the movements you can introduce are completely three-dimensional and multi-planar. Consider conventional training where you lift/press/pull a resistance in a linear movement, such as in a Bench Press or a Lat Pull Down, or follow a predicted movement arc, for example when using cables during a 'wood chop' movement. With ViPR Training there is no predetermined movement arc nor necessarily a definitive start or finish point to the exercise. Each exercise can be developed or progressed by adding more variables to the movement, such as a further twist, bend, force, or direction change.

The ViPR is essentially a cylindrical tube of rubber, of varying weight from 4 kg to 20 kg. It has handles for different grip positions and can be lifted, dragged, tilted, thrown, stepped on, rolled, carried and even flipped. The main principle behind the movements are that within each exercise the body works as a unit, rather than as in conventional resistance training whereby different muscles work in isolation. In ViPR all muscles have to work together, which is called Whole Body Integration.

SIX KEY STEPS

ViPR Training utilises the principles of integration, timing, three-dimensional movement and gravity with regards to the exercise and nature of movements used. In addition there are six key steps to consider when programming the nature of an exercise. These steps highlight what specific aspect you are applying within the exercise itself.

1. SERIES

The series is the nature of movement of the exercise and more importantly what you, the exerciser, are performing as a movement – are you performing a dragging movement, a lifting movement, are you rotating, throwing, or pulling the ViPR? Essentially, this describes what you are doing to the ViPR.

2. EXERCISE

This step relates to the exerciser and the gross movement pattern of the person in a particular exercise. This might be a locomotive pattern, such as a lateral step, walk, run or shuffle action. It might involve a level change such as a step up/down, lunge or squatting action. Also included is the stationary force production within the exercise. With the feet fixed, how is the ViPR being moved – is it being lifted against gravity, or being pushed or pulled across the floor? The opportunity with the exercise step is that a combination of aspects can be applied together. Perhaps the movement incorporates a locomotive movement pattern such as a lateral shuffle whereby at the end of the shuffle you drop into a lateral squat or twist into a lunge whilst applying rotation or tilting of the ViPR.

3. HOLD/GRIP

There are 33 different ways to grip the ViPR and, subject to the specific exercise, different grips might create a different force through the body.

4. FOOTPRINT

The footprint relates to where the feet are positioned at the beginning and where they finish at the end of the movement. You might choose a neutral stance or alternately have a staggered stance, with either the right or left foot forward. You might begin in a staggered stance but after various movements such as stepping, walking, hopping, jumping, turning, etc. you might finish in a very different footprint position, even possibly standing on one leg, depending upon the exercise in question.

5. HANDPRINT

Unlike the hold/grip aspect, the handprint relates to where the hands are positioned at the beginning of the movement and where they move to. They might reach forwards, reach overhead, tilt to one side, or a combination of all of these, finishing in a particular position.

6. THRESHOLD

This is the level that you achieve during the movement such as the repetition range, set range and motion range, together with speed of movement, as this will affect the force created and the complexity of movement. The threshold is obviously subject to the ability of the individual in question and whether they can maintain correct form throughout, before compromising form due to fatigue or poor motor skills.

Fundamentally, when performing any movement, always opt for a lighter weight initially to learn the correct form, keeping movements slow and controlled and within a smaller range before becoming more dynamic and covering a larger movement range. Dalcourt suggests that by applying the variable steps described above more than 9000 exercises are possible with the ViPR. In all honesty, as I believe the ViPR is in its infancy, the possible permutations of exercises are limitless, as subtle variations and progressions will continue to develop as a result of imaginative minds and utilisation of multiple fitness products – unstable bases, partner interaction, alternate resistance aids, etc. Below are just some examples of how the ViPR can be utilised but it would be impractical to list all the potential progressions for each exercise, as there would just be too many.

THE EXERCISES

Exercise 19.1 Squat: 'Thread the Needle'

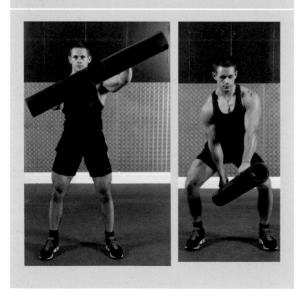

Starting position and action

- Begin holding the ViPR at arm's length, resting it on your thighs.
- Brace your abdominals and lift the ViPR to chest height and squat down, maintaining correct neutral spinal alignment as you rotate the ViPR 90 degrees clockwise, 'feeding' it between your legs leading with your right hand first.
- Decelerate the movement and, maintaining correct abdominal tension, reverse the action extending through your hips to drive the ViPR back up to chest height rotating it 180 degrees anti-clockwise at chest height with arms outstretched in front of you.
- Repeat movement by squatting down again, maintaining correct spinal alignment as you thread the ViPR between your legs, this time leading with the left hand.
- Repeat movement 10–20 times.

Progressions/adaptations

- To simplify movement, aim for 6–10 repetitions leading/feeding from one side only without rotating the ViPR, before switching sides and leading/feeding from the other. The squat technique and abdominal bracing applies throughout.
- To progress the exercise, after each feed lift the ViPR above your head before rotating 180 degrees and then squatting down to repeat movement.
- An alternate progression is to change your footprint by adding a quarter turn or half turn when the ViPR is above your head.
- Another progression is to jump into a quarter turn or half turn position thus rotating 90 or 180 degrees before repeating movement sequence.

OUTSIDE SWINGS

This is a variation on the previous exercise but instead of feeding the ViPR between your legs you swing it alternately to the outside of your torso.

Exercise 19.2 Outside Swings

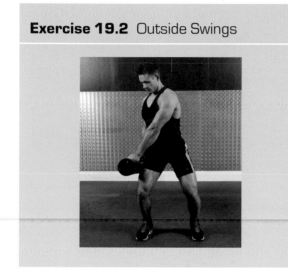

Starting position and action

- Begin holding the ViPR at arm's length, resting it on your thighs.
- Then brace your abdominals and lift the ViPR to chest height before rotating it, leading with your right hand down to your right side past your right hip.
- Make sure you absorb the torque force caused by the movement of the ViPR by rotating slightly to your right, while bending your knees.
- Decelerate the movement while maintaining correct abdominal tension, reverse the action to swing the ViPR back to chest height or higher in an arc, and continue leading with your left hand to swing the ViPR past your left hip.
- Repeat these arc movements with the ViPR, alternating sides 10–20 times in a continuous movement, before lowering the ViPR to waist height and then placing on the floor.

Exercise 19.3 Lateral Tilt/Flip with Lateral Step

Starting position and action

- Begin with the ViPR standing on its end vertically in front of you. Then with feet shoulder width apart and knees slightly bent hold on to the ViPR with your right hand.
- Tilt the ViPR to the right maintaining contact as the ViPR lowers to the floor.
- To ensure correct body positioning you will need to step/shuffle laterally to your right to

maintain contact. Just before the ViPR touches the floor, brace your abdominals and lift the ViPR by its end back to the vertical position and beyond.

- As the ViPR returns to the start position transfer your hands to hold the ViPR with your left hand to lower it to the left. This time to remain in correct body alignment you will need to shuffle to your left.

- Again, before the ViPR touches the floor, lift the ViPR back to the starting position and repeat alternating right and left 15–20 times.

Progressions/adaptations

- To modify this exercise, use the opposite hand to control the ViPR as it lowers to the floor. Thus the left hand reaches across the body to maintain contact when the ViPR is lowered to the right. Alternatively, use both hands to lower and lift the ViPR.

- One progression is to drop the ViPR completely to the floor before lifting it from a horizontal resting position back to vertical.

- Another option if there is sufficient space is to 'flip' the ViPR continually to the right for 8–10 flips/tilts before flipping/tilting it back again to the left for another 8–10 flips/tilts.

Exercise 19.4 Cylindrical Lift

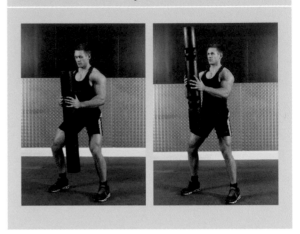

Starting position and action

- Position yourself behind the ViPR standing upright on its end.

- Brace your abdominals and maintain correct spinal alignment as you squat down and grasp the ViPR with both hands firmly and with elbows bent but fixed.

- Then, still holding the ViPR, forcefully return to a standing position to provide the force to lift the ViPR upwards, essentially driving it towards the ceiling.

- The force you exert with your legs should cause the ViPR to be 'thrown' upwards allowing you to grip further down the base of the tube.

- Slowly repeat the movement, squatting down again and maintaining your grip on the ViPR as you lower.

- Upon reaching the squat position drive upwards using your legs to power the ViPR towards the ceiling again, so that upon release you can grip the ViPR lower down the tube as you work your way to the ViPR's base.

- At all times maintain neutral spine and keep your abdominals braced, ensuring that the ViPR remains vertical throughout all the lifts.

Exercise 19.5 Uppercut Lunge

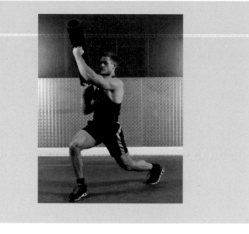

Exercise 19.6 Uppercuts to Block

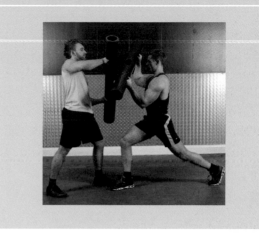

Starting position and action

- Hold the ViPR horizontally in front of your chest, abdominals braced, with your arms bent.
- Begin to rotate the ViPR towards 90 degrees into a vertical position with your right hand above your left hand.
- Continue the movement of the ViPR but step forward into a lunge position with your right leg as you push your left hand forwards to resemble an 'uppercut' boxing movement with your left arm.
- Decelerate this movement by pulling back with your left hand, maintaining core tension as you push back off your right leg from the lunge to return back to a neutral stance with feet shoulder width apart, and bring the ViPR back to the start position.
- Step forward into a lunge with your left leg, this time having rotated the ViPR so that your left hand is over your right and continue the movement to perform an 'uppercut' movement leading with your right arm.
- Decelerate this movement and return, pushing off your left leg back to the start position.
- Repeat 10–15 times each side, maintaining correct abdominal bracing throughout.

Starting position and action

- Begin holding the ViPR with both hands and elbows bent as in the Uppercut Lunge.
- Brace your abdominals and rotate the ViPR in a forceful and dynamic movement, bringing your right arm over your left.
- Continue this movement stepping forward without lunging with your right leg, but aim the ViPR pushing forward with your left arm in an 'uppercut' movement so that the ViPR contacts with force a ViPR held by your partner as a target.
- Reverse the direction, pulling back with your left arm and rotating the ViPR back through the start position in a continuous movement and then step forward with your left leg.
- As you step with your left leg continue your arm movement rotating the ViPR so you can push through with your right arm in an uppercut movement to forcefully contact your partner's ViPR.
- Repeat alternate uppercuts 12–20 times.

Progressions/adaptations

- Vary the exercise by altering the angle of strike and thus the need for rotation movement.
- Modify your stance to a neutral stance throughout without the stepping action described in this exercise.
- To intensify the action further try jumping into split/staggered stances alternating your lead leg with each uppercut contact.

CANOE/KAYAK ROW

The Canoe/Kayak Row mimics the arm action of a canoeist or kayaker but instead of holding a paddle you are using the ViPR.

Exercise 19.7 Canoe/Kayak Row

Starting position and action

- Begin standing in a neutral stance with feet shoulder width apart, holding the ViPR in front of you with arms bent.
- Keeping abdominals braced begin rotating the ViPR with a figure eight movement of your hands so that, leading from your right arm, the ViPR travels back pointing behind your right side.
- Then, by bringing your right arm around and over, your left hand drops down to point the ViPR behind you to your left. Continue the movement, this time bringing your left arm up and over as you drop your right arm ready to perform another 'stroke' on your right side.

- Repeat this alternating 'figure eight' movement 10–20 times before slowing the movement down and placing the ViPR on the floor.

Coaching point
- Due to the continuous movement and momentum of the ViPR, ensure you are maintaining abdominal bracing throughout and breathing regularly without losing correct spinal alignment.

Progressions/adaptations
- This movement can be progressed by increasing the speed of movement or regressed by reducing the speed and focussing on control.
- Alternatively, modifications might be to vary your stance or even add an alternate 90-degree turn on each 'paddle' movement.
- In addition to adding a cardio element you could 'jump' into alternate split stances for each paddle action (left foot staggered in front of your right foot, jumping to land right foot staggered and in front of your left foot).

Exercise 19.8 Integrated Clean and Press – with Lunge

Starting position and action
- Stand behind the ViPR in a neutral stance with feet hip distance apart.
- Keeping your back fairly straight, bend your knees and at the hips squat down ready to grasp the ViPR.
- Brace your abdominals and, holding the ViPR by the handles, extend through your hips and legs powerfully to perform a 'clean' action, lifting the ViPR initially to your chest before powering through your arms to press the ViPR overhead.
- With the ViPR held, arms extended, overhead and your abdominals braced, step backwards with your right leg into the reverse lunge position.
- As you lower toward the floor maintain correct tension in your core muscles and shoulders to keep the ViPR stable.

- Before your right knee reaches the floor behind you, pause briefly before powering through your left glutes and quads to return to a standing position with feet hip distance apart.
- Then lower the ViPR carefully to chest height and then to the waist before placing or touching it to the floor without letting go of the handles.
- When it touches the floor repeat the Clean and Press action, maintaining core stabilisation throughout to press the ViPR overhead and then continue with the reverse lunges before repeating the complete movement.
- Repeat complete movement 10–20 times.

Progressions/adaptations

- Instead of completing a Clean and Press action to lift the ViPR from the floor each time, a regression of this exercise is to start from a 'hang clean' position with the ViPR held at waist height instead of touching the floor.
- Continue the Clean and Press action and then the reverse lunges each side before lowering to waist height and repeating.

Exercise 19.9 Anterior Lunge with Multi-planar Tilts

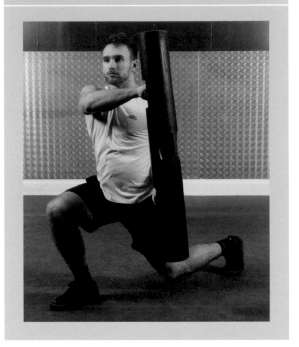

Starting position and action

- Begin holding the ViPR with both hands on the handles and stand in a neutral stance with feet hip distance apart.
- Hold the ViPR with arms slightly bent but with your elbows in a fixed position.
- Keep your abdominals braced and step forward into a forward lunge position with your right foot.
- As you bend your knees to lower yourself into the lunge position, keeping your abdominals braced, press or tilt the ViPR to your left to challenge your stabilisation muscles.
- Bring the ViPR back to the central position, before pushing through your right foot to step back to the start position.

- Repeat this movement with your left leg lunging forwards and tilting/pressing the ViPR out to the right of your body, maintaining core tension throughout.
- Repeat 10–20 times before lowering the ViPR to the floor.

Progressions/adaptations

- This exercise is about stabilising the core while absorbing the momentum and weight of the ViPR as it moves through different planes of motion as you lunge, so try varying the angle, distance, direction and speed of movement when tilting/pressing the ViPR.
- In addition, instead of a forward lunge, you could perform a lateral squat or multi-planar lunge whereby you are stepping in any direction, forwards, backwards, sideways or diagonally, again pressing or tilting the ViPR as desired with varying force.
- To add intensity instead of stepping forward into the lunge position you could try alternate split lunge jumps with varying pressing/tilting movements.

Exercise 19.10 Ice Skater with Tilt Rotation

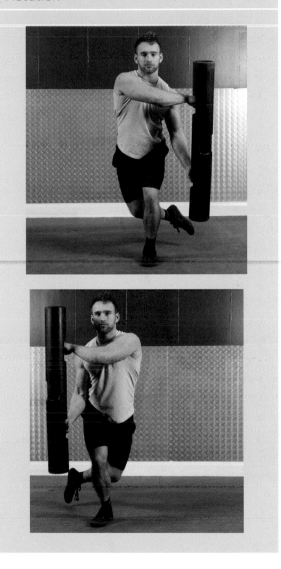

Starting position and action

- Begin holding the ViPR at arm's length in front of you, standing in a neutral stance with feet slightly wider than shoulder width apart and with knees bent slightly.

- Brace your abdominals and step with your left leg laterally to your left.
- As you step, rotate the ViPR from a horizontal position to almost vertical with the left hand above the right pushing down and to your left side with your right hand.
- Stabilise through your glutes and decelerate the movement of the ViPR before reversing the action, rotating in the other direction as you step laterally to your right.
- The ViPR rotates from the near vertical, through a 180 degree rotation to finish in a similar position, this time with your right hand above your left.
- Repeat these alternating lateral stepping movements whilst holding the ViPR 10–20 times each side.

Progressions/adaptations
- To intensify the exercise increase the dynamic movement by increasing the speed of pressing the ViPR to alternate sides.
- An alternative option is to increase the distance of the lateral step by hopping further on to each leg with each left and right movement.

Exercise 19.11 Overhead Squat with Tilt

Starting position and action
- Stand behind the ViPR in a neutral stance with feet hip distance apart.
- Squat down and take hold of the ViPR by the handles and, bracing your abdominals, perform a Clean and Press action to lift the ViPR overhead.
- Keeping the ViPR stable by stabilising your shoulders and keeping your elbows locked, squat down to a near seated position, with your thighs almost parallel to the floor, and with the ViPR held overhead.
- Pause briefly and then tilt the ViPR to your right to change the centre of balance and stabilisation required through your core muscles.
- Return the ViPR to an overhead central position before pushing through your glutes and legs to return to a standing position with the ViPR held overhead throughout.

- Repeat squat action, this time tilting the ViPR to the left while in the squat position before returning back to the standing position.
- Repeat the complete squat and tilt movement for a total of 10–20 repetitions.

Progressions/adaptations
- To regress this movement, try tilting the ViPR to the side, when standing upright with the ViPR held overhead instead of in the squat.
- When you reach the start position, tilt the ViPR laterally to your right, maintaining your core tension, before returning the ViPR to the overhead position. Repeat the squat movement before returning back to the start position and then tilting the ViPR overhead to your left.

- Another option is to perform the full Clean and Press action before each squat and tilt, making this a very demanding total body exercise.

These are just some examples of ViPR exercises that have been created. However, at the point of writing this book, ViPR training is in its infancy and, due to the possible variations and modifications to come, the potential number of exercise options is almost limitless. Dalcourt himself hints that some 9000 exercise options are possible and if you look to combine ViPR training with any permutation of other unstable base equipment or other fitness product, then it really comes down to the individual's imagination as to what can be attempted and achieved.

SUSPENSION TRAINING

20

One of the newest trends in gyms and with personal trainers is suspension training. This can take the form of modified suspension where part of your body is in contact with the floor, or another unstable base of some kind. Alternatively there is Total Body Suspension training whereby your entire body is supported, usually through your arms, by holding a set of rings, not dissimilar to those used in gymnastics.

For the purpose of this book I have referred to Total Body Suspension training, but while it is arguably a fantastic training tool for athletes, the demands and stresses it puts on your body even during the most basic of exercises are probably too challenging for the general user. Certainly it is a method of training to work up to, but it is not necessarily a training device I would utilise for mainstream gym users until I felt fully confident that they had enough shoulder stabilisation and strength to perform movements without fear of injury. While I am aware that there is still a trend for 'Circus Training', the utilisation of a trapeze or Olympic rings is probably going to excite only a small minority, rather than filter into mainstream demand.

Modified Suspension training however is something totally different as you can progress (intensify) or regress (make easier) almost every exercise very simply just by adjusting your body position to reduce/increase the load or resistance you are working with. In this form of suspension training you are partially supported by the suspension stirrups yet you have either your foot/feet or hand/hands secured on the floor or another unstable device such as a BOSU™, stability ball, medicine ball, etc.

TRX Suspension Training is leading the industry with its delivery of training courses and products. It was co-devised and created by Randy Hetrick, a former US Navy Seal who, working with his fellow commando teammates, searched for ways to stay in condition which required minimal equipment, space and time to set up. It was also vital that the product was easily portable. Initially the prototype of the TRX Suspension Trainer began its life as a parachute harness delivering a few dozen exercises, before being developed into the fantastic product that it is today, with an estimated repertoire in excess of 300 exercises.

Suspension training provides total body integration in that when performing a movement, all the muscles have to work together, not in isolation. This functional integration of muscles helps enhance not only core stability but muscular balance, joint stability and improved mobility. Weighing in at less than 2 lbs, with minimal set-up time, it is the perfect train-anywhere fitness tool as it can be used wherever you can secure it to create an anchor point, for example, to a tree, lamppost, climbing frame, etc.

The device itself consists of two nylon webbing cables, adjustable CAM buckles, grips, integrated handle/foot cradles and a carabiner to secure the locking mechanism. It can be shortened in length from 12 to 6 ft and only requires that the anchor point you hang or wrap it around is between 7 and 9 ft from the ground. After securing the carabiner and adjusting the cables to the correct length, ensure you weight-check the grips by hanging on to them and tugging them to test the cables.

Currently the device is predominantly used as a personal training aid for trainers and enthusiasts but, as its popularity develops, varying TRX Suspension Training class formats will begin to flood gyms and fitness studios. With progress the workouts will become multi-dimensional, utilising all forms of unstable base technology together with other resistance aids such as kettlebells and ViPRs.

Below are just a few of the many exercises that can be performed with TRX Suspension Training, movements within one workout. Imagination and creative development will mean that limitless ideas and concepts will be applied within the Suspension Training concept.

THE EXERCISES

Exercise 20.1 Chest Press

Starting position and action

- Begin by holding both handles around chest height, facing away from the anchor point, and position yourself so that you can lean forwards and extend your arms to support your body weight.
- In this position, adjust your feet so that, when leaning forwards in a modified press-up position, you are supporting your body weight through your arms and shoulders, keeping your abdominals braced to maintain rigidity through your torso with legs straight.

- In this position, while keeping your shoulders stabilised, separate your arms by bending through your elbows to lower yourself down so that your chest draws near to your hands, holding the handle grips.
- Maintaining core stability to ensure correct spinal alignment, press through the grips to take you back to the start position.
- Repeat 10–20 times.

Progressions/adaptations

- To intensify this exercise, walk your feet further back so that you are supporting more body weight when in the start position.
- To intensify further, take your legs all the way behind you while keeping your feet on the floor and perform the press-up movement, maintaining stabilisation of the core muscles and shoulder complex. Start in the same position, but intensify the exercise by putting your feet on a medicine ball, stability ball, etc.
- Another modification is to perform the chest press on one leg, with the other leg off the floor. This puts different demands on the core stabilisation muscles of the torso as the temptation is to drop the hips to one side to compensate the rotational forces involved.
- Try not to overcompensate, but remain in a neutral position with correct spinal alignment.

Exercise 20.2 Flye

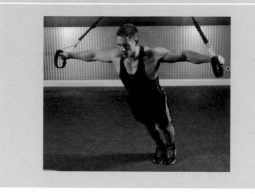

Starting position and action

- Begin holding both handles at chest height (as in the start position for the Chest Press) facing away from the anchor point and position yourself so that you can lean forwards and extend your arms to support your body weight.
- Keeping your abdominals braced to maintain rigidity through your torso with legs straight and keeping a slight bend in the elbows, open your arms, allowing your torso to lower forwards as the arms move out to the side.
- Maintain control of this movement, stabilising through your torso and shoulders and adjusting your foot position if the intensity is too great.
- When your arms are fully outstretched, pause briefly before you contract your chest muscles to bring your arms back together again, to push you back to the start position.
- Repeat 10–20 times.

Coaching points

- Because of the nature of the Flye do not attempt a movement that is too wide for you to control. Begin the first few repetitions at an easy incline before adjusting the foot position to a more challenging intensity.

Exercise 20.3 Double-arm Back Row

Starting position and action

- Stand holding the grips at arm's length facing the anchor point and lean back, so that your body weight is supported, while maintaining core stability through your torso muscles and shoulder complex.
- Keeping your feet together, from an extended arm position pull on the grips to bring your body toward the handles.
- The exact hand position can vary, either with palms up, palms inwards or palms down.

- This will affect the nature of the movement, but as long as the pulling action is constant and the elbows drive backwards, the focus will be on the back muscles rather than your arms.
- Maintain a rigid body throughout this movement.
- As your chest draws level with the handles, pause briefly before lowering your torso back to the start position, with arms extended, maintaining rigidity throughout your torso.
- Repeat 12–20 times.

Progressions/adaptations

- Vary this exercise by reducing the rigidity through the torso and dropping your hips during the lowering phase. Then as you begin the rowing, pull through your arms and engage the hips and glutes to push back to a straight torso position.
- To add intensity walk your feet further away so that you are supporting more of your body weight.
- To increase this intensity even further, develop the exercise into an elevated row position by placing your feet on an unstable base such as a BOSU™, medicine board or stability ball.

DELTOID RAISE

This exercise has a number of modifications, but there are three key movements: the T-Deltoid Raise, Y-Deltoid Raise and W-Deltoid Raise.

Exercise 20.4 T-Deltoid Raise

Exercise 20.5 Y-Deltoid Raise

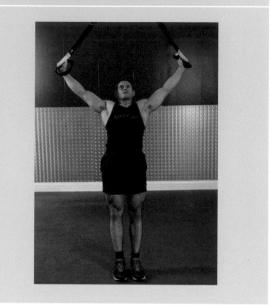

Starting position and action

- Stand facing the anchor point, holding the grips at arm's length, and with hands together lean back slightly so your body weight is pulling on the cables and they are taut.
- Maintaining core tension, beginning with palms facing each other retract your shoulder blades and then using your shoulder muscles open your arms wide to pull against the grips, lifting your body upwards.
- Maintain a rigid torso until you are in a 'crucifix' position with your arms outstretched, perpendicular to your torso.
- Pause briefly, before returning your arms under control to the start position, bringing your hands together again as your body lowers back down.
- Repeat the 'T' movement 12–20 times.

Starting position and action

- For this movement, follow the same steps as the T-Deltoid Raise, but for the lifting movement, take the arms upwards in a 'Y' position to finish midway between arms being overhead and the 'T' position.
- Pause briefly before returning to the start position.
- Perform 12–20 complete movements.

Exercise 20.6 W-Deltoid Raise

- Perform 12–20 complete movements.

Coaching points

- As with all Suspension Training, to add intensity position yourself so that more of your body weight is pulling on the TRX straps by adjusting your feet and stance.
- One exercise option is that you look to combine the above three exercises alternating between the T-Deltoid Raise, Y-Deltoid Raise and W-Deltoid Raise movement and aiming for 15–25 repetitions. Adjust your foot position to ensure each repetition has sufficient intensity without being so difficult that you lose form and stability.

Starting position and action

- Stand holding the grips at arm's length, facing the anchor point, and lean back so that your body weight is supported while maintaining core stability through your torso muscles and shoulder complex.
- Keeping your feet together, from an extended arm position pull on the grips to bring your body toward the handles, pulling back from the elbows with palms down.
- When your elbows draw level with your chest, bracing your abdominals and with your arms bent at right angles, rotate your forearms back to incorporate your rotator cuff muscles, bringing your hands level with your head with palms facing the anchor point.
- Pause briefly before lowering your hands back to chest level and then extend your arms to return to the start position.

Exercise 20.7 Single-arm Power Pull with Rotation

Starting position and action

- Interlock the handle grips so you are pulling on one handle.

- Hold one handle with your right hand in front of you and lean back so that you are supporting your body weight with your right arm.
- With your right arm fully extended, open up your chest, by rotating to your left side so that you can reach down with your left hand to touch the floor.
- Brace your abdominals and maintain rigidity throughout your body, pull yourself up towards the handle using your upper back muscles and arm.
- As you near the handle rotate your torso inwards so that you are facing the handle.
- Hold this position briefly before opening up and lowering back to the bottom position.
- Repeat 10–20 times before changing hands and repeating using your other hand.

Progressions/adaptations

- If you stagger your stance with one foot in front of the other this will affect the intensity of the exercise. To assist the movement, if holding the grips with your left hand have your left foot in front of your right. When holding with your right hand reverse your foot position.
- Alternatively, try standing on one leg. Be sure to stand on the leg on the same side as the hand which is holding the hand grip.

Exercise 20.8 Squat

Starting position and action

- Stand holding both grips with arms extended, with feet hip distance apart and leaning back so you are supporting your body weight, keeping your abdominals braced throughout the movement.
- Bend your legs to lower yourself into a squat position, holding the suspension cable handles to support you.
- Sit back keeping your torso and lower legs (shins) almost parallel to each other and so your upper thigh, flexing at the hips and knees, becomes almost parallel to the floor.
- Hold this squat position briefly before extending through your hips and legs to return to standing.
- Repeat 15–20 times.

Exercise 20.9 Single-leg Squat

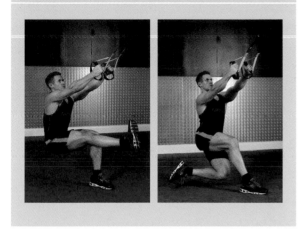

Starting position and action

- Stand holding both grips with arms extended, with feet hip distance apart and leaning back so that you are supporting your body weight, keeping your abdominals braced throughout the movement.
- Transfer your body weight on to your left leg with your right leg raised off the floor.
- While maintaining abdominal bracing and correct body alignment, bend your left leg to lower yourself into a single-leg squatting position, holding the suspension cable handles to support you.
- As your left leg flexes so that the knee is bent at almost 90 degrees, maintaining correct spinal alignment, push off your left leg and glutes to return to a standing position.
- Repeat 10–20 times before returning to the start position and repeating the entire movement with your body weight now on your right leg.
- Repeat movement on your left leg 10–20 times.

Progressions/adaptations

- As with all suspension training exercises, it is possible to increase intensity by adjusting your foot position to take more load.
- Another option is to transfer supporting legs in an alternating single-leg squat movement, thus after completing a repetition while on your right leg, swap legs and then immediately squat down on your left leg before returning back to a standing position. Repeat alternating single-leg squats 15–30 times.
- To intensify this movement further you can add dynamic power so you can jump with force from one single leg squat to the next, whether this is the alternate or same leg. Aim for power and height with each push. This variation is sometimes called a Pistol Squat (figure on the left). Another variation is the Balance Lunge (figure on the right, this page).
- Another variation is to add movement to the jump technique so that after each squat technique you push off with such force that you 'launch' yourself into the air, held by the suspension straps, and you travel 3–5 ft to your right side before squatting down on your right leg. Then, push back with force to land 3–5 ft to your left landing on your left leg and repeating the single leg squatting action. Repeat 15–30 times.
- Further modifications include the Balance Lunge, which is essentially a single leg squat but this time as you lower down your raised leg, instead of being held in front of you, it is extended behind and to the outside of your squatting leg.

Coaching points

- As you perform this movement, be very careful not to lose abdominal bracing and maintain a firm torso.
- The movement of your raised leg will affect your hip and pelvis alignment, so try not to extend your raised leg too far behind your squatting leg, especially if this means compromising your posture and spinal alignment.

Exercise 20.10 Sprinter's Start

Starting position and action

- Hold on to the grips facing away from the anchor point.

- Keep elbows bent and behind you, but keep grips close to your chest with arms fixed.
- Lean into the straps so that your body weight is partially suspended but then lower yourself down into lunge position, with your left leg behind you.
- In this position, maintain correct shoulder and arm tension by keeping your elbows fixed throughout.
- Contract through your right glutes and quads to provide the force to drive your left knee forwards from the lunge position upward in a dynamic movement so that your left knee comes to about rib height.
- Return the left knee back to the floor under control and repeat 10–20 times before changing legs and repeating using other leg.

Progressions/adaptations

- This should be a dynamic movement but to increase the force element, drive through your supporting leg to push off the floor into a partial hop, before landing and returning to lunge position with the trail leg.
- In addition, you can add some lateral perspective to the drive so that you power off at a partial angle to the anchor point to 'land' a few inches/ feet from where you took off.
- Always ensure the shoulder complex and core musculature are stabilised throughout this dynamic exercise.

Exercise **20.11** Hip Press

Exercise **20.12** Suspended Crunch

Starting position and action

- Initially sit on the floor facing the anchor point, with the foot cradles hanging about 8–10 in from the floor.
- Place your right foot in the foot cradle that hangs to the left, placing your toes through the cradle.
- Then lift your left leg over your right and place your left foot, toes first, through the right foot cradle.
- When your feet are in the cradles, rotate over to your right side to position yourself on your hands, placed shoulder width apart.
- In this position, lift your hips upwards and bring your knees in towards your chest to engage your abdominals in a crunching action.
- The core muscles will be involved throughout to maintain balance and stability.
- Repeat 20–30 times before resting or changing exercises

Starting position and action

- Sit on the floor facing the foot cradle and place your right foot, toes first, through the cradle. The cradle should be about 8–10 in from the floor.
- Extend your legs out while in a supine position lying on your back with arms by your side.
- Brace your abdominals and lift your backside off the floor, pushing your hips upwards to the ceiling.
- Hold briefly in the top position before lowering, either completely to the floor or just sinking down with your hips to recover before repeating.
- Repeat hip thrust and hold action 10–20 times before resting.

Coaching points

- Initially, due to the instability of this movement, you might want to keep your arms on the floor.
- As you become more experienced, try taking your arms off the floor and crossing them over your chest.

Exercise 20.13 Atomic Press-up

Starting position and action

- This is a combination of a Suspended Crunch and a Suspended Press-up
- Initially, sit on the floor facing the anchor point, with the foot cradles hanging about 8–10 in from the floor.
- Place your right foot in the foot cradle that hangs to the left, placing your toes through the cradle.
- Lift your left leg over your right and place your left foot, toes first, through the right foot cradle.
- When your feet are in the cradles, rotate over to your right side to position yourself on your hands, placed slightly wider than shoulder width apart.
- Keeping your abdominals braced draw your knees in towards your chest, lifting your hips and supporting your bodyweight through your arms and shoulders.
- Then extend your legs back behind you and when stable lower yourself by bending your arms, to lower your chest towards the floor.

- When your chest is about 6 in from the floor, push against the floor to push yourself back to the start position, maintaining correct spinal alignment throughout.
- Repeat alternating knees to chest action with full press-up for 10–20 complete movements.

Progressions/adaptations

- This knee-to-chest action can be changed by keeping the legs straight and going into a 'pike' position, lifting the hips high as you pull your feet towards your chest. Return feet to outstretched star position behind you before performing press-up. Repeat movements 10–20 times.
- Instead of a knee-to-chest or pike movement, you can perform an oblique pull, where the action is similar to a knee-to-chest movement but this time you draw the knees in and to your right side, before returning back to a straight leg start position and performing a press-up. Then bring the knees in again but obliquely to your left side, before extending your legs behind you and performing another press-up.
- Repeat this alternating left and right oblique crunch with full press-ups in between each for a total of 8–15 complete movements.
- Another modification is the Suspended Press-up. For this exercise you only focus on the 'press-up' aspect, yet you only have one foot in the foot cradle while the other foot is held adjacent and stabilised through leg, glutes, hip complex and core muscles – see Total Body Burpee.

TOTAL BODY BURPEE

This is a combination of a Suspended Press-up and a Suspended Lunge, yet it is performed in a very dynamic way.

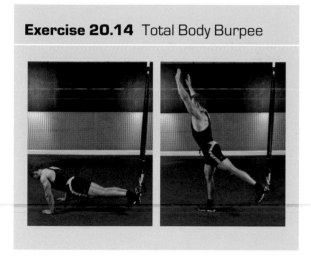

Exercise 20.14 Total Body Burpee

Starting position and action

- Interlock the handles to create a single handle to use as in Exercise 20.7 (page 189). Stand facing the anchor point and feed your right foot through the foot cradle so that when you turn around to your left to face the opposite direction, your right leg is bent and is supported by the TRX suspension band.
- Bend your left leg to lower yourself to the floor but as you do so place your hands on the floor slightly wider than shoulder width apart.
- Brace your abdominals and ensure your hips and right leg are stabilised and ready to take increased resistance.
- As soon as they contact the floor, lift your left leg off the floor and extend it back to draw level with your right leg.

- As soon as you lift your left foot off the floor your body will be supported through your arms and right leg.
- When you are stable, perform a press-up, lowering your chest to the floor by bending at the elbow.
- Push back up by extending the arms and then maintaining correct shoulder stabilisation and core control, bring your left knee back towards your chest and place your left foot on the floor.
- Pushing up through your arms and driving through your left leg so that you come into a standing position, continue the dynamic leg drive to push yourself off the floor in a hopping action.
- As you land, bend through your leg to repeat the movement as before, lowering back to the ground and repeating another press-up, etc.
- Repeat 8–15 times before changing your suspended leg and repeating, this time working the other leg.

Coaching points

- This is a very advanced and dynamic movement combining two different exercises.
- Always ensure you maintain correct form and do not try to compromise technique for repetitions.
- Reduce the exercise intensity by cutting out the jump at the end of the power lunge.
- To increase intensity further, try applying partial lateral movement with each lunge jump to introduce even more leg, hip and core stabilisation within the exercise.

4

PART **FOUR**

ALTERNATIVE TRAINING

In writing this book based on abdominal training I felt it was important to look at other forms of exercise that apply similar principles of core stability, or focus on improved movement and function. This book aims to provide you with exercises that will help you to achieve core stability and so enhance posture, sporting application and functional movement. While core stability is not necessarily the main goal in the disciplines described in this part of the book, the outcome of an enhanced and enriched life, with improved mobility, posture and sporting performance, is to a certain extent the same.

The current vogue in fitness, as in many sports, is 'alternative' training, which might be called holistic as opposed to specific. In some of these forms, such as Pilates, there are specific exercises that emphasise the core musculature, and include breathing techniques and specific movements of the limbs. Other disciplines, such as t'ai chi and yoga, encourage a more holistic approach, aiming for fluidity of movement combined with various postures that need to be maintained with correct form. This book only scratches the surface of these disciplines, many of which date back thousands of years, but it is interesting to see how many different disciplines in fact have a similar approach, albeit with varying amounts of meditative emphasis.

More recently, the Feldenkrais and Alexander techniques have taken the concept of functional movement with correct form a step further. They look at the genesis of movement in relation to a final outcome, and aim to overcome incorrect form, which has a negative effect at every stage in between.

This type of relearning, regrowth or rebirth, when applied to movement and function, follows similar pathways despite originating from different continents and spanning millennia. Some of the following disciplines, while touched on only briefly here, might be of interest to you and you may wish to find out more about them for yourself.

ALTERNATIVE TRAINING AND EXERCISES

21

PILATES

HISTORY

Joseph Pilates was born in Munchengladbach, Germany, in 1880. He was a small child who suffered from asthma, rickets and rheumatic fever. His father was a gymnast and his mother a naturopath, and Pilates himself was so fascinated by the body and movement that he even studied Zen Buddhism and yoga. He was a competent boxer, gymnast and skier, and as a youth used various body-building methods to assist his training.

He was interned in England during the First World War, where he taught wrestling and self-defence. Later on he was transferred to the Isle of Man, where he began assisting as a nurse and, to help rehabilitate immobilised patients, he designed exercise apparatus by attaching springs to hospital beds. Many of these machines would have been comparable in design to other devices used in the world of gymnastics and early fitness training.

After the war, Pilates returned to Germany and began coaching the Hamburg Military Police in self-defence and physical training, applying many of the techniques he had used during the war. However, dissatisfied with the political climate there, he decided to sail to New York. It was during this journey that he met his future wife, Clara.

In America, Joseph and Clara opened their first Pilates studio in 1926. There were several dance and rehearsal studios in the same building, and this proximity allowed Pilates to work with many dance students, not only towards their rehabilitation, but also to help strengthen their bodies for dancing and movement. He designed more than 500 specific exercises, using five major pieces of unique equipment.

Word spread within the dance community of his training talents, and soon Pilates was asked to train a host of renowned dancers and performers. In addition, many choreographers and teachers began to incorporate specific 'Pilates' exercises into their lessons.

The Pilates principles of training are not dissimilar to other early training methodologies developed by leading fitness exponents of the era. Vladislav Krayevsky, a Polish-born physician, founded the St Petersburg Amateur Weightlifting Society in 1885 and much of his work has parallels with many of today's current training methods, including the use of cables, variable resistance, springs, cams, levers, and so on. Some of the world's strongest men at that time used his principles and training methods.

Eugene Sandow, born in Russia in 1867, was not only a respected strongman and trainer in the late nineteenth century, he was also recognised as one of the leaders in the field of scientific fitness training. His book, *Life is Movement*, was well received by the kings and queens of Europe, as well as US presidents. He was even appointed Professor of Scientific Culture to His Majesty George V.

The Pilates adaptations and principles were aimed primarily at the world of dance, so differed somewhat from the exercise progressions of other fitness gurus and specialists. The exercises and machines used were geared to nurture intrinsic strength and conditioning, both in a rehabilitative nature and for injury prevention, and improved quality of movement in general.

Unfortunately, Joseph Pilates was a somewhat autocratic man and did not officially train anyone to teach his technique. When he died, his disciples scattered themselves across the globe, teaching their own versions of his original technique. As a result, several variations on Pilates are taught worldwide today.

WHAT IS PILATES?

Pilates is a body-conditioning technique designed to create inner strength and flexibility without building bulky muscles. It concentrates on strengthening the core postural muscles, namely the transverse abdominus and internal obliques (corset muscles) and multifudus (muscles of the lower back). By learning to keep these muscles stabilised while executing slow, controlled, flowing movements, tight overstrained muscles will learn to relax and lengthen and weak muscles

will be strengthened. Not only does the participant begin to look and feel better, the risk of injury is greatly reduced by the focus on balancing and aligning the body, ultimately improving posture.

Pilates concentrates on strengthening the core postural muscles to achieve stability in the trunk. Each exercise is executed with correct postural alignment. You are taught to recognise unwanted tension and release it; then, with your core stability maintained, you can think about stretching those muscles that are too tight, strengthening those that are weak, and increasing flexibility and mobility. In this way balance is restored to the body.

A way of life

The Pilates method is more than just a series of exercises; it is an entire approach to exercise, a way of moving the whole body.

Pilates has been around for many years and, until recently, the technique was practised almost exclusively by dancers. Over the last few years, however, modifications have been made to the technique, enabling everyone to benefit.

It can take a while to get the hang of Pilates and, at first, it can seem as if you are doing very little. First, the participant needs to learn how to pull their navel towards their spine, making the connection between the ribcage and the pelvis, while maintaining neutral or natural spinal alignment. Next, the breathing needs to be focused into the ribs and thoracic region of the spine to enable the participant to remain stabilised while executing the exercises. Finally, the participant needs to strive for stability of the shoulder girdle by gently pulling the shoulders down into the back without throwing the ribcage forwards; this takes practice. You can practise combining all these elements almost anywhere – walking down the street, sitting at your desk and even driving your car. The art of stabilising the core needs to become automatic, without conscious thought. The only way to make this happen is first to practise as often as you can.

Pilates is a complete body and mind conditioning system, incorporating many principles from eastern exercise programmes; its essence is training the mind to control the body. By developing the participant's sense of body awareness and co-ordination, they are taught to control every aspect of their body, and so improve alignment and postural fitness.

Pilates is currently used internationally by individuals at all levels of fitness as well as by dance companies, students at performing arts schools and universities, sports teams, spa clients, and fitness enthusiasts at private health clubs and gyms. There are two different types of class: mat-based and equipment-based. The mat-based class is exactly that: executed either seated or lying on a mat, using gravity as resistance. An equipment-based class can be far more challenging (as well as expensive) as highly specialised apparatus may be used to increase resistance.

THE BENEFITS

The ability to stabilise the core, while at the same time being able to move the limbs effortlessly, not only reduces the risk of injury (especially to the spine) but improves our posture, giving us that longer, leaner look. Remember that Pilates is not a cardio-vascular or fat-burning workout – in order to lose body fat and work your heart and lungs, you will still need to engage in large body movements or activities that make you breathless and sweaty.

Who can benefit?

Everyone can benefit from Pilates – from experienced sportspeople to the complete beginner, from pregnant and new mothers to the mature individual and, of course, the chronic back pain sufferer. If you have special needs, which might include any of the categories mentioned above and several others, it may be wise to seek individual tuition, especially in the early stages. Make sure you find a reputable instructor with the knowledge and experience necessary to cater for your individual needs. Once you have a basic working knowledge of your limitations and any modifications you need to make, you can safely attend a more mainstream class.

We now know, through research, that the Pilates method of body conditioning is not only fundamental in preventing injury for people in all walks of life but can also be used to help rehabilitate people suffering with many types of injury.

PILATES EXERCISES

Exercise 21.1 Supine Neutral Pelvic Alignment with Stabilisation

Starting position and action

- Lie down on the floor, face up, with your knees bent and your feet on the floor approximately hip distance apart.
- Rock your hips backwards and forwards a few times and be aware of the two extremes: (i) the hip bones pushing up towards the ceiling as the middle back flattens into the floor; (ii) the hip bones pushing forwards and down as the back arches away from the floor.
- Now try to find neutral spine alignment by just allowing your pelvis to flop into a position that feels natural to you.
- Take a breath, deep into your back, trying to visualise your ribcage expanding sideways.
- As you exhale, draw the navel towards the spine, without tilting the pelvis (i.e. pushing the back into the floor).
- Continue to breathe into the ribcage while maintaining the intra-abdominal pressure.
- Try to increase the duration of each contraction, building up to one minute.

Coaching points

- If you rest your fingers just 'inside' your hipbones, you should be able to feel your core muscles contracting.
- Remember to keep breathing throughout, into the ribcage.

Exercise 21.2 Supine Shoulder Stabilisation

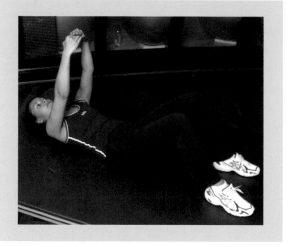

Starting position and action

- Lie down on your back, in the neutral position, with your knees bent and your feet flat on the floor, approximately hip width apart.
- This time, maintaining pelvic stabilisation, reach both arms directly above your shoulders towards the ceiling, shoulder width apart and with your palms facing inwards.
- As you inhale, pull your shoulder blades apart, closing the chest.
- Try to keep the back of your head in contact with the floor.

- Feel the muscles of your neck and shoulders tighten and shorten.
- As you exhale, keep your arms where they are, but pull your shoulders down into your back, opening the chest and lengthening through the back of the neck.
- Try to maintain pelvic stabilisation throughout the exercise, keeping your arms extended and taking 4–5 complete breaths.
- Then, after the last exhalation, lower the arms to the side of the body, palms down.

Coaching points
- If you have maintained shoulder stabilisation you will find that your arms will naturally lower to the floor, with the elbows slightly relaxed and away from the sides of the body.

Exercise 21.3 One-leg Circle

Starting position and action
- Lie down, face up, with neutral spine alignment, your shoulder girdle stabilised and your arms by your side with palms down.
- Keeping one leg extended along the floor, bring the thigh of the other leg perpendicular (at right angles) to the floor, without losing neutral alignment.
- Bend the knee of your elevated leg slightly, and slowly make small controlled circles.
- Try 10 circles in one direction and then ten in the other.
- The object of this exercise is to make the largest circle possible while preventing any movement in the trunk or tilting of the hips.
- Exhale as the leg moves away from the mid-line of the body, inhale as the leg moves towards the centre.

Coaching points
- Don't forget to do an equal number of circles in both directions with each leg.
- As you improve, you can extend the working leg further at the knee.

Exercise 21.4 Leg/Hip Slide

Starting position and action

- Lie down on the floor, face up, with your knees bent and your hips and pelvis in neutral alignment.
- Take a deep breath and pull your navel in towards your spine, bracing your abdominals. As you exhale, slowly slide your right foot along the floor, extending the leg so that it lies flat on the floor.
- Maintaining your alignment, return your leg to the start position by sliding it slowly back.
- Keeping your abdominals braced, repeat the movement, this time sliding the left leg.

Coaching points

- Try not to tilt your pelvis or press down on the floor with your bent leg.

Exercise 21.5 Leg Slide with Arm Extension

Starting position and action

- Lie down on the floor, face up, with your knees bent and your pelvis in neutral alignment.
- Brace your shoulders by pulling your shoulder blades down without expanding your ribcage.
- Inhale, bracing your abdominals, and exhale as you extend your right leg along the floor.
- Simultaneously bring your left arm up in an arc movement to reach over your head and down towards the floor, or as far as is comfortable, while preserving the spinal alignment.
- Then, keeping the tension through your abdominals, breathe in as you return the leg and arm to the start position.
- Repeat, sliding your left leg along the floor and lifting your right arm up and over your head.

Coaching points

- If you find performing both arm and leg movements simultaneously too difficult, begin by performing the leg actions for 10–15 repetitions and then perform the arm actions, maintaining shoulder stability and spinal alignment.
- Another option is to slide the same arm and leg simultaneously to create a bias on one side, before repeating on your opposite side.

Exercise 21.6 Spine Curls

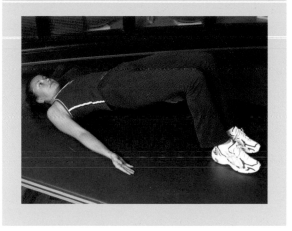

Starting position and action

- Lie on the floor, face up, with your knees bent, keeping your hips and pelvis in neutral alignment.
- Breathe in and pull your navel towards your spine to maintain tension.
- Keep your feet, knees and hips in line and your knees bent.
- Slowly curl your lower back off the floor, lifting your buttocks into the air.
- As you lower back again, try to lengthen your spine by lowering the back one vertebra at a time.
- Begin with small movements, lifting just your buttocks and lower back off the floor, and gradually increase your movement range.

Coaching points

- Be careful not to arch your back or lose correct alignment as you lift.
- Do not lift any further than your shoulder and upper back.

Exercise 21.7 Pillow Squeeze

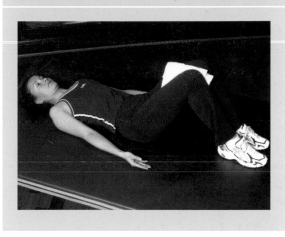

Starting position and action

- Lie on the floor, face up, with your knees bent and your hips and pelvis in neutral alignment.
- Place a cushion or folded towel between your knees.
- Without tilting your pelvis, squeeze the cushion with your thighs and contract your pelvic floor muscles by trying to lift and tighten them.
- Hold this contraction for 5–10 seconds and then release. Repeat 5–10 times.

Coaching points

- Do not tense your neck as you squeeze, and maintain your abdominal tension, breathing throughout.

Exercise 21.8 Prone Leg Lengthening

Starting position and action
- Lie face down with your hands or a cushion under your forehead, keeping your neck in correct alignment.
- Brace your abdominals, pulling your navel in and up away from the floor.
- Lift your right leg so that your toes are 2–5 cm off the floor, and try to push the heel away from you, without tilting your pelvis.
- Maintain this stretch for 5–10 seconds before lowering and repeating with the left leg.

Coaching points
- Do not lift your leg too high, as this will cause your pelvis to rotate out of alignment.
- Keep breathing throughout and remember to maintain your abdominal tension, relaxing briefly only when you have lowered the leg to the floor.

Exercise 21.9 Standing Roll-downs

Starting position and action
- Stand with your back to a wall, leaning back slightly to rest against it, with your feet shoulder width apart and your buttocks and shoulders in contact with the wall.
- Keep your hips and pelvis in neutral and keep your spine in alignment.
- Breathe in and, as you breathe out, drop your chin to your chest and try to roll your back off the wall, bending down as you do so.
- Try to imagine peeling yourself away from the wall, one vertebra at a time.
- Allow your arms to hang down to the side as you lower, bringing your head towards your knees.
- At the lowest point, pause briefly and then slowly return to the start position, rolling yourself back up to a standing position.

Coaching points
- Allow your back to flex comfortably but try not to force any movement as you lower.

- You might prefer to support your back by keeping your hands on your thighs as you lower.
- This movement can also be performed free-standing, but be careful if you have a lower back injury or suffer from lower back pain.

T'AI CHI CH'UAN
HISTORY

The origins of t'ai chi ch'uan go back to the Taoist study of Chi Kung, a form of physical health and spiritual growth. In the tenth century, the introduction of a self-defence component, blending healing, martial arts and meditation, formed what is now known as t'ai chi ch'uan (often abbreviated to t'ai chi). One aspect of the art was to develop concentration and become focused, or centred.

This is the foundation of t'ai chi: without this centring on the present moment, or the 'now', it is not possible to alter or heal anything. In order for change or healing to take place, a location in the abdomen called the Tan T'ien is thought to be the true body centre, and from this central 'feeling point' all movement and distribution of feeling occurs.

The practice of t'ai chi as an art form does not focus on the physical characteristics or self-defence applications. Rather, it should be viewed as an opportunity to experience and understand change as it occurs in our lives and in the world around us.

What is the aim of t'ai chi?

T'ai chi emphasises the need to achieve harmony between body, mind and spirit. Considered a 'movement art', it seeks to cultivate an understanding of change as a natural life process, believing that we should accept change as it is inevitable.

WHAT IS T'AI CHI?

To an outsider, t'ai chi may seem a slow-moving choreography of positions, interlinked by adjustments in the participants' balance and stance. The movements should be carried out slowly; they should flow smoothly and rhythmically, enhancing balance and posture. Several main principles underlie the practice of t'ai chi; one of these is 'lift the head', which encourages participants to lengthen their neck and spine consciously during the movements. Slow and low transitions are more difficult to perform as the body weight is over a single leg for longer. The goal is to achieve a smooth transition from one stance to another. In order to do this the participant needs to focus on their posture and muscle bracing. The 'push hands' style encourages an active release of this braced position while supporting the body with the weight biased to one leg (the hand actions emphasise t'ai chi's martial arts element).

T'ai chi encourages fluidity of joint movement rather than specific muscle strengthening. This continual movement improves circulation and can help patients suffering from arthritis and rheumatism.

The role of t'ai chi in core stability training is in its pursuit of the ability to remain balanced, with the appropriate spinal posture. Taoist monks believed that there is an important relationship between the body and gravity, and that we should utilise the energy that gravity provides to move the body through this force with good posture. This physical 'good balance' then transcends into a similar ability to be well balanced, both physically and emotionally, in life.

T'ai chi is renowned for its therapeutic qualities, both on a physical and functional level.

Stress affects the body in many ways – tightening of muscles, tension, irritability, and so on – and t'ai chi uses a combination of deep breathing techniques, fluidity of motion, and the relaxing of both mental and physical tensions that helps restore balance throughout the body. This cleansing of tension seems to help dissipate stress.

WHO CAN BENEFIT?

Because t'ai chi focuses on balance at every level, it is an effective training aid for older people. The entire body is recruited into each movement, and on so many levels that it seems there is a symphony of sensation, perception and ability, integrated into a centrally balanced and fluid consciousness.

The joints of the ankle, knee and hip are constantly challenged, so body awareness, posture and balance are all improved. This leads to a greater sense of confidence with regard to movement, which helps those practising t'ai chi to lead a more active life. The fitness level required before embarking on a t'ai chi course would quite simply be the ability to walk unaided (however, in certain circumstances even this inability can be overcome through modification of technique).

One interesting aspect mentioned by students of t'ai chi is that it draws together 'opposites of movement'. For example, it can be considered to be a soft art but extremely powerful: you are exercising while remaining calm and relaxed. T'ai chi can really make you think; it challenges your preconceptions of how you exist in relation to gravity, your inner self and your relationships with others.

One important point demonstrated by practising t'ai chi with older people is that, whatever age you are, there is still much to be learned. Improvements in balance, core function and mobility can be achieved, while the cognitive functioning of the brain (both in terms of learning and with regard to movement skills) is stimulated. Such 'growth' occurs at many different levels – spiritual, physical, mental and emotional – and encapsulates what t'ai chi is all about: movement, change and rediscovery.

YOGA
HISTORY

Yoga is a spirituality involving physical and mental discipline. Although it originated in India over 5000 years ago, its roots are still uncertain. It has three major cultural influences: Hindu yoga, Buddhist yoga and Jaina yoga. In 1893 the missionary Swami Vivekananda is credited with the introduction of yoga to western societies after speaking at the Parliament of Religions. Just over a century later, the current western yoga movement has some 20 million devotees.

Three influences

The philosophy of yoga suggests that creation and life is subject to the influences of activity (Rajas), inertia (Tamas) and clarity (Sattva).[9]

WHAT IS YOGA?

The word yoga means union, and yoga teachings aim to educate the mind to control the body. This control occurs through five principles:

- proper breathing
- correct diet
- relaxation
- exercise
- correct thought and meditation.

Yoga poses encourage you to maintain a specific posture and hold it, while relaxing, so that the mind can be undisturbed. This emphasis on bodily posture, or 'asana', probably sums up the main idea western societies have of yoga and its principles. The 'asanas' are taught in sequence, emphasising varying levels of spirituality, meditation and dynamic movement, according to the specific style.

For some people, the word yoga may conjure up images of wiry Indians in contorted postures, levitating above the ground and meditating incessantly. In reality it is a physical and spiritual discipline where you transcend to a higher state of consciousness through the use of meditation, different postures and breathing techniques.

Yoga seems to be everywhere, and many of its current 'derivatives' use the term 'yoga' as a prefix to assist their marketability. How closely these alternative concepts really relate to yoga is questionable, yet they all serve the purpose of combining mindful movement with postures that require elements of abdominal bracing to maintain form.

WHO CAN BENEFIT?

Yoga is practised by people of all ages, and benefits can be gained throughout your life, whatever your age. Many fitness texts identify with the benefits that yoga can provide, including recovery from injury, and improved concentration and mental discipline. At a deeper level, yoga has been praised for its ability to heighten spiritual awareness and enlightenment, both of which can result in stress reduction.

Yoga assists with co-ordination in children and can help to improve concentration and mental focus. The asanas can help relieve backache during pregnancy and increased mobilisation of the joints in the stances can help improve posture and circulation in older people. Sportspeople can benefit too, as yoga can help to regulate any muscular imbalances and improve flexibility, leg strength, balance and concentration.

In the western world, Hatha yoga is the most common form practised. Devotees are drawn to this style in the understanding that the different postures and movements are combined to increase flexibility, improve relaxation and enhance spirituality. Its therapeutic effects – improved strength and flexibility, together with vitality, and improved concentration and immune system function – are now well known.

While it may be true that Hatha yoga can enhance all these functions, this is simply a by-product of the bigger picture of what yoga really is and what it can do for you. Yoga is about clarity of mind and body; it tries to peel away the layers of obscurity that surround us, helping us achieve an unclouded view, and the ability to see and perceive things clearly.

The benefits of yoga may be reaped by anyone, and while different styles will have a different emphasis and identify with different elements – being geared towards spirituality, meditation or well-being – many forms encourage body awareness to facilitate these elements. Heightened body awareness and the ability to maintain form in various postures is an excellent way of achieving inner strength from the deep stabiliser muscles, either directly or indirectly.

THE ALEXANDER TECHNIQUE
HISTORY

Frederick Matthias Alexander was born in Tasmania, Australia, in 1869. He spent a while in Melbourne and devoted much time to acting and giving recitals – his voice suffered as a result. On self-examination he discovered that the position in which he held his neck and head affected his larynx and consequently his voice. This led Alexander to hypothesise that the manner of 'doing' could ultimately affect function. He concluded that habitual patterns of movement might not be the 'most appropriate' for optimum function and that it would be wise to reconsider movement as a whole based on the desired function or outcome. This meant relearning many everyday tasks.

In the early twentieth century he moved to London and set up a practice, treating many actors and actresses. Over the next 50 years he gained the respect of many influential people, including George Bernard Shaw.

WHAT IS THE ALEXANDER TECHNIQUE?

The Alexander technique identifies with the correct functioning of the human body, its natural movements and how to perform them with minimal ease and causing minimal disruption. The Alexander principle states that certain ways of moving are preferable to others and that not applying these 'better' movements has a negative effect on the functioning of the body.[11]

In his book, *The Use of Self*, published in 1932, Alexander specifies movements as 'Use and Mis-use'. He proposes that some of the resultant conditions of mis-use of the body's natural movement and function are poor postural effects that can, in their most severe form, cause breathing disorders, arthritis, backaches, headaches and gastro-intestinal conditions.

WHAT ARE THE BENEFITS?

The Alexander technique offers a way of changing your everyday habits to re-educate your mind and body to achieve improved movement, balance, support and co-ordination. The emphasis is not just on mind/body interaction but on looking at the entire process of movement and function. The focus is to release unnecessary muscular tension, in the belief that, as the result of modern living, our muscles are continually being tightened and our bodies distorted and unbalanced. This increase in tension, located in the neck and upper back, restricts the head's freedom of movement and interferes with our posture and functional movement. By creating harmony of movement you can gain harmony of function.

During an Alexander class, your teacher will probably use a hands-on technique to feel your breathing and movement patterns, and to locate any tension by touching your neck and upper back. This hands-on technique is beneficial because your teacher can literally 'feel' your tension and movements while moving and manipulating you into the appropriate position. Initially, it is advisable to attend classes regularly during the first few weeks, even as regularly as two or three times a week, as there is much new information to be learned. Later on, though, attending on a weekly basis should be fine.

The process of learning new movement, together with an understanding of sensory appreciation and control of inhibition, offers one explanation of the principles of the Alexander technique. The correct use of functional movement and posture to encourage a beneficial link between health and well-being is perhaps another.

THE FELDENKRAIS METHOD
HISTORY

Moshe Feldenkrais introduced his method of integrated movement and function in the middle of the twentieth century, believing that humans do not live at their full potential but that, through gentle movement and the development of self-awareness, they could aid self-healing and transformation.

Working in unison with the nervous system, the Feldenkrais method was designed to improve flexibility and enhance well-being. The underlying principle behind the method is that one should relax into the postures with fluidity. Correct posture should be approached with minimal effort. The idea behind this is that a relaxed yet aware body will form a natural alignment in gravity.

Muscles should help align the skeleton, allowing movement where necessary. The focus is that of natural balance rather than correct posture. A constant emphasis on developing self-awareness with regard to alignment and balance is taught.

WHAT IS THE FELDENKRAIS METHOD?

The Feldenkrais method explains that there are three factors that contribute to postural problems:

- poor balance
- unnecessary effort
- lack of self-awareness.

Poor balance can create tension in the muscles, which in turn can compound the postural problem itself. Tension in the neck and ribs can cause the body to assume a posture that is off-centre and so balance is affected. As a result, the muscles are compromised and this in turn leads to worsening posture and increased tension.

WHO CAN BENEFIT?

Feldenkrais believed that neuro-muscular disorders such as strokes, cerebral palsy or spinal injury could benefit from this alternative system of functional movement and self-healing. In addition, he believed that there were benefits to be gained for those suffering from the discomfort of skeletal problems, neck pain and stress. The method was less about curing any conditions, and more concerned with looking at better ways of dealing with them. Feldenkrais believed that, often, the discomfort was based on the body's response to a specific condition rather than the condition itself.

If they can apply functional integration and awareness of movement, human beings have an enormous capacity for self-correction and self-improvement. Many students of this technique experience improvements in posture and a reduction in discomfort.

Feldenkrais teaching is, like the Alexander technique, largely based on touch. The teacher demonstrates new movement patterns and neuro-muscular organisation using, literally, a hands-on approach.

The Feldenkrais method is a system in which correct body movement and functional alignment can help reduce the effects of physical or emotional discomfort. It has been shown to help enhance functional movement in athletes and dancers.

CORE STABILITY TRAINING FOR SPECIFIC AGE GROUPS

22

CORE STABILITY TRAINING FOR OLDER PEOPLE

Participation in any of the disciplines described in the previous chapter can lead to increased mobility, improved posture and possible core strength gains. The inclusion of various forms of holistic and mind-focused exercise will certainly be of benefit to older people. The baby-boomers will soon be entering their golden years and there is a growing need for activity-based exercise routines that will benefit this growing age group.

At the end of the twentieth century, the number of people aged 65 or over neared 20 per cent of the population; indeed, in the next 30 years the size of the 50+ age group will have increased by another 74 per cent.[12] Research has indicated that fitness and strength gains, together with reduction in body fat, increased mobility and many other health gains have been achieved in people in their sixties, seventies and eighties. Yet one area that is often forgotten when designing training programmes for the elderly is that of balance.

Impaired balance can result in falls, and these are the leading cause of death in older people, especially from the age of 70 onwards. With this in mind, exercise programmes should link specific leg, lower back and core trunk-strengthening exercises with dynamic movements that improve co-ordination such as standing on one leg, throwing and catching balls, and exercising with a stability ball or something similar.

T'ai chi (see page 207) has a low risk of injury and is renowned for its ability to instil a feeling of relaxation and improve cognitive function. Yet it has also been shown to develop excellent balance and mobility in the elderly.[16,17]

Other forms of therapeutic exercise, such as yoga, and the Alexander and Feldenkrais techniques, could play a valuable part in an overall health and well-being training programme for the elderly. Any activity that requires mobilisation, balance and co-ordination, while simultaneously paying attention to posture, will have definite benefits for core stability. Ballroom dancing is one option, depending on taste and musical preference. I have even been fortunate enough to experience a hip-hop street-dance class at a health club, in which the majority of the participants were over 55, the oldest being 76 years of age – a true inspiration.

As the percentage of older people in the population grows, more thought needs to be put into expanding current training ideologies.

Humans are not automatically destined for retirement homes and institutions. If the appropriate training principles can be developed to cover a more functional approach, older people's lifestyles can be enriched dramatically.

One possible approach is a specific emphasis on core stabilisation, which can enhance balance and posture, leading to enhanced integrated function, improved mobility and an enriched life.

CORE STABILITY TRAINING FOR CHILDREN

Core stability training is not just for adults. In fact, many children's games require core stability and balance at various levels. One aspect of core stability is the capacity to keep a specific posture while in unstable positions; another is to overcome momentum by using appropriate abdominal contraction and incorporation of the stabiliser muscles to minimise further movement. You only have to think of children's games such as musical statues or hopscotch to realise the level of proprioceptive adjustment called for to maintain balance.

It is only relatively recently that balance and agility training has been introduced to sports training drills both at senior and youth level. While it is generally understood that sports training ultimately needs to be sport-specific, many of the fundamentals of balance, agility training and core stability can be achieved simply by having fun and playing games. Consider the motor skills, functional strength training and neuro-muscular control developed and improved when climbing a tree or swinging on a rope.

All too often when designing core stability programmes, trainers focus on drills with a purist emphasis. As a result, they sometimes miss the bigger picture of functional design and conditioning relative to certain activities or sports.

It's all too easy to forget the games and activities of our own childhood and adolescence; back then, we spent an enormous amount of time just playing. Why not recapture those very same ideals, the very same spontaneity and zest for life that was apparent in your long-forgotten youth?

By disguising exercises and fitness principles, making them look like play activities, you can achieve a more intense workout because, often, you won't even realise how hard you are working. Some of the activities are quite deceptive and it is easy to get carried away – the relative intensity won't become apparent until later.

Below are some ideas based on classic children's games that require varying degrees of abdominal bracing, balance, agility and stabilisation.

TAG (STUCK-IN-THE-MUD, MUSICAL STATUES)

- This is simply any kind of tag game, where restrictions are put on either the chasers or those being chased: for example, hopping only, backwards movement only, walking only.
- Once tagged, the person remains still, waiting to be un-tagged (a version of stuck-in-the-mud).
- The winner is the last person to be tagged.

Modifications

- You can modify this drill by making everyone 'freeze' on a command or when the music stops. In this case, the stabiliser muscles have to work overtime to decelerate you, yet keep your balance.

HOPSCOTCH

- To begin, draw some lines on a path with chalk, or use the pattern of the slabs on your patio.
- Throw a stone ahead of you on the floor, then hop towards it, one hop on each paving stone. Bend down on one leg, pick up the stone and hop back.

PATIO MADNESS

- Get into a sports stance with your abdominals braced and your feet shoulder width apart.
- Try touching every paving stone on the path/ patio with each foot, without touching the cracks, as quickly as possible.
- Make sure the emphasis is on keeping your torso in a braced position throughout, and keep breathing.
- Time how long it takes you to cover every stone. Rest and repeat.
- This is a fantastic way of developing co-ordination, balance and agility.

LEAP-FROG/LEAP-FROG RACES

- Working with a partner, leap-frog over each other to a desired distance; or leap-frog over a partner and then crawl through their legs – they then follow suit. Aim either to achieve a total number or a certain duration.
- Make sure that, as you go to jump over your partner, you brace your abdominals to assist with the force required in the jumping movement.
- In addition, when bending over waiting to be leap-frogged, you will need to brace your abdominals, torso and legs to avoid collapsing.

'SPIDERMAN'

- Position yourself on all fours with your weight evenly spread between your toes and your hands.
- Keep your feet and knees turned out slightly to minimise hip flexor involvement.
- Brace your abdominals and keep your torso as rigid as possible. Keep your spine in neutral throughout.
- With small movements of your hands and feet, 'crawl' yourself forwards, making sure you preserve neutral spine and with minimal movement through the hips and pelvis.
- Aim to cover a distance of 10–20 m before resting briefly and repeating.

WHEELBARROW RACES

- Start in the push-up position with your legs behind you and your feet together.
- Your body should remain perfectly rigid throughout.
- Your partner then lifts your legs off the floor, holding your ankles.
- This might be hard enough for most people to maintain, but to make it harder still try to walk forwards on your hands over about 3–10 m, keeping your body and legs straight.
- Make sure you keep your abdominals tensed throughout.
- Don't let your back sag at any stage, as this will mean loss of tension through your abdominals.
- An excellent workout for your upper body, shoulder stabilisers, abdominals and back.

HULA-HOOP

- If you can beg, buy or borrow a large hoop that is big enough to fit around your waist probably twice over, then learning to hula-hoop can be a fun way of toning up your tummy.

- By keeping the hoop spinning around, using a rotating movement of the hips and torso, all the abdominal muscles are activated. This will help tone and tighten your entire mid section.

PIGGY-BACK RACES

- As well as being an excellent calorie-burner and great for the leg muscles, this activity requires you to brace your abdominals and torso in preparation for your partner to jump/climb on to your back.
- Without the appropriate abdominal bracing and correct breathing during movement this exercise can cause injuries. Care and common sense must be applied at all times.

- Make sure you can maintain your partner's weight in a relatively upright posture to avoid any discomfort or risks to your lower back.

SPACE HOPPERS

- Bouncing on a space hopper can be an excellent way of training balance with fun.
- Sit on a space hopper, leaning forwards slightly, and aim to cover a set distance without falling off or losing correct abdominal tension.
- Be careful if using a child-size hopper, as this is likely to be too small for you and could put unnecessary strain on your lower back and knees.

ABDOMINAL TRAINING IN WATER

23

When you train in water your body has to overcome different principles to those encountered on land, namely buoyancy, water resistance and hydrostatic pressure. Archimedes, an Ancient Greek mathematician, discovered that when an object is immersed in water, the amount of water displaced is equal to the mass of the object immersed. This displacement causes the water to have a buoyancy effect on the object immersed and, consequently, the gravitational effects are minimised.

THE BUOYANCY EFFECT

Putting this into context, when you get into a swimming pool, the water has a buoyancy effect on your body. The deeper you are the greater the buoyancy effect and the less effect gravity has on your body. If you stand in water to waist level, the gravitational forces are reduced by 50 per cent, whereas with water at chest level gravitational forces are only 20 per cent of those on land.[18]

These buoyancy effects mean that less stress is placed on the bones and joints. There is reduced pressure on the skeleton, muscles, ligaments and discs. For these reasons, water-based activity offers an effective form of rehabilitation for those with muscular, joint or spinal injuries, who would find it difficult to exercise 'normally'. In addition, those returning to exercise after a long break, and anyone who is overweight or elderly, can benefit too. The buoyancy effects of water-based exercise make it ideal: the participant will be supporting only a fraction of their body weight and this minimises the risk of injury.

On land, when lifting your arms or holding a specific position, you have to work certain muscles to hold your limbs or move them against gravity. When immersed in water, gravity will not have the same effect – quite the reverse in fact. If you are immersed up to your neck, the buoyancy of the water will naturally lift your arms to its surface. This is useful as, in addition to the benefits mentioned above, it also enables you to achieve a resistance effect when working against upward buoyancy forces. This effect can be enhanced if you work with specific flotation devices, which increase the buoyancy effects.

HOW FAT STORES AFFECT BUOYANCY

Buoyancy is affected by the amount of body fat you have, its relative distribution around your body and also the air in your lungs. The more fat you have the easier it will be for you to float but, often, your stability and speed of movement in deeper water will be harder to maintain. The less fat you are carrying the less buoyant you will be, yet while it will be harder for you to float in deeper water, you will be more stable and your movement faster in slightly shallower water.

Where you store fat is also important. Men tend to store more fat around their waists and upper body, whereas women tend to be more pear-shaped and often store more fat on their legs and buttocks and around their hips. If you have greater fat stores in your upper body, maintaining a vertical position is relatively easy, yet a more horizontal position is harder, as your legs will tend to sink. Exercises that require a vertical position, however, will be more challenging for those with excess fat distributed around their hips and lower body. In these situations the abdominals have to work much harder simply to remain upright.

RESISTANCE IN WATER

When exercising in water there are three different resistances to deal with:

- frontal resistance
- eddy resistance
- viscous resistance.

Each of these has a different effect on the body. Water is approximately 12 times more resistant than air, so when you perform movements in water, you need to consider the speed, surface area and lever length used.[18] For example, if your movement is too slow there will be minimal resistance effects against the water, as the greater the speed of movement through the water, the more force is required by the muscles.

FRONTAL RESISTANCE

The dragging effect of frontal resistance should also be considered. This occurs when an object with a large surface area moves through water. Take your hand, for example: if you slice through water with an open hand and your fingers together there will be much less resistance than if you have a clenched fist or if you 'cup' your palm. The larger an object's surface area, the harder it will be to move that object through the water. In addition to the surface area of an object, the lever length used in the movement is also a factor. Think about making a running movement, using bent arms, in deep water. The water resistance against the relatively short levers will be much lower than if your arms were straighter, creating a longer lever.

EDDY RESISTANCE

Eddy resistance is a drag effect created as you move an object through water. It is a form of turbulence where, when movements are performed at speed, the water creates currents that affect your movement. To overcome these currents you have to engage your stabiliser muscles to maintain your balance. When performing large movements in a class environment ('aquafit', etc.), these eddy currents will be much greater due to the number of bodies affecting the water and creating currents.

VISCOUS RESISTANCE

The last sort of resistance to mention when thinking about exercising in water is the viscous effect. However, this is not as important as the other types of resistance because even though water, like any liquid, has a viscosity that is affected by temperature, most swimming pools are of a similar temperature throughout, so the viscosity of the water remains relatively consistent.

HOW EXERCISING IN WATER CAN BENEFIT CORE STABILITY

When performing movements in water, your stabiliser muscles have to act constantly to maintain posture or correct form against the multi-dimensional forces that are acting on your body. All movement will require strong reinforcement from your abdominal muscles, so you should focus on both the appropriate contraction during the movements and on allowing sufficient time after each exercise to relax your muscles and let them recover.

It is very effective to perform powerful and dynamic movements in water due to the resistance effects already described. However, before you embark on a water-based training programme you should consider your own fitness level and strength. As with any fitness plan, start each exercise at beginner or basic level before you increase the intensity by using longer levers or floats, and before you increase your speed of movement.

Certain equipment can be used in water exercise to aid buoyancy, improve your grip on the pool floor and make movements harder by increasing the surface area to be moved through the water. Some of these are described below.

'GRAVITY'/BUOYANCY VESTS

These are vests worn around the chest, which have a buoyancy effect that allows you to perform deep-water exercises without having to worry about sinking. These have been shown to be excellent devices when used to achieve fitness gains by athletes who cannot perform impact exercise due to injury.

AQUA DUMBBELLS OR FLOATS

These are foam or polystyrene floats in the shape of dumbbells. They can act as a floating aid when placed under your arms or as a resistance tool when immersed in water. Their large surface area means that they restrict movement in the water and their buoyancy effect means that there is increased resistance when you press them downwards.

AQUA SHOES

Aqua shoes are worn in the pool and offer excellent traction on the pool floor, allowing you to get a much firmer grip, which can assist your stance and body position in the water. Aqua shoes are excellent when changing direction in the water or when you need to 'brake' or stop quickly.

WATER EXERCISES

Exercise 23.1 Rocking Horse

Exercise 23.2 Single-arm Punches

Starting position and action

- This is a good warm-up exercise as the movement can be graduated easily.
- Stand with one foot in front of the other, with your weight on your rear leg and your front leg slightly raised.
- Brace your abdominals to maintain a strong torso, and rock forwards, hopping on to your front foot and lifting your rear foot as you do.
- Bend your front leg then extend it, pushing you back to 'hop' back on to your rear foot, raising your front knee as you land on your rear foot.
- Continue this rocking action, maintaining abdominal tension, and gradually increase your range of movement as you rock.
- Change your legs after 15–20 rocks so that your front and rear legs are reversed.

Coaching points

- This is a good movement to help beginners get to know the feel of the water and its effects on their relative body weight and movement potential.
- Start with a small movement at a leisurely pace and gradually build up momentum and your range of movement as you feel more confident and begin to warm up.

Starting position and action

- Stand in water to chest or shoulder height, holding a float or aqua dumbbell in your right hand next to your right shoulder.
- Keep the float under the water, brace your abdominals and extend your arm in a punching action.
- At full extension, pull it back towards your shoulder and repeat.
- Perform 15–30 punches, making sure not to lock out your arm before swapping hands and repeating with your left arm.
- Keep the movement slow to start with, gradually gather pace to increase the intensity.

Coaching points

- If using an aqua dumbbell is too difficult, reduce the intensity by using a cupped hand instead. Be careful not to over-rotate or over-reach during this exercise.
- Try the exercise with a rigid posture, keeping the torso still. By applying a small rotation, a fuller range of movement can be achieved in the punching phase and the retraction, or pulling, phase. This can also be performed with both arms working alternately, but greater stabilisation is required when working unilaterally.
- You might find that a split stance, with one foot in front of the other, makes your balance easier to maintain.

Exercise 23.3 Arm Pulls

Starting position and action
- Stand as before, in water to shoulder level, holding an aqua dumbbell or float.
- Hold the float at arm's length in your right hand with the float on the surface of the water.
- Brace your abdominals and, keeping your torso upright, pull the float down towards your waist in an arc, keeping your right arm slightly bent.
- Then return the arm to the surface.
- Aim for 10–20 repetitions, change hands and repeat with the float in your left hand.
- As you pull down, focus on contracting your abdominal muscles and squeezing the muscles of your back and between your shoulder blades.

Coaching points
- When you return the float to the surface, the buoyancy effect will make this easy, yet when the exercise is performed at speed, the surface area of the float will provide resistance and the frontal shoulder muscles will be forced to work.
- A variation is to perform the movement using both arms together, cupping your hands. This will reduce the lateral and torque forces to your torso, but increase the stabilisation necessary to maintain an upright position.

Exercise 23.4 Alternate Bear Hugs

Starting position and action
- Stand in water to chest height with your arms out to your side but still in the water.
- Brace your abdominals and maintain an upright stance.
- Sweep your right arm inwards in a large arc to cross the centre of your body, using your chest muscles in a forceful action at speed, pushing the water across your body to the front. Then slowly lower your arm and let it move outwards and back to the start position with much less force.
- As your right arm crosses the centre of your body, perform the same forceful movement with your left arm, as your right arm returns to the start.
- Repeat these forceful movements, alternating your arms in large sweeping actions, much like a front crawl action in swimming yet without any twisting of the torso.
- Perform 15–20 'hugs' with each arm.

Coaching points
- Make sure the arm is not locked but is slightly bent at the elbow during the sweeping action.
- As the movement is performed with a long lever you might tire quickly. Remember, the more force or speed you apply to the movement, the more resistance you will feel and the harder the exercise will become.

- This exercise can be performed with both arms together and, if required, using dumbbells to increase the resistance effects. Using both arms will, however, alter the direction emphasis of force to the torso.

Exercise 23.5 Alternate Outward Scoops

Starting position and action
- This exercise is similar in nature to the alternate bear hugs but the force is in the opposite direction.
- Stand in water to shoulder height and begin with your arms outstretched in front of you under the water.
- Extend your right arm horizontally in a sweeping action to bring it out to your right side in a half-crucifix position, pulling the water behind you, then bend your arm and slowly return it forwards to the start position.
- As you begin to bend your right arm, repeat the forceful outward-sweeping movement with your left arm and return slowly to the start position.
- Perform 15–20 alternate scoops with each arm.

Coaching points
- The action is similar to the breast-stroke in swimming, but with the arms alternating.

Exercise 23.6 Trunk Rotations

Starting position and action
- Stand in water to chest or shoulder level.
- Clasp your hands together, outstretched in front of you.
- Stand with your feet sturdy and brace your abdominals.
- Rotate through your waist to turn to one side, keeping upright, then just before reaching full rotation, turn back the other way, forcing your arms through the water.
- Perform 15–20 double-arm rotations.

Coaching points
- Begin this movement slowly and gradually increase your pace and movement range.
- The 'eddy drag' effects will make the change of direction difficult.

Progressions/adaptations
- This exercise can be performed with both arms outstretched to the sides in a 'crucifix' position, and keeping the arms under the water's surface. Care should be taken not to over-rotate in these exercises.

Exercise 23.7 Single-leg Swings (Hip Extension/Flexion)

Starting position and action

- Stand so that the water level is at about chest height, holding on to the pool-side with your right hand.
- Brace your abdominals prior to and throughout all movements to keep your torso still.
- Drive your left knee forwards and up, bringing your thigh to a horizontal position, then pull it back, extending your hip and leg to push the leg out behind you.
- Be careful not to arch your lower back or tilt your pelvis excessively during the movement.
- Perform 10–15 leg swings before changing legs.

Coaching points

- Begin this movement with a bent leg to reduce intensity, then gradually extend the leg, without locking it at the knee, to increase the lever length and intensity.
- Performing the movement faster will also increase intensity.

Exercise 23.8 Twists

Starting position and action

- With your back towards the pool wall and your torso pressed against it, hold on to the pool side with your arms outstretched to each side and bring your knees up so that your thighs are approximately parallel to the floor.
- Brace your abdominals and rotate through your torso to twist your legs first to one side and then the other.
- Be careful not to tilt your pelvis or twist your lower spine.
- Perform 15–20 twists each side at moderate pace.

Coaching points

- Due to the 'eddy drag' effect, make sure that you keep your abdominals tightly braced when you change the direction of the leg movement.

Exercise 23.9 Deep-water/Supine Twist-ups

Starting position and action
- Position yourself so that you are in deep water using either floats or a gravity vest to help you stay afloat in an upright position.
- Brace your abdominals and lift your knees towards your chest, twisting slightly so that you pull your knees up and to one side before lowering them and repeating to the other side.
- Keep this movement at a moderate speed so you feel the resistance effects of the water.
- Perform 15–20 twist-ups to each side.

Coaching points
- Unlike the previous exercise, which emphasises rotation, this exercise incorporates a simultaneous lifting and twisting action.
- As you lift and rotate, bring your knees to each side, being careful not to twist from your lower back, or tilt the pelvis excessively.

Progressions/adaptations
- This exercise can be modified by lying on your back, face up, with your legs outstretched in front of you. (You should be able to 'scull' with your arms to stay afloat and should not need a buoyancy vest.)
- Bracing your abdominals as before, pull your knees in towards your chest, twisting slightly so that your knees are pulled in, first to your right side and then to your left.
- The faster the action of bringing in the knees, the greater the resistance effects of the water.

Exercise 23.10 Pull-throughs

Starting position and action
- Roll forward so your torso and head are in a prone (face down) position with your legs outstretched behind you in a near-horizontal position.
- Have your arms forwards and your palms 'sculling' to maintain your position.
- Contract your abdominals and draw your knees in towards your chest.
- As you do this, rapidly sweep your arms together in an arc to give you the propulsion necessary to rock yourself on to your back, to face upwards.
- Extend your legs out to the front with your toes up and your arms by your side, sculling to help you stay afloat.
- Then contract your abdominals again and pull your knees up, but this time tip forwards to rock on to your front again and extend your legs out behind you as they were in the start position.
- Aim to change positions 10–20 times, making controlled movements throughout.

Coaching points
- Keep your head in line with your spine throughout and avoid arching your lower back when in the prone position.
- Increasing the speed of movement will increase the difficulty of the exercise. If you find this movement uncomfortable in deep water, use a float or hold onto the side for assistance.

5

PART **FIVE**

PROGRAMME IDEAS AND CLASS STRUCTURE

This part of the book is aimed at the fitness instructor or personal trainer rather than the individual exerciser. However, some of the general points raised may provide food for thought for all types of reader.

When introducing abdominal stabilisation exercises within a class environment there are a number of practical factors to consider. The first includes the size of your class and also the space available as, when using stability balls, say, the range of exercises and space required will sometimes limit numbers.

Space is not the only limiting factor regarding the size of class, however. For instance, would you feel confident commanding a class of 25 participants or more? More importantly, do you feel that you can explain and teach all the necessary posture adjustments in a large-class environment?
There is a big difference between teaching abdominal stabilisation techniques on a one-to-one basis and teaching in a class environment.

The difficulty is in the explanation and application of contraction methods that are necessary to train your group. If your group is constantly changing, with new participants turning up every week, you will still have to go through the education process from the start, which can be unnecessary, and rather dull, for regular participants.

The trick is to have a short series of exercises that cover different principles of stabilisation and each of which has a number of progressions. In this way, when teaching an exercise, your regular attendees can quickly move on to the more advanced progressions as they will already be aware of the basic body positions and bracing techniques. This will leave you more time to concentrate on the newcomers. After the first three or four weeks, you should introduce one new exercise a week and then keep this exercise for at least four to six weeks to allow both re-education of newcomers and potential progression for your 'regulars'.

THE BASIC STRUCTURE OF A CLASS

24

WARMING UP

The warm-up section of a core stability class should include various forms of rotation, flexion and extension movements. The joints need to be mobilised and the heart rate elevated slightly. Yet the emphasis, as with any warm-up, is on performing reduced-intensity movements that relate to the movements that will be performed in the class itself.

To begin, stand with your feet shoulder width apart and make various graduating twists and flexions of the trunk to help mobilise the torso. Graduate the exercise intensity by performing a few repetitions of each exercise that will be performed in the class yet, as mentioned above, at a reduced intensity. This will not only help mobilise the muscles and joints prior to the exercises themselves, but will also stimulate the brain and nerve endings to rehearse the desired movement. The neuro-transmitters in the brain send messages to the muscles to move, then messages are sent back to the part of the brain that detects sensory movement to confirm the actions that have taken place. This two-way movement of messages is ongoing and continual yet, when introducing new movements, constant rehearsal is important to help establish a movement and achieve proper form.

Consider, for instance, learning how to ride a bike. The objective is to move the bike forwards by using muscles in the leg to work the pedals. The muscles in the trunk need to be stabilised to allow force, and the hands have to grip the handlebars. In addition, the neutraliser muscles and sensory nerves responsible for maintaining balance have to work hard to stop the rider falling off. When learning, this involves constant adjustment and re-adjustment: the neural pathways have to be created and reinforced continually until the ability is second nature and the necessary adjustments work subconsciously. The process of learning new stabilisation exercises works in much the same way.

SERIES OF EXERCISES

The stabilisation exercises should always be introduced first within a class environment, because they require greater explanation so that participants can achieve the correct position and contraction emphasis, and also because the stabiliser muscles have a greater endurance potential compared to the larger mobiliser muscles. That said, from experience I strongly believe that a core stability class should consist of flexion, rotation and extension movements that involve the mobiliser muscles at some stage. My reasons for this are that there will always be some participants in larger classes that simply do not grasp the action of bracing and so will come to a class and gain nothing. When working with participants that find the new information and movements too difficult, it is important not to blind them with science or persist with teaching movements they cannot do. Take a break from the mental focus required from time to time, and introduce simpler movements or movements that have been learned previously, to reassure the group or particular exerciser.

It is very easy to give up on a task if you cannot see the 'light at the end of the tunnel', so always aim to provide positive comments on what your participants can do well and where there are opportunities to improve. This will reassure them. If there is even a small portion of the class that can identify movements in which the participants feel confident they are doing well, this will encourage them to return. Hopefully, on their next visit, they should gain a better understanding of the contractions required during bracing activities, and will begin to identify with the stabilisation principles more readily.

If you are lucky enough not to have to worry about class numbers, or if you have the opportunity to work with a smaller class (e.g. 8–15 people), this will mean you can place your emphasis solely on stabilisation exercises initially, if you wish. Because you have a smaller class, you can work on a much more 'individual' basis with all the participants regularly, thus literally getting a feel for their kinaesthetic awareness and contraction ability through hands-on work.

TIMINGS/REPETITIONS

Core stability training may be a new concept for novices and athletes alike. The intensity of certain exercises and movements will be relative to the skill or ability of the individual participant, yet no matter who you are working with, the fundamentals of stabilisation still need to be applied. If your athlete can identify with appropriate bracing and stabilisation principles then you can move on to the more intermediate exercises, but only when you are satisfied that correct spinal alignment, breathing and muscle contraction has been achieved.

For the initial exercises, repetitions should be performed slowly and rhythmically, focusing on a timing of 2–5 seconds for the movement and 3–10 seconds for any holding or static positions. As the stabilisers begin to lose correct tension and posture, or correct form falters, the participant should rest. Participants should aim for up to 10 repetitions performed well before moving on to more advanced movements. The focus is on quality of movement rather than quantity of ineffective repetitions.

INTENSITY

The relative intensity of any exercise depends on many factors, not least of which is your own fitness level together with the level of resistance used, the duration of the static contraction, lever lengths, and so on. Intensity can be adjusted up and down to suit the individual, and this should be done on the basis of technique. With most of the exercises in this book the underlying emphasis is on improving core musculature to assist function. With this in mind, any increase in the intensity of a particular exercise should be geared towards increasing the duration of hold rather than the level of resistance overload. The core muscles, as we have seen, are 'slow twitch' and work throughout the day, so the training of them should be structured with a functional focus in mind.

However, provided that the correct technique has been mastered in one specific movement, then overload needs to be progressive in order to stimulate the muscles and nerves effectively. As in any training programme, progressive overload should be graduated in small increments, utilising the different overload principles one at a time. Only when a movement of exercise becomes relatively easy to perform for the necessary number of repetitions and/or duration should you increase the intensity. Do not forget that intensity itself can be split into two characteristics: increased stabilisation and increased resistance.

When performing an exercise that has a sport-specific application, the question of increasing intensity should be considered solely on the basis of whether this will enhance performance in the sport itself as opposed to just increasing the resistance or duration for the sake of it.

WORKING WITH MIXED ABILITIES AND SPECIAL POPULATIONS

When working with the deconditioned client, those suffering from injury or pregnant women, in other than the latter case it is important to ascertain the nature of the injury or problem. Without any knowledge of the condition it is possible that you could aggravate it and cause pain. Always seek advice from a doctor or refer your client to a professional therapist for guidance on the nature of their problem.

It is fine to do stabilisation exercises during pregnancy as long as the exercise intensity is at the appropriate level for the participant and they have already been exercising prior to and throughout their pregnancy without problems. While it is not wise to begin training during pregnancy, most forms of bracing and pelvic floor work will help train the core musculature without any risk to the foetus. Once again, though, exercise intensity should be minimal to start with and should progress only very gradually, relative to the condition of the participant.

During pregnancy, any exercise in a prone (face down) position should be avoided, as this will place pressure on the foetus. It should be remembered that, as the foetus develops, balance will also be affected, as the pregnant woman's natural centre of gravity will have changed. An example of a suitable programme for a pregnant woman is shown on page 235.

SAMPLE
// PROGRAMMES

BASIC CLASSES

Following a suitable warm-up, as described in the previous chapter, a class aimed at beginners, where there is no equipment available, might include the exercises listed in Table 25.1.

When incorporating stability balls, the two class structures outlined in Tables 25.2 and 25.3 might be suitable.

If you are lucky enough to have a Reebok Core Board™ or BOSU™ available, then the exercises outlined in Tables 25.4 and 25.5 can be introduced in a class format.

Table 25.1	Class suitable for beginners (no equipment available)			
No.	Exercise	Reps	Static hold	Sets
1	Prone abdominal hollowing	5–8	5 sec	1–2
2	'Superman'	5–8	5 sec	1–2
3	Lateral bridge on knees (right)	3–5	10–15 sec	1–2
4	Supine bridge	5–8	5 sec	1–2
5	Reverse curl/hip lifts	5–8		1–2
6	Four-count leg lift	5–8		1–2
7	Oblique reach	8–12		1–2
8	Lateral bridge on knees (left)	3–5	10–15 sec	1–2
9	Prone bridge on knees	3–5	10–15 sec	1–2
10	Abdominal curl	8–15		1–2
11	Standing balance	3–5	10–15 sec	1–2

Table 25.2   **Stability ball class, suitable for beginners**

No.	Exercise	Reps	Static hold	Sets
1	Pelvic tilting	10–15		1–2
2	Figure of eight	10–15		1–2
3	Seated leg lift	5–8	5 sec	1–2
4	Stability ball curl	5–8		1–2
5	Lying torso rotation	10–12		1–2
6	Oblique curl	5–8		1–2
7	Prone roll-in (on knees)	5–8		1–2
8	Back extension	8–10		1–2
9	Prone press-ups (on hips)	5–8		1–2
10	Lateral flexion	5–8		1–2

Table 25.3   **Stability ball class, suitable for intermediate/advanced levels**

No.	Exercise	Reps	Static hold	Sets
1	Lying torso rotation	20–30		1–3
2	Supine lateral ball roll	8–12*		1–3
3	Stability ball power drive	10–12*		1–3
4	Prone arm extension	10–15		1–3
5	Stability ball press-up	10–15		1–3
6	Prone roll-in (alternate legs)	8–12		1–3
7	Supine bridge alternate roll-in	8–12*		1–3
8	Prone stability ball roll-out	8–15		1–3
9	Lateral crunch	8–12		1–3
10	Kneeling balance		10–30 sec	

Note: * refers to performing the movement to each side or with each leg.

Table 25.4	BOSU™ class, general level			
No.	Exercise	Reps	Static hold	Sets
1	Kneeling 'Superman'	10	5 sec	1–2
2	Prone cobra	10–15		1–2
3	Press-ups, one leg raised	10–15		1–2
4	One-leg balance		20–30 sec	
5	Squats	10–15		1–2

Table 25.5	Reebok Core Board™ class, general to intermediate level			
No.	Exercise	Reps	Static hold	Sets
1	Standing tilts	20–30		1–3
2	Squats	15–20		1–3
3	Forward lunge	10–15*		1–3
4	Squat thrusts	20–30		1–3
5	Press-ups with rotation/twist	10–15		1–3
6	Bicycles	20–30*		1–3
7	Press-ups with knee pull	8–12*		1–3
8	Abdominal curl	15–20		1–3
9	Lateral squats with leg lift	10–15*		1–3
10	Reverse lunge lift/jump	10–15*		1–3

Table 25.6	Sports-specific class			
No.	Exercise	Reps	Static hold	Sets
1	Oblique twists (kneeling)	20–30		2–3
2	Partner statues	5–10	5–10 sec	2–3
3	Dynamic plank (using medicine ball)	3–5	45–60 sec	2–3
4	Give and receive	20–30		2–3
5	Wobble board (single-arm throw)	10–15		2–3
6	Interactive wobble board passing	30–40		2–3
7	Wobble board (chest passes)	20–30		2–3
8	Reverse throw	10–15		2–3
9	Dynamic medicine ball press-up	15–20		2–3
10	Goalkeeper drill	20–30		2–3

An advanced sport-specific class or training session using medicine balls and wobble boards might include the following exercises to apply core strength, specific power and stabilisation training.

The above are just sample programmes for classes that can be structured, but the nature and intensity of exercise is essentially dependent on the ability of your group, as well as the equipment and space available.

Provided that your group is willing to be adventurous and all participants have reached a sufficient level of ability, then any number of interactive sessions can be developed.

One word of warning, though: if you have a regular group with members returning each week, their ability will improve rapidly. With this in mind, be careful not to allow an elitist atmosphere to develop, in which new exercisers feel somewhat intimidated. Always demonstrate some exercises that are multi-level in intensity but follow similar teaching curves. In this way your advanced participants will have something to be getting on with, and you can spend more time with the beginners.

DESIGNING A PROGRAMME FOR // INDIVIDUALS

26

One of the main advantages when working on a one-to-one level, whether as a personal trainer or in a rehabilitation environment, is the connection you get with your client. You have an ideal opportunity to educate them in the necessary muscle contraction techniques, while making sure they are positioned correctly and identifying neutral spine through both hands-on and observation techniques.

Of course, this is also the perfect environment for them to communicate with you about any difficulties they are having with any of the contraction or bracing techniques, without the fear of embarrassment sometimes experienced in a group exercise setting.

The relationship you develop with your client should allow them to tell you when they feel the exercises are working and when they are not, due perhaps to incorrect postural alignments or muscle contraction emphasis. It is important to gradually increase the intensity of the exercises and only progress on the basis of satisfactory achievement of the previous exercise progressions rather than simply changing exercises after a certain time to reduce monotony.

As mentioned in Chapter 3, it is important to understand the needs of your client and identify any imbalances they might have through the use of appropriate screening tests. It is then possible to identify the specificity and extent of any corrective exercises and flexibility work that needs to be structured before embarking on more advanced exercises.

A number of training organisations have recognised the need for corrective work prior to more generalised training and I would strongly recommend reading or studying further with organisations such as the National Association of Sports Medicine or the CHEK Institute. Before you begin developing programmes for individuals who might have possible imbalances, it would be wise to be studying at a level that goes much further than this book. This will give you the confidence and knowledge to create your own structured programme. I hope the exercises, ideas and principles in this book will be a useful reference guide should you need some new exercises to work with.

It must be said that, while this book has tried to identify many elements of core stability from 'old school' to 'new school', the sheer nature and progression of the fitness industry means that not every possible variation could be described or demonstrated.

Below are some examples of training programmes for sports people and special populations. These training programmes are not exhaustive and should be used purely as a guide. Each programme has scope for further restructure relative to the specificity of the sport and the individual in question. In addition, the specificity of a certain position within a team sport will demand different exercises. As such, further development of the programme will be necessary.

No.	Exercise	Reps	Static hold	Sets
Table 26.1	**Programme for pregnancy 1st and 2nd trimester**			
1	Abdominal hollowing	8–12	Hold for 5 sec	1–2
2	'Superman' variations	8–12	Hold for 5 sec	1–2
2	Standing balance	8–12	Hold for 10 sec	1–2
3	Single arm cable press	8–12 E/A		1–2
4	Step up to balance	8–12 E/S		1–2
5	Single arm cable row	10–15 E/A		1–2
6	Woodchop	8–12 E/S		1–2
7	Lat pull down on stability ball	10–15		1–2
8	Reverse woodchop	8–12 E/S		1–2
9	Wall squat (partial)	10–15		1–2
10	Single leg lateral raise	10–15		1–2

No.	Exercise	Reps	Static hold	Sets
Table 26.2	**Golf training plan**			
1	Standing single leg balance on stability disc	6–10 E/L	Hold for 10–15 sec	1–2
2	Stability ball cobra	6–10	Hold for 3–5 sec	1–2
2	Standing single leg chest press	8–12 E/L		1–2
3	Standing single leg cable row	8–12 E/S		1–2
4	Kneeling golf swing	8–12 E/S		1–2
5	Walking lunge with rotation	10–15		1–2
6	Wood chop	10–15 E/S		1–2
7	Medicine ball chest pass (single leg)	10–15		1–2
8	Reverse woodchop	10–15 E/S		1–2
9	Oblique medicine ball throw (kneeling)	10–15		1–2
10	Overhead reverse throw	10–15		1–2

Table 26.3 **Racquet sports**

No.	Exercise	Reps	Static hold	Sets
1	'Superman' exercise on a BOSU™	6–10 E/L	Hold for 5–10 sec	1–2
2	Stability ball cobra	6–10	Hold for 3–5 sec	1–2
2	Multi-direction lunge with overhead press	8–12 E/A		1–2
3	Standing single leg low row/bent over row	8–12 E/A		1–2
4	Overhead throw to floor	8–12		1–2
5	Walking lunge with rotation	10–15		1–2
6	Wood chop with lunge	10–15 E/S		1–2
7	Medicine ball rotation and throw (single leg)	10–15		1–2
8	Single arm throw to floor (medicine ball)	10–15 E/S		1–2
9	Oblique medicine ball throw on Core Board	10–15 E/S		1–2
10	Overhead reverse throw	10–15		1–3

Table 26.4 **Volleyball**

No.	Exercise	Reps	Static hold	Sets
1	Step up to balance with curl and press	6–10 E/S		1–2
2	Stability ball cobra with medicine ball catch	6–10 E/S		1–2
2	Single leg touchdown to overhead press	8–12 E/A		1–2
3	Standing single arm cable row	8–12 E/A		1–2
4	One arm d/b snatch	8–12 E/A		1–2
5	Walking lunge with rotation	10–15		1–2
6	Wood chop	10–15 E/S		1–2
7	Overhead throw to floor	10–15		1–2
8	One arm clean and press	10–15 E/A		1–2
9	Single arm throw to floor on Core Board	10–15 E/S		1–2
10	Overhead reverse throw	10–15		1–2

No.	Exercise	Reps	Static hold	Sets
1	Standing single leg balance with medicine ball pass	10–15 E/L		1–2
2	Clean and press	8–12		1–2
2	Cable squat and dead lift	10–12		1–2
3	Standing single leg chest press	10–12		1–2
4	Goalkeeper drill	20–30		1–2
5	Walking lunge with ball catch	10–15 E/S		1–2
6	Wood chop	10–15 E/S		1–2
7	One arm snatch	10–15 E/A		1–2
8	Multi-direction lunge with overhead press	10–15 E/S		1–2
9	Oblique medicine ball throw (kneeling)	10–15 E/S		1–2
10	Overhead reverse throw	10–15		1–2

Table 26.5 Field sports (soccer, rugby, hockey etc.)

APPENDIX: SMR TECHNIQUES

For descriptions of these exercises, please see pages 50–51.

Latisimus Stretch

Rhomboids Stretch

Quads Stretch

Hamstrings Stretch

Gastrocnemius Stretch

IT Band Stretch

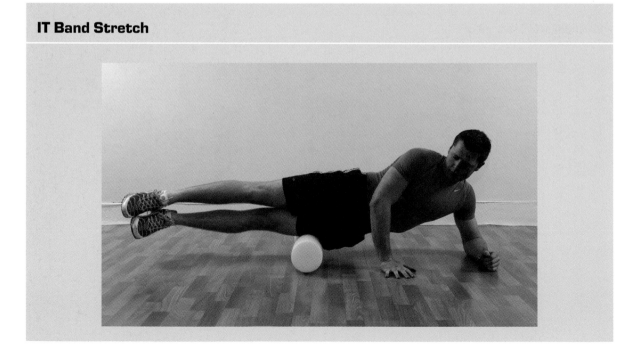

Tensor Fascia Latae Stretch

Piriformus Stretch

Abduct To move away from the centre line. For example, when abducting the shoulders, the arms move out to the side.

Aerobic With oxygen present. (Anaerobic means without oxygen or in the absence of oxygen.)

Alexander technique A retraining technique to reduce postural problems.

Atrophy The wasting away of a muscle.

Autogenic inhibition A reflex muscular relaxation that occurs in the muscle when the Golgi tendon organ is stimulated.

Biomechanical disadvantage The point at which a muscle has to deal with the greatest effort because of leverage.

Blood pressure The force of the blood on the walls of the arteries as it circulates through the system.

Bracing A tensing or contracting of muscles.

Cables These are attached to the weights on a cable-pulley machine.

Calorie A unit of energy equal to the amount of heat required to raise the temperature of one gram of water by one degree centigrade.

Central nervous system Comprises the brain, nerves and spinal cord and regulates all conscious movements.

Coccyx The bones at the base of the spine, forming the 'tailbone'.

Compound exercise An exercise that involves multiple muscle groups and usually two or more main joints.

Concentric contraction A movement in which the muscle shortens as it contracts against a resistance.

Cross-gravitational force A lateral or angled force that acts on the body during certain power movements or when using pulley cables and medicine balls, and so on.

Diaphragm The muscular partition between your lungs and your abdomen.

Dynamic movement Movement involving power, speed or force.

Dynamic stabilisation Stabilisation while balancing on an unstable base or moving platform.

Eccentric contraction A movement whereby the muscle lengthens while in tension.

Extension A straightening movement about a joint caused when the joint angle increases.

Facet joints Joints between one vertebral arch and another.

Fascia A tough sheet of fibrous tissue supporting and separating skeletal muscles.

Fast-twitch fibre A muscle fibre with low endurance that responds better to speed, strength and power movements.

Flexion A movement that reduces the angle between two joints.

Foam roller A cylindrical tube, usually made of foam, used as a tool within self-myofascial release exercises.

Force The power that causes an object to move.

Functional exercise Any exercise that relates to a specific movement or function in daily life.

Golgi tendon organ A sensory receptor found near the junction of tendons and muscles that is sensitive to increased tension within the muscle.

Gravity The downward force acting on our bodies at all times.

Hip flexors The group of muscles crossing the hip joint that assist in flexing this joint, i.e. when lifting the leg or bending the torso.

Hyper-extension The over-extension of a joint.

Hypertrophy Occurs when muscle filaments increase in number and strength, increasing the cross-sectional size of the muscle.

Integrated functional unit The collective outcome of related muscles, nerves and bones working together in synergy to create a specific movement.

Intervertebral discs Flexible cushioning pads that lie between the vertebrae.

Intra-abdominal pressure The pressure created within the abdominal cavity during abdominal bracing and muscular contractions of the abdominal stabiliser muscles.

Isokinetic contraction A contraction whereby the speed of movement is controlled regardless of the force applied.

Isolation exercise An exercise or movement focusing on a specific muscle or muscle group.

Isometric contraction A muscle contraction during which there is no change in its length.

Isotonic contraction A muscle contraction that causes the muscle to increase or decrease its length against a resistance.

Kinaesthetic awareness Being aware of the body's movement and function in relation to the bones and muscles.

Kinetic chain The result of muscles, tendons, ligaments, fascia, nerves and bones working together in synergy.

Ligament Band of fibrous tissue connecting bones to other bones.

Lumbar The area in the lower back between the thoracic spine and the sacrum.

Lumbar curve The normal curve of the lumbar spine that gives it flexibility.

Lumbo-pelvic–hip complex The group of muscles, nerves and bones that are involved in movement and stabilisation around the hips, pelvis and lumbar spine.

Metabolism The total amount of chemical changes or reactions in the body.

Motor skill The co-ordination ability to perform a task.

Muscle A group of muscle fibres bound together by connective tissue.

Muscle fibre A muscle cell.

Muscle spindle A sensory receptor within the muscle that senses when the muscle is being stretched.

Muscle trauma Damage to a muscle, often through injury.

Muscular endurance The ability of a muscle to overcome a resistance for an extended period.

Muscular imbalances This is when one muscle is overly strong in comparison to a weaker localised muscle.

Muscular strength The ability of a muscle or group of muscles to overcome a resistance. This is often referred to as the ability to perform a single repetition to overcome a resistance.

Myotatic stretch reflex This reflex action causes the muscle to contract to prevent over-stretching the joint.

Nerves Elongated cells that transmit information between different parts of the body and brain.

Neural canal Space between the vertebrae that allows the nerves through.

Neuro-muscular Relating to the nerves and muscular systems.

Neuro-muscular efficiency The ability of the neuro-muscular system to allow agonists, synergists, stabilisers and neutralisers to work together efficiently as an integrated functional unit.

Neuro-transmitters Chemicals that allow communication of information between nerves.

Neutral spine The natural alignment of the spine.

Normal length The optimum length of a muscle relative to its normal training movement requirement.

Osteopath Specialist who treats the joints and soft tissues through manipulation.

Overload Exercising a muscle with a greater resistance than normally encountered.

Overload principles The rules or principles that enable overload to occur.

Pelvic floor The group of muscles at the base of the abdominal cavity responsible primarily for bladder control.

Pelvis Bones fused together at the base of the abdomen.

Posterior chain The name given to the muscles that run down your lower back and legs to include the lower back muscles, glutes, hamstrings and calves.

Postural deviations These occur when muscular and/or postural imbalances cause natural alignment to be compromised from the normal or neutral position.

Posture The relative positioning of your body.

Power The rate of doing work, essentially the force multiplied by the velocity, or the strength required to overcome the resistance multiplied by the speed of the movement.

Prime mover The muscle directly responsible for a movement or joint action (also called the agonist).

Progress To intensify a movement or exercise.

Progressive overload Increasing the resistance as a muscle adapts during a training programme.

Proprioception The communication of messages from the muscles to the brain to determine body position and movement.

Range of movement The amount of natural movement about a joint.

Regress To modify/make easier or reduce the intensity of an exercise.

Repetitions Often shortened to 'reps', the number of times you perform a complete movement in an exercise.

Resistance tubes Tubes that increase in resistance as they are stretched. They often come in different colours to denote thickness and potential resistance intensity.

Rotation The rotational movement about a joint.

Sacrum Five vertebrae at the base of the spine fused together to form the pelvic basin.

Sciatic nerve The largest nerve in the human body, originating in the sacrum area and travelling through the gluteal muscles down the back of the leg to the ankle.

Screening test A posture test with movement to identify any postural deviations that may be caused by potential muscle imbalances.

Self-myofascial release A stretching technique that can improve the flexibility around a joint through pressure on stretch receptors within the muscle that reduce muscle tension and allow increased movement.

Slow-twitch muscle The fibres of these muscles have a high aerobic capacity and greater endurance.

Spinal cord The nerves from the brain that pass down through the neural canal in the spine.

Split stance A standing position where one foot is placed a stride's length in front of the other.

Sports stance A 'ready' stance, as in a sporting movement when the body is braced and balanced in preparation for the next movement.

Stability The synergistic co-ordination of muscle contractions around a joint to assist stabilisation.

Super-sets Two or more sets of an exercise working either the same or different muscle groups.

Synergistic dominance This occurs when a muscle or group of muscles (agonists) is weak and when one or more synergists take over the function of the agonists to assist a specific movement.

Synergy Harmony or balance between muscles and/or joints.

Tendon Bundle of collagen fibres connecting muscles to bones.

Thoracic Related to the chest.

Vertebrae The bones that make up the spine.

Yoga An exercise regime originating in India, which aims to enhance both life force and flexibility.

REFERENCES

1 Richardson, C., Jull, G., Hodges, P. and Hides, J. (1999) *Therapeutic Exercise For Spinal Segmental Stabilisation in Low Back Pain – Scientific Basis and Clinical Approach.* Edinburgh: Churchill Livingstone.

2 Gracovetsky, S. (1988) *The Spinal Engine.* Vienna and New York: Springer-Verlag.

3 Chek, P. (1999) A new frontier in abdominal training, *IAAF Technical Quarterly: New Studies in Athletics* 4.

4 Chek, P. (2000) Understanding spinal stability, *Fitness Network* Oct/Nov, 12–14.

5 Bompa T.O. (1983) *Theory and Methodology of Strength Training.* Dubuque, IA: Kendall/ Hunt Publishing Company.

6 Chek, P. (2001) Functional or not? *Fitness Network* Oct/Nov, 8–11.

7 Schmidt, R.H. (1991) *Motor Learning and Performance.* Illinois: Human Kinetics.

8 Norris, C. (1999) *The Complete Guide to Stretching.* London: A&C Black.

9 Stewart, M. (1992) *Yoga.* London: Hodder & Stoughton Ltd.

10 Mohan, A.G. (1993) *Yoga for Body, Breath and Mind.* Portland, Oregon: Rudra Press.

11 Barlow, W. (1973) *The Alexander Principle.* London: Gollancz, 24.

12 Eckmann, F. (1997) IDEA 'Exercise and Aging Future Visions Conference': Introduction.

13 Lord, S.R., Ward, J.A. and Williams, P. (1996) Exercise effect on dynamic stability in older women, *Archives of Physical Medicine and Rehabilitation* 77, 232–6.

14 Kallinen, M. and Markku, A. (1995) Aging, physical activity and sports injuries in the elderly, *Sports Medicine* 20(1), July, 41–52.

15 Means, K.M. (1996) The obstacle course: a tool for the assessment of functional balance and mobility in the elderly, *Journal of Rehabilitation and Research Development* 33(4), Oct, 413–29.

16 Wolfson, L. et al. (1996) Balance and strength training in older adults: intervention gains and tai chi maintenance, *Journal of the American Geriatric Society* 44, 498–506.

17 Wolf, S. et al. (1996) Reducing frailty and falls in older persons: an investigation of tai chi and computerized balance training, *Journal of the American Geriatric Society* 44, 489–97.

18 Lawrence, D. (1998) *The Complete Guide to Exercise in Water.* London: A&C Black.

19 Clark, M. *Integrated Training for the New Millennium.* Thousand Oaks, CA: National Academy of Sports Medicine; 2000.

20 Clarke, M., Lucett, S., Corn, R., Cappucio, R., Humphrey, R., Kraus, S., Titchemal, A., Robbins, P., *Optimum Performance Training for the Health and Fitness Professional.* Thousand Oaks, CA: National Academy of Sports Medicine; 2004.

21 Russell, A., Wallace, T., *Self-Myofascial Release Techniques.* – Articles – Continuing Education. Thousand Oaks, CA: National Academy of Sports Medicine; 2002.

FURTHER INFORMATION

READING

ABDOMINAL TRAINING
Christopher Norris, *Abdominal Training – 2nd edition* (A&C Black, 2001)

ALEXANDER TECHNIQUE
Richard Brennan, *The Alexander Technique Manual* (Little, Brown, 1996)

Michael Gelb, *Body Learning: An Introduction to the Alexander Technique* (Aurum Press, 1994)

PILATES
Lynne Robinson, *The Official Body Control Pilates Manual* (Macmillan, 2002)

T'AI CHI
Master Lam Kam Chuen, *Step-by-step Tai Chi* (Gaia Books, 1994)

Bill Douglas, *The Complete Idiot's Guide to T'ai Chi and QiGong* (Alpha Books, 2002)

YOGA
Georg Feuerstein and Larry Payne, *Yoga for Dummies* (John Wiley & Sons Inc., 1999)

Howard Kent, *The Complete Illustrated Guide to Yoga* (Element Books, 2003)

Beryl Birch, *Power Yoga: The Total Strength and Flexibility Workout* (Prion Books, 1995)

FELDENKRAIS
Moshe Feldenkrais, *Awareness through Movement: Easy-to-do Health Exercises to Improve Your Posture, Vision, Imagination, and Personal Awareness* (HarperCollins, 1991)

GENERAL
Anita Bean, *The Complete Guide to Strength Training* (A&C Black, 2001)

Paul Chek, *How to Eat, Move and Be Healthy* (CHEK Institute, 2004)

Paul Collins, *The Body Coach: Functional Fitness* (Meyer and Meyer Sport, 2009)

Michael Clark, *Integrated Training for the New Millennium* (National Academy of Sports Medicine, 2000)

Debbie Lawrence, *The Complete Guide to Exercise in Water* (A&C Black, 1998)

Rex Hazeldine, *Fitness for Sport* (The Crowood Press, 2000)

USEFUL CONTACTS

GENERAL

American College of Sports Medicine
P.O. Box 1440
Indianapolis
IN 46206–1440, U.S.A.

C.H.E.K. Institute
609 South Vulcan Avenue
Suite 101
Encinitas
CA 92024, U.S.A.
www.chekinstitute.com

Faster Health and Fitness Training
2 East Foscote
Grittleton
Chippenham
Wiltshire
SN14 6AE
United Kingdom

National Academy of Sports Medicine
26632 Agoura Road,
Calabasas
CA 91302, U.S.A.
www.nasm.org

National Strength and Conditioning Association
1885 Bob Johnson Drive
Colorado Springs
CO 80906, U.S.A.
www.nsca-lift.org
www.acsm.org

Premier Training
Premier House
Willowside Park
Canal Road
Trowbridge
Wiltshire
BA14 8RH
United Kingdom
www.premierglobal.co.uk

TRX – Suspension Training
755 Sansome St
6th Floor
San Francisco
CA 94133, U.S.A
www.trxtraining.com

ViPR Training – Contact Fitness Professionals
FitPro
107-113 London Road
London
E13 0DA
United Kingdom
www.fitproshop.com

YMCA
111 Great Russell Street,
London
WC1B 3NP
United Kingdom
www.ymcafit.org.uk

PILATES SITES

Pilates Foundation
www.pilatesfoundation.com
Body Control Pilates
www.bodycontrol.co.uk
Pilates Institute
www.pilates-institute.co.uk
Pilates Search Site
www.pilates.co.uk

EQUIPMENT

Physical Company Ltd
2a Desborough Industrial Park
Desborough Park Road
High Wycombe
Buckinghamshire
HP12 1BG
United Kingdom
www.physicalcompany.co.uk

INDEX

abdominal exercises, 66–9
  abdominal curl, 66
  internal oblique
    basic crunch, 68
    lateral crunch, 68
  oblique reach, 67
  reverse curls/hip lifts, 67
  slow eccentric curl, 69
  super-slow bicycles, 69
  see also entries under conventional
    training
abdominal training in water *see* water, abdominal
  training in
adductors, 12
adjustable cable pulley machines, 104
aerobic exercise, 29
aesthetics, 38
Alexander technique, 210–11
  benefits of, 210–11
  definition, 210
  history, 210
  for older people, 212
alternative training, 199–223
  see also specific training techniques
aqua dumbbells, 218
aqua shoes, 218
autogenic inhibition, 50

back exercises *see entries under* conventional
  training
balance, 15
basal metabolic rate (BMR), 37

bicep exercises *see entries under* conventional
  training
bio-mechanical considerations, 35
bio-motor skills, 14–15
blood pressure, 31
body types, 38
Bongo Boards™, 97–8
BOSU™, 97–102
  abdominal curl, 101
  alternating jumps (across), 100
  kneeling 'Superman,' 100
  lateral crunch, 101
  one leg stance, 99
  press-ups one leg raised, 102
  prone cobra, 102
  sample programmes, 232
  squats, 99
bracing techniques, 3
breathing, 31
buoyancy effect, 216–17
buoyancy vests, 218
bus surfing, 28

cardio-vascular workouts, 37
cervical vertebrae, 4
chest exercises *see entries under* conventional
  training
children's games, 213–15
  hopscotch, 214
  hula-hoop, 214–15
  leap-frog/leap-frog races, 214
  patio madness, 214

piggy-back races, 215
space hoppers, 215
'Spiderman,' 214
tag (stuck in the mud, musical statues), 213
wheelbarrow races, 214
coccyx, 4
compound exercises, 15–16
concentric contractions, 31, 32
contra-indicated exercises, 39–40
conventional training, 103–23
    abdominal exercises
        cable crunch (kneeling), 120
        cable crunch on stability ball, 120–1
        cable crunch (supine), 123
        cable machine wood chop, 121
        cable resisted oblique reach, 123
        overhead lateral flexion, 119
        reverse golf swing, 122
        reverse wood chop, 122
        stability ball oblique curl, 121
    back exercises
        kneeling stability ball one-arm row, 111
        lateral pull-down, 110
        reverse cable press, 111
        seated single-arm row (cable), 110–11
        standing single-arm row, 112
    bicep exercises
        lying cable curl, 117
        prone stability ball concentration curl, 117
        seated bicep curl, 116
    chest exercises, 103–23
        cable chest press, 108
        cable flye, 106
        cable press/single arm press, 109
        chest press on stability ball, 105
        dumbbell flye, 106
        stability ball press-up, 107
        stability ball pull-over, 107

    leg exercises
        lunge (foot on stability ball), 116
        single-leg wall squat, 115–16
        wall squat, 115
    shoulder exercises
        prone bent-over laterals (on stability ball), 114
        prone frontal extension, 114
        seated lateral raise, 113
        seated shoulder press, 113
    triceps exercises
        kneeling tricep kickbacks, 119
        lying tricep extension, 118
        tricep dips, 118
core stability, 2–3
    benefits, 22–5
    definition, x
    importance of, 14–21
    mechanisms of, 7–13
    teaching/learning, 26–9
crunches, x, xi

dance, 22–3
diaphragm, 7, 9, 11
diastasis, 24
diet, 29, 37
discs, intervertebral, 4
double leg raises, 39–40

eccentric contractions, 31, 32
ectomorphs, 38
eddy resistance, 217
elderly
    benefits of exercise, 23
    core stability training for, 212–13
electrical muscle stimulation (EMS), 40
endomorphs, 38

endurance, 30
equipment, 27
exercise classes, 227–37
   advanced programmes, 232
   beginners programmes, 230–1
   BOSU™, 232
   intensity, 228–9
   intermediate programmes, 231–2
   mixed abilities, 229
   one-to-one, 234–7
      field sports, 237
      golf training, 235
      pregnancy, 235
      racquet sports, 236
      volleyball, 236
   Reebok Core Board™, 232
   series of exercises, 227–8
   special populations, 229
   sports-specific, 232
   timings/repetitions, 228
   warming up, 227
external obliques, 7, 9, 10, 12

facet joints, 4–5
fast-twitch fibres, 9
fat stores, affect on buoyancy, 216–17
Feldenkrais method, 211, 212
field sports training, 237
floats, 218
frontal resistance, 217
functional fitness, 14–16

gastrocnemius, self-myofascial release,
   51, 240
gluteals, 12
golf training plan, 235
Golgi tendon organ, 49–50
'gravity' vests, 218

hamstrings, 12
   self-myofascial release, 51, 239
hands-on partner work see partner work
hip flexors, 10, 11
hydraulic amplifier effect, 12–13
hypertrophy, 30

iliopsoas, 10, 11
illiotibial band (IT), self-myofascial release, 51, 240
individual exercise programmes see exercise
   classes, one-to-one
inertia, 35
intercostal muscles, 8
internal obliques, 7, 9, 10, 11, 12
intervertebral discs, 4
intra-abdominal pressure, 9, 12
isokinetic contractions, 30
isokinetic exercises, 31
isolation exercises, 15–16
isometric contractions, 30, 32
isometric exercises, 31
isotonic contractions, 30
isotonic exercises, 31, 32
IT band, self-myofascial release, 51, 240

kettlebell training, 161–71
   clean and press, 166–7
   clean and rack, 164–5
      double-arm, 165
      single-arm, 164
   figure eights, 169
   overhead lunge, 168
   overhead squat, 169
   snatch, 167
   swings, 162–3
      alternate single-arm, 163
      double-arm, 162
      single-arm, 163

Turkish get-up, 171
   windmills, 170
kinaesthetic awareness, 3
kinetic chain, 16
kyphosis, 17

latissimus dorsi, 12
   self-myofascial release, 50, 238
leg exercises *see entries under* conventional training
lever/bio-mechanical considerations, 35
life movement skills, 14–15
lordosis, 17
lumbar vertebrae, 4

martial arts, 22–3
medicine balls, 132–45
   dynamic stabilisation and balance
      dynamic medicine ball press-up, 137
      dynamic plank/bridge, 136
      interactive passing drill, 138
      press-ups on a medicine ball, 137
   flexion and rotation
      basic curl, 133–4
      give and receive, 135
      goalkeeper drill, 136
      Russian twist, 134
   power and speed, 138–45
      chest pass, 138–9
      interactive chest pass with movement, 145
      kneeling oblique throw, 140
      overhead flat throw, 142–3
      overhead throw to floor, 142
      reverse overhead throw, 143–4
      single-arm throw/pass, 144
      stability ball chest pass, 139
      stability ball oblique throw, 141
   see also entries under multi-joint and plane
      movements

mesomorphs, 38
momentum, 35
motor skills, 15
multifidus, 8, 10, 11
multi-joint and plane movements
   ball cobra – interactive catch on stability ball,
      154
   cable dead lift and row, 155
   cable lat pull down with squat/lunge, 156
   cable press with part lunge, 151
   kneeling clock drill with medicine ball, 153
   lunge to side with medicine ball overhead
      press, 157–8
   multi-direction lunges, 156–7
   single leg touchdown with overhead press,
      150
   stability ball wood chop, 152
   step up to balance with overhead press,
      149–50
   walking lunge with interactive catch, 160
   walking lunge with twist, 158–9
   wood chop with side lunge, 151
muscle fibres, 9, 30
muscle(s)
   contraction, 30–1, 32
   hypertrophy, 30
   imbalance, 16, 18
   inner and outer units, 11–12
   overloading, 30–6
   overworking, 18
   repetitions/sequencing, 33–4
   resistances, 31–3
   strength, endurance and power, 30
   trunk, 7–13
   workings of, 11
muscle spindles, 49–50
myotatic stretch reflex, 49–50
myths, 40

nerve fibres, 5
nerves, spinal, 5
neural canal, 5
neuro-muscular adaptation, 33
neuro-muscular efficiency, 16
neutral spine, 5–6

older people *see* elderly
one-to-one exercise programmes *see* exercise
    classes, one-to-one
overload principles, 29, 32

partner work, 124–31
    back extension off bench (feet held), 129
    back extension off bench with rotation (feet
        held), 129
    kneeling oblique twist, 126
    partner twist (statues), 125
    resisted ab curl, 126–7
    resisted flexion (lateral), 130–1
    resisted stability ball abdominal curl, 130
    resisted standing flexion (vertical), 127, 128
    resisted tennis shots (forehand/backhand), 128
pelvic floor, 8, 9, 11
Pilates, 3, 199–207
    benefits of, 201
    definition, 200–1
    exercises
        leg/hip slide, 204
        leg slide with arm extension, 204
        one-leg circle, 203
        pillow squeeze, 205
        prone leg lengthening, 206
        spine curls, 205
        standing roll-downs, 206–7
        supine neutral pelvic alignment with
            stabilisation, 202
        supine shoulder stabilisation, 202–3

history, 199–200
piriformis, self-myofascial release, 51, 241
posture, 16–19
    causes of poor, 18–19
    deviations, 18
    improving, 19
    kyphosis, 17
    lordosis, 17
    overhead squat test, 19–21
    scoliosis, 17–18
    testing your, 18–21
power, 30
power training, 35
pre-exhausting, 34
pregnancy, 23–5, 235
programme design, 35–6
    see also exercise classes
progressive overload, 33
proprioception, 28–9
psoas, 8, 10, 11
purposeful movement, 172
pyramiding, 34

quadratus lumborum, 8, 9, 10
quads, self-myofascial release, 50–1, 239

racquet sports training, 236
recovery, 34
rectus abdominis, 7–9, 10, 11
Reebok Core Board™, 27, 90–8
    alternate squat thrusts, 92
    bicycles, 97
    incline/decline squats, 94
    lateral squat with leg lift, 95
    lunges, 95–6
    press-up, 92
        with rotation and knee pull, 93
        with rotation/twist, 93

reverse lunge/lift/jump, 96
    rotations/tilts, 91
    sample programmes, 232
    squats with leg lift/raise, 94
repetitions/sequencing, 33–4
resistance, 29, 31–3
    in water, 217
resistance tubes, 104
rhomboids, self-myofascial release, 50, 238

sacrum, 4
sciatic nerve, 4
scoliosis, 17–18
self-myofascial release (SMR), 49–51
    gastrocnemius, 51, 240
    hamstrings, 51, 239
    IT band, 51, 240
    latisimus, 50, 238
    piriformis, 51, 241
    quads, 50–1, 239
    rhomboids, 50, 238
    tensor fascia latae, 51, 241
sensory proprioceptive skills, 65
shoulder exercises *see entries under* conventional
    training
sit-ups, x, xi
    myths, 40
    straight-leg, 39
six-pack, x, xi
slow-twitch fibres, 9
SMR *see* self-myofascial release (SMR)
soleus, 20
spinal cord, 3, 5
spinal erectors, 8, 10, 11, 12
spine, 3–6
    extension, 3
    facet joints, 4–5
    flexion, 3

intervertebral discs, 4
    neutral, 5–6
    rotation, 3
    spinal column, 5
    vertebrae, 4
sport, 22–3
stabilisation exercises, 57–65
    'Superman' variations, 60
    within conventional training *see* conventional
        training
    four-count leg lift, 58
    four-count leg lowering, 59
    horizontal balance, 65
    knee stabilisation work, 63
    lateral bridging, 62
    prone abdominal hollowing, 57
    prone bridging (plank work), 61
    scissors, 60
    'Spiderman,' 64
    standing balance, 64–5
    supine bridge, 63
    two-point bridge, 62
stabiliser muscles, 9
stability balls, 27, 70–89
    advanced exercises, 86–9
        'dive' hip extension, 87
        kneeling balance, 88
        kneeling 'Superman,' 89
        prone arm extension, gripping ball, 86
        stability ball power drive, 86–7
        stability ball 'Superman,' 88
        standing balance, 89
    beginner exercises, 74–80
        ab curl using ball as resistance, 76
        back extension, 77
        lateral flexion/crunch, 77
        lying torso rotation, arm extended, 79–80
        oblique curl, 76

prone press-ups (hips/knees/feet on ball), 78

prone roll-in, 78–9

seated leg lift, 74–5

seated pelvic tilting, 74

stability curl, 75

intermediate exercises, 80–5

prone extension with leg rotation, gripping ball, 81

prone hip extension, 82

stability ball roll-out, 81

supine ball rotation, 83

supine bridge ball rolls, 80

supine lateral ball roll, 82–3

two-ball prone balance, 83–4

two-ball prone pec dec, 85

two-ball supine balance, 84

sample programmes, 231

warm-up exercises, 72–3

rotations, 73

seated pelvic tilting/rotation/figure of eight, 72

squat and press, 73

see also entries under conventional training; *entries under* multi-joint and plane movements; *entries under* partner work

stability discs, 97–8

static stretches, 52–6

abdominals, 55

bent leg crucifix, 54

cat stretch, 53

hip flexor stretch, 54

knee hugs, 52

seated spinal twist, 53

shoulder girdle and chest, 55

upper back, 56

straight-leg sit-ups, 39

strength, 30

stretching/stretches, 49–56

self-myofascial release (SMR) *see* self-myofascial release (SMR)

static *see* static stretches

super-setting, 34

suspension training, 184–95

atomic press-up, 194

chest press, 185–6

deltoid raise, 188–9

T-deltoid raise, 188

W-deltoid raise, 189

Y-deltoid raise, 188

double-arm back row, 187

flye, 186

hip press, 193

single-arm power pull with rotation, 189–90

single-leg squat, 191–2

sprinter's start, 192

squat, 190

suspended crunch, 193

total body burpee, 195

synergistic dominance, 16

t'ai Chi ch'uan, 207–8

benefits of, 208

definition, 207–8

history, 207

for older people, 212

tempo/rhythm, 34–5

tendons, 11

tensor fascia latae, self-myofascial release, 51, 241

thoracic vertebrae, 4

thoraco-lumbar fascia, 8, 12

total caloric expenditure, 37

transverse abdominus, 8, 9, 10, 11–12, 26

triceps exercises *see entries under* conventional training

trunk muscles, 7–13
TRX suspension training *see* suspension training

unstable base training *see* Bongo Boards™;
    BOSU™; Reebok Core Board™; stability
    balls; stability discs; wobble boards

vertebrae, 4
ViPR training, 172–83
    anterior lunge with multi-planar tilts, 180–1
    canoe/kayak row, 178–9
    cylindrical lift, 176
    ice skater with tilt rotation, 181–2
    integrated clean and press: with lunge, 179–80
    key steps, 173–4
    lateral tilt/flip with lateral step, 175–6
    outside swings, 175
    overhead squat with tilt, 182–3
    squat 'thread the needle,' 174
    uppercut lunge, 177
    uppercuts to block, 177–8
viscous resistance, 217
volleyball training, 236

warming up, 46, 227
warm-up exercises
    lateral flexion, 48
    rotations, 47

supported cat flex, 49
up and overs, 48
water, abdominal training in, 216–23
    benefits of, 218
    buoyancy effect, 216–17
    exercises, 219–23
        alternate bear hugs, 220–1
        alternate outward scoops, 221
        arm pulls, 220
        deep-water/supine twist-ups, 223
        pull-throughs, 223
        rocking horse, 219
        single-arm punches, 219
        single-leg swings (hip extension/flexion),
            222
        trunk rotations, 221
        twists, 222
    resistance in water, 217
weight control, 37
Whole Body Integration, 172
wobble boards, 27, 97–8

yoga, 22–3, 208–9
    benefits of, 209
    definition, 208–9
    history, 208
    for older people, 212